RED HAWK

BOOK THREE

A CHARADE OF MAGIC

HELEN HARPER

HUMMINGBIRD RECAP

The Story of *Hummingbird*

Scotland is a troubled land ruled by the Mages, men with magic who abuse their power and position. Each Scottish city has its own Mages and an Ascendant who leads them. Every night, as soon as darkness falls, the Afflicted take over – men and women who were once human but who have been transformed by disease into something very different.

Mairi Wallace lives and works in a small tartan shop in Glasgow owned by Belle and Twister, a humourless and unkind couple. Mairi dreams of studying at university to become an apothecary so she can use her knowledge of herbs to help people, but she is held back by her lifelong inability to speak.

Mairi's best friend, Isla, sends word that she needs help at the orphanage where they both grew up. Mairi risks venturing out at night to go there and help a young, orphaned girl who is sick. Isla tells her that a baby girl has gone missing and she suspects that the Mages have taken her.

On her return journey to the tartan shop, Mairi is confronted by a daemon called Nicholas who has been enslaved by the Mages. Instead of giving her up to his Mage companion, he helps her hide by way of magic. As a slave, Nicholas is physically unable to refuse a direct order from a Mage, but there are often loopholes and he possesses some limited freedom.

The following week, Belle and Twister are given a large order for tartan to be delivered to the Mages at the City Chambers. A woman called Fee comes to the shop and tells Mairi to visit her because she possesses secrets about Mairi's true nature. Mairi decides to ignore this, but then Isla is publicly executed for asking too many questions about the missing baby girl. Devastated by grief and shock, Mairi resolves to avenge her friend. She walks away from Belle and Twister and her apothecary dreams and seeks out Fee.

Fee, together with her two wards, Flora and Jane, and a strange old man called the Gowk, tell Mairi that they are part of a resistance movement against the Mages. They also reveal that women can wield magic just like men but the Mages prevent them from doing so.

Mairi learns that she possesses magic; although she cannot speak, she can pull on her considerable power by humming. However, strong emotions can dampen the effects of magic and a magic-wielder must be in control of themselves to control their power.

After learning this, Mairi sneaks away from Fee and the others to go to the City Chambers. Using a connection she has already made with a Mage called Noah, she gains employment as a servant.

Once working there, Mairi meets Billy, a young man who tends a garden inside the Chambers. She also meets the daemon Nicholas again, who initially appears displeased that she has found her way into the City Chambers. Mairi learns that Nicholas's real name is Laoch; the Mages renamed him when they enslaved him. She also meets a grumpy old Mage called Angus, who is very different to his cohorts.

After a secret message is passed to her by Trish and Lottie, two servants who also work for the Mages, Mairi meets the Gowk in a local park. He tells her that she cannot kill the Ascendant on her own but, if she can find incontrovertible proof of the Mages' wrongdoings, the city might be spurred into action against their magical leaders.

Mairi reluctantly agrees. She tries to find incriminating evidence but doesn't discover anything useful until she follows a small group of Mages one night. She realises that they have captured and imprisoned one of the Afflicted, though she doesn't understand why.

Noah continues to flirt with her and asks her out for dinner. There is a rumour that if a male Mage has sex with a woman who possesses magic, some of the Mage's magic will transfer to her during the act. To test this knowledge, Mairi has sex with Laoch. She discovers that the rumour isn't true, but their intimacy results in a sudden and unexpected ability for them to communicate telepathically. Laoch tells her that he is on her side and he will help her.

Mairi finds a strange garden inside the City Chambers that is macabre, reeking of death and powered by magic. Laoch gifts Mairi with a spell that allows her to transfer herself into the body of a mouse, which she christens Mungo. While in Mungo's body, she finds a hidden basement beneath the Chambers.

After she returns to human form, she finds the Afflicted man who was taken prisoner inside a tiny cage. He has obviously been tortured, but Angus confronts her before she can release him from the cage. Instead of raising the alarm, the old Mage helps her to free him. As she escapes the basement with the Afflicted man, they go through the strange garden where the man digs up some loose earth and uncovers the mutilated corpse of Mairi's friend, Isla.

Shaken by the gruesome discovery that the Mages use female corpses to boost their magical powers, Mairi takes the Afflicted man to a back door near the kitchens. The house-keeper, Ailsa, is there and, after some discussion, helps Mairi to free him. Ailsa tells her that the Mages don't kill the baby girls they kidnap; she doesn't know why they take them, but she knows that they are adopted by good families. Mairi later finds out that the Mages drain the babies of their natural magic.

The following day, Mairi witnesses the Ascendant blaming a Mage called Ross for the Afflicted man's escape and brutally punishing him. The Ascendant mentions someone called Farris, who has provided crucial information about the resistance. The Ascendant has received details of a powerful female, and he instructs the Mages to find her. Mairi initially believes he is talking about another baby girl but later realises that she is the target.

When Mairi goes to meet the Gowk again, she overhears him being called by his real name, Farris; *he* has been passing information to the Mages. Mage Ross discovers who Mairi is and what she can do. He immediately attacks her, but Belle and Twister appear and stab him in the back.

Ross's death and the revelation about the Gowk mean that all the Mages are now after Mairi, but several people in nearby streets help her escape. She learns that the Gowk didn't know-ingly pass on information and that the Mages have been using him for years. She also realises that those who have helped her, including the Gowk, Belle and Twister, may now be the Mages' prisoners. She resolves to return to the City Chambers and try to release them.

Using Mungo the mouse's body, Mairi returns to the City Chambers and persuades Ailsa to help her. They locate the

Gowk and the people who helped Mairi escape but they are confronted by the Ascendant and Noah before they can escape.

The Ascendant tells Mairi that women are not allowed to do magic because the existence of female Mages caused the disease that affects the Afflicted, then he orders Laoch to kill her. Before Laoch attacks her, he tells her telepathically that he loves her. Something inside Mairi breaks and she finally finds her voice. She uses her magic to hold back Laoch and kill the Ascendant. Noah is wounded and beaten back.

Mairi frees Laoch and he disappears back to his own realm before she and her companions escape into the night.

NIGHTINGALE RECAP

The Story of *Nightingale*

After killing the Glaswegian Ascendant, Mairi has become the face of the growing resistance against the Mages. The Mages, however, are fighting back and have called in reinforcements from Edinburgh, including a vicious Mage called Lord Aspen.

In a bid to stay safe, Mairi and her friends hide in a basement belonging to a Glaswegian man called John McAllan. When Mages start knocking down doors and searching nearby properties, they are forced to separate and flee. Thanks to a diversion created by a young boy, Mairi manages to get away and hide herself in a crowded market. While she is there, Noah uses magic to project his voice across the city and inform the citizens that if they do not find her, the Mages will begin random executions at regular intervals.

Mairi reaches the next safe house, a small church. On her way there she notices a strange rune. She reunites with her friends but knows that the only way to prevent the upcoming executions is to hand herself over to the Mages, so she sneaks out in the middle of the night to do just that. When enters the City Chambers, she goes first to speak to Mage Angus and ensure the future safety of the resistance before she gives herself up. He persuades her that her idea is foolish and repeats what the Glasgow Ascendant told her before his death: the Afflicted are a natural by-product of the existence of female Mages like her, and that is why women with magic are killed.

The City Chambers is attacked, both by the servants within and the people outside. Angus and Mairi flee, together with Mungo the mouse. The Afflicted also appear and launch an attack. One Afflicted man speaks to Mairi and says, 'He Is Coming,' as chaos reigns through the city's streets.

Mairi escapes to the church with Angus and Mungo, but her friends have vanished. The next morning Laoch appears without warning, returning from his own realm to be with her. Together they travel to the City Chambers to see the aftermath of the previous night's events. Once there, they discover another rune that is identical to the one near the church. Neither of them understand what it means or where it has come from.

The Mages come out of the half-ruined City Chambers and Lord Aspen addresses the crowd of people who have assembled in front of it. He offers an apology for the Mages' actions and manipulates the situation by forcing Mairi to accept a place in the upcoming Ascendancy Challenge in Edinburgh, where the best person will be selected to lead Glasgow. Mairi knows that it is a trap and will likely lead to her death, but she has no choice but to accept. She reunites with her friends and spends the next few days preparing her magic.

Limited as to who she can take to Edinburgh to support her, Mairi takes Angus and Belle, with Laoch hidden in Mungo's body in her bag. The Mages arrange for their carriage to be attacked en route to Edinburgh so they can test Mairi's magical capabilities. Aware of their plan, Mairi holds back as much power as she can.

Once the attack is over she realises that Noah, who was travelling with them, has disappeared together with the carriage driver. She finds the driver's dead body some distance away before realising that Noah has been knocked unconscious and is being dragged away by a group of the Afflicted. Worryingly, the Afflicted have never been seen outside in daylight before.

Against her better judgment, Mairi rescues Noah with Angus and Laoch's help. However, Noah is now Afflicted. Mairi spots another rune at the cave where the Afflicted were hiding and realises that they have been drawing the runes. She transports Noah to Edinburgh to prove what happened to him to the other Mages.

Noah's advancing disease proves that Mairi is telling the truth about the Afflicted's attack. She is led to a small room within Edinburgh Castle. Laoch is exhausted after using so much magic to remain in Mungo's body, so while he rests Mairi takes the opportunity to transfer her own consciousness into the mouse. She escapes the room to investigate the castle and spy on the Mages.

In the Edinburgh Ascendant's study, she discovers some information about the first round of the Ascendancy Challenge but she is forced to flee when several Mages come into the room. She escapes but is grabbed in the corridor by a female daemon who is called Frederica by the Mages but whose real name is Teasag. Teasag helps Mairi by taking her to the Mages' garden to gather some herbs to help Laoch's recovery before returning her to her room.

The following day, a friendly young Mage called Andy and

his companion take Belle and Mairi out of their room for a tour of the castle. They don't get far before they are stopped by the Edinburgh Ascendant who fakes kindness and interrupts the tour to show them the battlements at the top of the castle. Once there, he shows them three hanging bodies: Billy, the gardener from Glasgow; John McAllan, who hid Mairi in his basement, and a young boy who helped her escape from a raven. The Ascendant uses the bodies to threaten Belle and encourage her to leave, but she stands her ground and refuses. Later Andy gives Mairi information to help her in the Challenge.

At midnight, Aspen escorts Mairi to the first Challenge. As they leave the castle, she notices yet another rune. Aspen questions the guards about it; when he doesn't receive a satisfactory answer, he attempts to kill the most senior one. Angus stops him. Not long afterwards, the guard deserts his post.

Faking a poison attack so that the Mages will not see the full extent of her magic, Mairi takes part in the first Challenge. She has to run from one end of Princes Street to the other while being attacked. She struggles and is the last person to succeed, but she survives while more than half of the other competing Mages are knocked out.

Mage Andy offers Mairi some healing ointment to help with the injuries she sustained in the Challenge and also gives her a page ripped from an old book. It depicts the rune she has seen in various places and its translation – *He Is Coming*.

In the second round of the Ascendancy Challenge, Mairi has to answer three riddles. Although she doesn't hear the first one, she manages to solve it with Laoch's help; he is hiding in Mungo's body and can communicate with her telepathically. At the end of the round, only eight participants remain.

Lord Aspen is suspicious that Mairi received help and searches her room. As Laoch is in Mungo's body, he isn't discovered. Belle and Angus are taken away, and Laoch and Mairi get to spend the night alone together. They admit their love for each other.

The next day Mairi takes part in the third Challenge. Every competitor has their magic temporarily stripped from them then must take part in hand-to-hand combat without the use of special powers. Most of the audience are on her side, but Mairi knows she is not as strong as the Mage she must fight. In the seconds before the fight starts, Aspen interrupts, reveals Mungo and forces Laoch to show himself before enslaving him again while Mungo the mouse runs away.

Mairi is forced to fight. She beats her competitor and kills him when he doesn't abide by the rules. When Andy escorts her back to the castle, he tells he's discovered that the runes are about a Mage called Cadal Righ. A hundred and twenty years ago, Righ staged a coup against the Mages. He was eventually beaten and disappeared before he could be executed. A month later, the Afflicted first appeared.

Before Andy can say anything more, guards appear and take Mairi to the Edinburgh Ascendant. He offers to send her and her friends to an uninhabited island where they can live in freedom as long as Mairi never returns to the mainland. When she refuses, the Ascendant puts her in a dungeon beneath the castle. She discovers someone else in the dungeon: Noah, who is now almost fully Afflicted. She realises that the Mages want Noah to afflict her and she tries to run. As a result of the last round in the Ascendancy Challenge, she still doesn't possess any magic with which to defend herself.

Noah keeps repeating over and over again, 'He Is Coming.' Instead of attacking Mairi, he climbs the stairs and breaks down the locked door. Angus, Belle, Andy and Teasag appear to help Mairi just as the castle comes under attack. Noah changes his words to 'He Is Here'.

Mairi and her friends run. When they reach the Ascendant's

study, Mairi looks out of the window and sees thousands of Afflicted approaching the castle. The walls are breached and a man who introduces himself as Cadal Righ appears. He kills the Edinburgh Ascendant and claims that Scotland now belongs to him.

ONE

Built on a towering volcanic hill, Edinburgh Castle overlooks the entire sprawling city. Rather than one solid, crenellated structure, it is a complicated collection of separate buildings located inside a fortress of high stone walls. The fortress is surrounded on three sides by a sheer rocky drop that is impassable for most people, while the main route into the castle trails through the narrow, cobbled street of the Royal Mile and its imposing terraced buildings, higgledy-piggledy shops, hidden wynds and shadowy snickets. There is also a gentler approach where visitors can curve around the long road that wanders up from the open drama of Princes Street to join the Royal Mile at its zenith just before the castle's main entrance.

Unfortunately, making use of either of those roads presupposes it is possible to stroll through the main gate of the castle and under the heavy iron portcullis. When thousands of groaning, shuffling Afflicted men and women congregate there, together with the magical bastard who appeared from nowhere and declared himself the new King of Scotland, neither of those routes is viable. Not if you wish to remain healthy and sane with all your limbs in their rightful place.

We didn't want to get into Edinburgh Castle. We needed to get out. Quickly.

'That Cavalry bampot blasted a hole in the castle wall. Can we no' just make a run that way instead of hiding in this wee room?' Belle demanded.

I glanced at her. Her face and clothes were covered in a thin layer of sooty ash, and her fine brown hair was escaping its usual confines and sticking up in several directions, but despite her unkempt appearance, she still looked in better condition than the rest of us.

'Cadal Righ,' I said absently. 'Not Cavalry.'

'Tha's what I said.' She crossed her arms over her chest and glared at me, as if all this were somehow my fault.

'Stupid woman,' Aspen muttered.

Belle didn't miss a beat. She turned to him and slapped him hard on his face. The sound cracked across the small, packed room where we'd hidden in our bid to escape the sudden appearance of Cadal Righ.

Both Mage Andy and Angus winced. I shrugged. As far as I was concerned, Belle could saw off Aspen's penis with a pair of rusty old scissors if she so wished. He was the least of our concerns.

'Nicholas!' Aspen barked. Wanker. I despised every moment that damned name was used. The Mages had given it to Laoch in the same way they'd forced the name of Frederica upon Teasag. They did everything they could to strip the daemons of their identities. 'Kill that woman now!'

I glared. Laoch, who remained under Aspen's yoke, had no choice but to obey a direct order and he started to move towards Belle. She squeaked and darted behind me.

'Rescind that order,' I told Aspen.

The Mage sniffed and his moustache quivered. 'I will not.'

'Rescind it, or I'll shove you out that door and you can deal with the hordes of the Afflicted and Cadal fucking Righ on your own.' I regarded the older Mage implacably. After having my magic drained from me as part of the Ascendancy Challenge, it was only now starting to trickle slowly back through my veins. But I wasn't standing alone against the might of the Mages because, for once, Aspen wasn't in full control. His magic was as depleted as mine.

Laoch raised his hands and his slave cuffs jangled as he tried to reach around me to get at Belle. Beads of sweat glistened on his skin, highlighting his tattoos and dampening his inky curls. I blocked him as best as I could. 'Aspen,' I warned.

The Mage rolled his eyes. 'Fine. Forget that order, Nicholas.' He paused. 'For now.' He beckoned to the two daemons, who shuffled towards him and took up position on either side of him.

Regardless of the horrors that were taking place outside our door, Teasag's eyes were bright and her cheeks were flushed. At this very moment, the patterns of power in Scotland were shifting and anything that might topple the Mages seemed to count as a win as far as she was concerned.

Laoch, however, was forbidden to look at me or communicate with me in any way, and his expression told an entirely different story. His emerald eyes were dull and there was a line of tense pain to his jaw. The pallor of his skin also worried me. Pain and guilt stabbed at me because it was my fault that he was enslaved again. I'd brought him here. I'd allowed this to happen.

I lifted my chin and met Aspen's eyes. 'You need to release them. You can't keep the daemons as your slaves, not now. Not with everything that's happening out there.'

The bastard Mage didn't deign to answer and I gritted my

teeth. We all knew that the only thing standing between Aspen and certain death was those two daemons, but he would face the gnashing multitudes of hell before he'd release them. I inhaled deeply and stayed calm. I'd force his hand sooner or later and see Laoch and Teasag freed. It was only a matter of time.

There was a sudden guttural howl from the hallway, and I wondered how many of the Afflicted were now within the castle walls. Were those narrow stone corridors and open courtyards completely overrun? I drew in a deep shuddering breath.

'We can't stay here for much longer.' I looked at Belle. 'We have to get out of this room and leave the castle. There's no chance we can get through the front gate or the hole that's been blasted in the wall because the Afflicted will tear us apart or we'll end up infected ourselves.' I swallowed. 'Does anyone think we can make some sort of deal with Cadal Righ?'

Angus pulled at his straggly grey beard. 'The Afflicted are his to command. We have no bargaining power.'

Belle snorted. 'We could hand over that bampot,' she jerked her hand towards Aspen, 'in return for our escape.'

'I'd like to see you try,' Aspen snarled.

Angus scratched his chin. 'I don't know who this Cadal Righ is, but he won't settle for one Mage. Even if he is willing to bargain, he'll want Andy and me as well. He'll be as happy to kill the both of us as he was to skin the Ascendant.'

The image of the Edinburgh Ascendant, his bloodied flesh exposed as a result of one brief incantation, sprang unbidden to my mind. Whoever Cadal Righ was, and whatever he truly wanted, he had more power in his little finger than any of us could dream of.

'The enemy of my enemy is my friend,' Belle muttered.

Unfortunately, I didn't think that was true.

Andy, who had been silent until now, started to tremble though his eyes remained focused. 'I'm willing to step up if it means the rest of you will be safe. I'll turn myself over to him.'

'Fuck off,' Angus replied mildly. 'So we're clear, *I* will not hand myself over. I will not give myself up to that madman.'

'We're not giving up either of you.' I set my jaw. 'For one thing, we're going to need all the magic we can lay our hands on to get through this. For another, he,' I pointed at Andy, 'is the only person who knows anything about Cadal Righ and where he's come from. The rest of us have been too focused on the Ascendancy Challenge to pay attention.' Andy's cheeks flushed.

'Do you have a plan?' Teasag asked.

I licked my lips. Not really, though I had a few ideas. 'There are lots of innocent people inside this castle. Servants, ordinary folk who were here to watch the Ascendancy Challenge—'

'And Mages,' Aspen interjected.

I didn't look at him. 'We need to round up as many of them as possible and get them to the battlements, where we'll have a good view of the city and the castle surroundings. We can find the best route and use magic to get everyone down into the city. We can't stay here –we'll be sitting ducks. We'll end up Afflicted ourselves.'

'Or we'll become dinner,' Angus muttered.

Belle flapped her hands. 'The Afflicted are out there. They're in the city.'

I regarded her calmly. 'The Afflicted are in here too.'

Belle's mouth tightened. 'Aye,' she said. 'They are. Whit about Glasgow? Do you think they're okay there? Do you think Twister is okay? He's no' much of a fighter and—'

I couldn't worry about Glasgow or Belle's husband right now. 'Let's concentrate on one problem at a time.' She bit her lip and nodded. I took a moment to appreciate her sudden silence then looked at the others. 'Does anyone else have a better idea? Or any objections?'

Andy drew in a ragged breath. 'Let's do it.'

'So be it,' Aspen said. 'Let's go.' I turned my head towards him and he grinned with considerable malice. 'The daemons are mine to command. If you want them to escape too, then I must come with you.'

Angus pursed his mouth. 'We could kill him now. He's weak after the Ascendancy Challenge. Andy and I can take him.'

Belle sniffed. 'I'll help.'

It was tempting. *Very* tempting.

'I'll release the daemons from their service once we're out of the castle,' Aspen said. He crossed his heart with his index finger. 'Promise. Try and kill me now and I'll squeal like a stuck pig. I'll bring half the Afflicted running into the castle. You won't get out of here alive if I don't.'

I sighed. In less than a few hours, the world had spun on its axis and I was still being plagued by a damned Mage on a power trip. I didn't want to have to worry about Aspen at my back. Neither did I want to waste time trying to kill him. It was too risky. 'He can come.'

The others didn't look impressed. Aspen's grin took on an edge of smugness. 'You're not always a stupid bitch.' He paused. 'We should take advantage of your temporary clarity. You must realise that we don't have time to rescue other people. It's every man for himself. The others can find their own way out.'

'You can come with us,' I snapped. 'For now. But you don't get a vote on anything else.' I nodded at Angus. 'Watch him,' I ordered, pointing at Aspen.

The old Mage bowed. 'Whatever my magnificent mistress commands.'

I frowned in irritation but Angus only smirked. Honestly, with this motley crew it would be a miracle if we made it out of Edinburgh Castle alive.

I glanced at Laoch, who was continuing to look everywhere but at me. His body remained tense and stiff but I thought I saw a glimmer of something in his eyes. Approval, perhaps. I sent him three words: *I love you.*

He didn't respond, just blinked. For now, that would have to be enough.

I tied back my hair, ignoring the snags and unruly red curls, then moved to the door. 'I'll take the lead,' I said. 'The rest of you stay close.'

I SLIPPED into the empty hallway with the others trailing behind. Although the corridor was empty, the stale smell spoke of rot and disease. The Afflicted were permeating the castle; even their stench was taking over. With Cadal Righ at the forefront, they'd won Edinburgh Castle in minutes. So much for the solid stone defences.

Unwilling to risk crashing into groups of marauding Afflicted, I took my time and only moved when I was sure it was safe. I paused at the first closed door, double-checked we were okay then knocked gently. 'Hello? Is anyone there? We're here to help.'

I held my breath then opened the door to reveal a small chamber that was identical to the one we'd been hiding in. There was a table, several chairs, a bookcase rammed with leather-bound tomes – and two huddled figures squeezed into the far corner. The man was brandishing a candlestick while the woman held a heavy-looking vase. Neither of those implements would do them any good against a single Afflicted man or woman, let alone the likes of Cadal Righ.

'You know who I am,' I said softly. 'My name is Mairi. Together with my friends here, I'm mounting an escape. I strongly recommend you come with us. I can't guarantee we'll make it out of here alive, but if you stay in this room you will either die or be Afflicted by nightfall. Your best bet is with us.'

The couple exchanged glances then their bodies sagged with relief. 'I'm Polly,' the woman said. 'This is Jones. You can bet your sweet Glaswegian arse that we're coming wi' you.'

I managed a smile as the pair of them sprang forward and joined our little gang.

We continued down the hallway, checking every room. Some were empty, others packed with frightened people, none of whom required persuading to leave. We all knew what would happen if we stayed.

Less than twenty minutes after we'd left our tiny bolthole, our numbers had swelled to almost thirty with a smattering of castle servants, shaky guards and people who'd been watching the Ascendancy Challenge. Everyone was scared, whether they were used to maintaining order for the Mages or simply sweeping the floors. With the Afflicted running amok, we were all now on equal footing. We were all in peril.

'We should head to the battlements,' Aspen grunted from somewhere towards the rear as I finally reached the winding staircase. 'There are already too many people here. We can't save them all.'

Eejit. We could certainly try. I ignored him and beckoned Andy. He hurried forward. 'The best way to the main battlements is up this way?' I asked. He nodded. 'And if we go down?'

'There's a small courtyard and access to the other castle buildings.'

Good. 'Angus,' I said, 'take these people and Belle up to the battlements and wait for us there. I'll go with Aspen and Andy and see who else we can round up.'

'Not happening. I'm going up to the battlements, too,' Aspen said. 'It's time to get the fuck out of here.'

I stayed calm. 'There are more people down there, including Mages. We need to help as many of them as we can. And we need their help in return.' I tilted my head. 'I don't know about you, Lord Aspen, but I barely have a quarter of my usual magic. My power is taking its time to return after your buddies took it from me for the last Ascendancy Challenge. You might struggle on your own.'

He glared at me. Given the ferocity of his expression, I doubted he'd recovered as much of his innate power as I had. But then I was younger, so perhaps I healed faster.

'I'm not alone. I have two daemons,' he snarled.

If ever there was a time to put on an act, it was now. I shrugged and affected an air of insouciance. 'If you think two daemons can stand between you, Cadal Righ and fifty thousand Afflicted souls, then on you go. Run away. Save yourself.' I paused. 'I'm sure you'll be absolutely fine.'

Several emotions flitted across Aspen's face, then he seemed to realise that three dozen people were watching him. He pulled back his shoulders. 'I still aim to be the Glasgow Ascendant. I am still the best man for that job. The Ascendant helps his people. He does not run away like a shivering child. I will come with you. I will help those poor souls in danger from the Afflicted – and *my* daemons will help *me*.' It would have been a finer speech if he hadn't been trying to run away on his own moments earlier.

I looked again at Laoch and wished that he could meet my eyes. I needed his warm reassurance. I turned to Angus. 'Thirty minutes,' I said. 'If we don't re-join you in thirty minutes, do what you can to leave with these people.'

'Aye, my Queen.'

I clenched my teeth. I was growing tired of Angus's jokes, which were neither appropriate nor amusing. Then I saw his expression; for once, it was both serious and concerned.

'Come back safe,' he said. 'We'll need you.'

This time all I could do was nod.

I waited until the group had disappeared up the stairs then beckoned Aspen, who gestured in turn to Laoch and Teasag. He didn't need to do so; both daemons were already in his thrall and following his footsteps. He only made the gesture to remind me that the daemons were his to order.

Despite my earlier efforts to put on an act, Aspen wasn't stupid; he knew they were important to me. We were fortunate that he hadn't yet realised exactly how important Laoch was to my aching heart. Aspen's cruel machinations would continue, regardless of the apocalyptic horror taking place on his doorstep. He was, I concluded, simply that sort of black-hearted bastard.

Bracing my shoulders and preparing for the worst, I started to descend. It wasn't far to the ground floor and our path was unimpeded. Before I reached the bottom step, however, I heard the snuffling grunts of several Afflicted people. I sucked in a breath, ducked out of sight and only peered around the corner of the winding stone staircase when I was certain that they were gone. Even so, they'd left enough of themselves behind to send a shiver of trepidation down my spine. Bloodied footprints left a shaky, winding trail all the way down the long corridor. It wasn't clear whether the blood was from the Afflicted or some other poor souls. I suppressed a shudder.

There were three rooms to my right and a door leading to the outside on my left. With Aspen, Laoch and Teasag at my back, I tiptoed to the first room and peered inside. It was empty, although it showed considerable signs of a struggle. Several pieces of furniture had been overturned and there was a smear of blood by the cold fireplace.

I hesitated then continued to the second room. I waited for a beat, listening for signs of life before looking inside. As soon as I poked my head past the doorframe, there was a muttered whisper, '*Ins veil.*'

Shite. I pulled out of the way in the nick of time and narrowly avoided the blast of attack magic. Whirling around, I grabbed Aspen's sleeve. 'Deal with this,' I hissed.

A nasty gleam of light flashed across his eyes and my soul hardened further. 'What is true for you is true for me.' I glared. 'I can bring the Afflicted running in this direction as quickly as you can. Until we get out of this fucking castle, we have to work together.'

Aspen pursed his lips as he thought about it. 'Aye, I suppose so,' he said finally.

There was no suppose about it; we were all in this apocalyptic quagmire. Even so, I'd have to watch Aspen like a hawk. He'd take every opportunity to put me down regardless of the brutal, bloody chaos around us.

'Stand down, lads,' Aspen called cheerfully. You'd have thought we were playing a child's game of tig.

There was a beat of silence. A second later, it was followed by a shaky voice. 'Lord Aspen?'

'The one and only. You can come out now. I'm here to save you.'

'I thought, Lord Aspen,' Teasag said in an innocent tone that was anything but, 'you believed it was every man for himself and we should escape instead of helping others.'

Aspen spun towards her with his fist raised. From his expression, there was no doubt that he'd have killed her on the spot for her insolence if he'd had any magic left to use.

I stepped between them. 'We don't have time for this.'

Laoch gazed ahead. 'She is right. We cannot delay. Not if we are to survive this day.' He spoke in a monotone that stabbed at my heart.

Before Aspen could say anything more, three grubby Mages appeared from the doorway. From their near-identical expressions, they genuinely believed that Aspen had appeared to rescue them from a grisly death. I gritted my teeth. If they were foolish enough to believe that Aspen was their saviour, let them. I'd expend my energy on worrying about what was real rather than imagined.

With a grandiose flourish that was very much out of place Aspen said, 'We are heading up to the battlements to make our escape from there. You three still have magic?'

The trio of Mages nodded, their focus wholly on him. At that point, I wouldn't have been surprised if they'd thrown themselves at his feet in gratitude for his appearance.

'Good,' he said. 'We'll need it to get everyone away from here. Conserve your strength, lads. You'll need your magic for what's to come.' He turned on his heel and returned down the hallway towards the staircase.

I barely glanced at his departing back. Instead I moved in the opposite direction towards the open doorway that led to the outside and one of the castle's many courtyards. There were plenty of other scattered buildings within the castle walls and that meant there were probably plenty of other people hiding who needed help.

'Is Queen Mairi attempting to rescue more people?' Teasag enquired loudly.

Queen Mairi? I shook my head in dismay. She was following Angus's lead but that wasn't going to help. Far from it.

Aspen whirled around. From the way his eyes narrowed at Teasag, he knew exactly why she'd chosen that particular moniker. She would pay for it later. 'You will not speak again, Frederica, unless I directly ask you a question or give you permission,' he barked.

Teasag's mouth closed but her iridescent horns trembled with undisguised fury.

Aspen sniffed and glanced at me. 'We are returning to the battlements to make our escape. It is time to leave. There are less than twenty minutes before the others go over the edge.'

'Aye, alright. Off you go.' I turned once more and continued to the doorway.

A second later, Andy joined me. 'I'm with you,' he said. His words were considerably quieter than Teasag's had been but there was no mistaking his intent. 'I'll help you save the others.'

The other three Mages looked from Aspen to me and back again. 'Lord Aspen?' the youngest one asked uncertainly.

This time I didn't bother to check what Aspen was doing. I sidled up to the open doorway and risked a quick peek through it. Shite. There were several clusters of shuffling Afflicted figures out there. Getting past them would be almost impossible.

'It's getting too dangerous,' I heard Aspen say. 'I don't want more people to die.'

Neither did I – that was the point. I scanned the courtyard for a second time. If I timed it right, I might be able to squeak past the Afflicted while they were looking the other way. They weren't known for their intelligence, so a sneaky diversion could work. I chewed on my bottom lip and considered.

'My brother is out there somewhere,' one of Mages said. 'I have to see if I can find him. I have to try.'

'Your brother is probably already gone,' Aspen growled

I spied an open sash window on the third storey of the building to our right. It was propped up by a thick hardback book. Hmm. It might work.

The young Mage drew in a breath. 'I'll meet you at the battlements shortly, Lord Aspen, but first I'll go with her and look for my brother.'

Aspen was nothing if not adaptable. 'We'll go together. We'll find Adam.'

'Aaron,' the Mage said. 'His name is Aaron.'

I stifled a brief, sad smile and turned to Andy. 'You see the window up there? With the book?'

Andy peered out. I could feel his body shaking next to mine. 'Aye,' he said. 'I see it.'

'Can you use your magic to bring down the book? It looks like a heavy volume and it'll cause a racket when it falls. The Afflicted will head for it and we can use the distraction to sprint the other way.' I pointed to a building on the left. 'There might be more survivors hiding in there.'

Andy nodded. 'Good plan.'

'It's a stupid plan,' Aspen said.

'Keep your voice down!' I hissed. 'They'll hear you.'

Aspen rolled his eyes, but when he spoke again it was in more muted tones. 'We can use the daemons. I'll send Frederica out. She can create the distraction.'

Out of the corner of my eye, I saw her flinch. I resisted glancing at Laoch, who remained as silent as the grave. 'We're saving lives,' I said. 'Not risking them.'

Aspen snorted. 'You could have fooled me.'

I clenched my jaw.

'I've got it, Mairi,' Andy said. 'On a count of five.'

I braced my body, tensing for the run. 'We move quickly and quietly,' I whispered. 'We don't want any of them to see us.'

Aspen pushed forward to insert himself in the space in front of me. 'I'll go first,' he said. 'The rest of you can follow.'

'You shouldn't risk yourself like that, my Lord,' one of the other Mages said.

Aspen smiled beneficently. 'I'll be fine.' He nodded at Laoch and Teasag. 'You two are with me.'

I opened my mouth to protest but Laoch jerked his head in warning, telling me to stay quiet. I grimaced, but I didn't argue. When he moved a step behind Aspen, I let my fingers brush against his. His skin felt cold and he didn't react. Sharp pain stabbed my heart.

'Five,' Andy said. 'Four. Three. Two.' He sucked air noisily into his lungs. 'One.'

Magic juddered out of his fingertips. Despite my temporary lack of power, I sensed the energy emanating from Andy. He wasn't a particularly powerful Mage, but for this he didn't need to be.

Tendrils of his magic looped around the book and tugged it forward. The window creaked. For a moment I didn't think he'd succeeded but then the book sprang free. The window crashed down and, a second later, so did the book.

'Now,' I whispered urgently to Aspen.

The bastard didn't move. There was a guttural roar from several of the milling Afflicted men and women. I heard rather than saw the momentary stampede towards the right as they rushed to investigate the sound.

'Aspen. For fuck's sake! Move!'

He remained stock still. 'I can't. Three of them are looking this way. If I go out now, they'll see us.'

I tried to get around him but he was blocking my way. Cursing, I pushed myself up onto my tiptoes. The way was clear;

nobody was looking and there was a direct path to the other building.

'It's fine!' I nudged Aspen sharply. 'Get out of the way and I'll go!' If we didn't make a run for it now, we'd lose our chance.

There was a groan from behind me and a hand shoved me roughly to one side. My body slammed into the wall as the Mage who was worried about his brother barrelled past. When Aspen continued to block the doorway, he murmured a single incantation, '*Ins veil.*'

Aspen's body jerked to the side, together with both Laoch and Teasag, and the young Mage – whose name I didn't know – darted into the courtyard.

Unfortunately, it was already too late.

I pushed away from the wall, ignoring the dull ache down my side from where I'd collided with the hard stone, and ran after the Mage. Half a dozen Afflicted, realising that a fallen book was of no interest to them, had swung around in his direction. Within a heartbeat there were several whoops and they sprinted after him.

I lurched forward, not sure how I could deal with this latest threat but knowing that I had to try, when my toe caught on a loose flagstone. Instead of pelting forward, I was thrown downward.

As I put my hands out instinctively to brace against the fall, the first of the Afflicted reached the hapless Mage. I watched helplessly as a woman with dirty brown hair that fell in uneven clumps from a balding scalp grabbed the Mage and screamed in joyful, anticipatory delight. Her jaws snapped down on his bare hand. It was the Mage's turn to scream but there was no delight in the sound that he made.

I scrambled to my feet, preparing to run towards him. This time a different hand yanked me back: Andy's. I jerked away from him. 'Stop that! We have to help him!'

'You can't. It's already too late. There's too many of them, Mairi.'

He was right. More and more of the Afflicted were loping towards the Mage. Some, I thought queasily, looked hungry; others were too slack jawed to display any expression whatsoever. 'Use your damned magic!' I hissed.

'I'm not strong enough, not against that many of them. None of us are strong enough.'

'If I had full use of my powers—' Aspen began.

'It still would not be enough,' Andy muttered. 'We can't win here.' He met my eyes. 'We have to retreat. That Mage is already lost.'

The Afflicted were swarming over the Mage now and I could no longer see him. More of them were pouring into the courtyard. Everywhere I looked, the Afflicted were appearing.

I turned my head and looked at the Mage's two companions, then at Aspen and Andy and Teasag. Finally, I looked at Laoch. He didn't return my gaze because he couldn't, but his hands were bunched into tight fists and his knuckles were white.

My shoulders slumped. 'Alright,' I whispered. 'Let's go. Head for the battlements.'

Before I'd finished speaking, Aspen had disappeared back inside with the two weeping Mages and both daemons. I nodded to Andy, who traipsed after them. I sent the screeching mêlée of Afflicted men and women one final glance and started to follow.

I'd barely taken a step when a deep boom tore through the air. I froze – and so did all of the Afflicted. The crowds parted, creating a path that led from the other side of the courtyard to the bedraggled heap that had once been a Mage. Was he still alive? I couldn't tell, but I could see his blood staining the cobbles around his body.

Mage or not, he was still a living being. I reached inside myself, searching for enough magic to do something to help him, but I hadn't recovered enough power. Any spell I attempted would fail. I pulled back into the dubious safety of the doorway.

And that was when Cadal Righ emerged.

When he'd first appeared and flayed the Edinburgh Ascendant with a single breath, he'd looked pale enough to be barely alive. Now there was colour in his sunken cheeks but, if anything, the spots of red only gave him a creepier appearance. They matched the red of his eyes and made him even more of a monster in human form.

He was short, only about five feet tall, and he was still wearing the tattered Mages' cloak that he'd had on earlier. His light brown hair was as long and matted as any of the Afflicted, but he'd tied it off his face with a narrow tartan ribbon. I dreaded to think where – or rather from whom – he'd taken that.

Despite his lack of height and gruesome appearance, Cadal Righ exuded authority. Magic seemed to throb from him. The hordes of the Afflicted prostrated themselves on the ground at his feet as he swept through them. His proximity seemed to give them far more consciousness and control than they usually displayed.

I knew that I should turn tail and run but, for reasons that I couldn't explain, I felt compelled to stay and watch. Nevertheless, I drew further back into the shadows where I was less likely to be seen.

Cadal Righ marched on towards the fallen Mage. He stretched out his hands as he walked and occasionally brushed his fingertips across the bowed heads of the kneeling Afflicted, but he didn't slow down until he reached the Mage's crumpled body. He jerked his hands towards an Afflicted man, who beamed like a rabid dog and jumped towards the Mage to hold him up for Cadal Righ's inspection.

It was clear that the Mage was still breathing. He raised his head and his bloodshot eyes widened as he registered Cadal Righ standing in front of him. 'No,' he said. 'No. No, no, no, no, no, no.' The word became a ceaseless litany.

Cadal Righ smiled slightly and placed his thin, bony fingers on the Mage's forehead.

'No, no, no, no, no, no.'

'Wheesht now,' Cadal Righ murmured. 'All will be well.' He half-closed his eyes. 'This is inevitable. As long as magic exists in Scotland, I too shall exist. I am the king you deserve. I am the king you need.'

The Mage stopped his desperate chanting and his mouth opened wide in a silent scream. As Cadal Righ's fingers flickered with pale blue magic, I remained stock-still, unable to tear my eyes away. I didn't understand what was happening but I knew it wasn't good.

All the fight had gone out of the young Mage's expression. His eyes grew vacant and his body slumped. When Cadal Righ finally pulled away his hand, the Mage dropped to his knees and lowered his head until it touched the ground.

When I turned my gaze back to Cadal Righ, I saw that there was even more colour in his cheeks. I swallowed hard, then I finally turned and ran after the others.

THREE

My feet pounded down the hallway then slapped hard on the stone stairs as I sprinted up towards the battlements. While I ran I told myself I shouldn't feel sorry for that Mage. He was a Mage; even if he himself hadn't executed innocent men, women and children, or used magical violence and intimidation to get his own way, he was part of the group that had done so. He had given tacit approval. The Mages had subjugated Scotland. They ripped magic from female children. They took everything and gave nothing in return.

But Andy was a Mage, and Angus was a Mage. I wasn't so far gone that I wanted to see every Mage in Scotland suffer horribly. I'd never succeed against any of them if I couldn't retain the humanity that they had lost. And now Cadal Righ was on the scene, whoever the fuck he was, the Mages weren't the source of my greatest fear.

I shook my head and put on a spurt of speed until I reached the last flight of stairs and pushed through the door to the open battlements. With the exception of Laoch, every face turned towards me.

Most of them seemed relieved to see me. I tried not to feel a surge of childish satisfaction when Aspen looked disappointed; this was hardly the time for such vindictive behaviour. I failed. Even now, in the face of almost certain doom, it appeared I could still be petty. I flashed the sour-faced Mage a grim smile and hurried to join Angus.

'I told you to come back safe,' he snapped, his thin grey hair flying in several directions because of the strong wind.

'I am safe.' I patted his arm.

'You're the last to arrive – by quite some distance.'

'I'm still safe, Angus. It's all good.' As I leaned forward and looked down, my stomach flip-flopped. Half an hour ago this had seemed like a good idea but now I wasn't so sure. I gazed at the sickly green moss and the sharp pointed rocks below us while the cold wind shivered through me. 'That's a long drop.'

He grunted. '*Folis* is a handy spell.'

It was the first one I'd learned. 'Aye,' I said. 'It is.' I glanced around at the people huddling together for warmth and comfort. There didn't seem to be as many of them as before.

Angus seemed to know what I was thinking. 'It seemed wise not to wait,' he said. 'One of us has to display *some* dregs of intelligence, so it's lucky I possess enough for all of us.' He waggled his eyebrows and I realised he was attempting a weak joke to lighten our situation. Once he realised his humour had failed, he shrugged. 'We've already managed to lower at least half our number to ground level.'

When I squinted, I made out a small cluster of people sheltering by a ramshackle building not far from Princes Street. 'I told them to keep clear of the castle. We don't know what the Afflicted are going to do,' Angus said.

'That was wise indeed,' I said with a faint smile.

Angus didn't smile back. 'What did you see down there?'

Cadal Righ's grim features flashed into my mind. 'I'll tell you later.' I looked down again. 'Let's get out of here first.'

'Amen to that, lass.'

Without enough magic of my own to be of use, I could only watch while Angus, Andy, the other Mages and Laoch and Teasag used their powers to lower people down from the battlements. Aspen strode around the parapet barking useless orders – he had no more magic than I did, so we were both more of a hindrance than a help. Still, the others worked quickly and, despite the terror on the faces of the ordinary folk and the castle servants, they allowed themselves to be lowered magically to safety.

In less than ten minutes, only a few of us remained. Belle, who had been uncharacteristically quiet, sidled up to me. 'I'm no' a big fan of heights.'

She wouldn't be a big fan of becoming Afflicted either. I bit back my irritated response when I saw her expression. Belle used to terrorise me, as well as her husband and most of the other shop owners on our street. Now she was the one who looked terrorised. Her skin was almost as pale as Cadal Righ's and she was shaking.

'You've seen everyone else get down safely,' I said.

'Aye,' she whispered.

'It will be the same for you.'

She stared at me, wide-eyed. She shuffled her feet, opened her mouth and then closed it again.

'What is it?' I asked.

'Everyone else got down safely.'

'They did.'

'How do we know they've still got enough magic left to get me down? What if their power runs out when I'm hanging in mid-air?'

'It won't.'

'How do you ken?'

Actually, I didn't. I had no way of knowing how much magic had been expelled so far or how much was left. Laoch and Teasag had strong reserves and I suspected they'd be fine, but the Mages were another story.

I cast an eye across them; they were all showing signs of strain. *Folis* wasn't a difficult spell – that was the reason that it was the first one I'd learnt. But those Mages had been forced to use it over and over again in quick succession and that had to be draining. Angus looked as if he'd aged ten years in ten minutes, and Andy was sweating profusely. The other two Mages gave the impression that a strong gust of wind would knock them over.

'It'll be fine,' I reassured her. 'There's no reason to worry.'

Belle gave me a flat look. 'Edinburgh Castle is overrun by the Afflicted and their murderous master. Our only way out is to float down to the ground with the help of the Mages who were trying to kill you stone deid until a few hours ago. So fuck off, Mairi. I'm going to worry.' She had a point.

'Can you do it? Do you have enough juice inside you to bring us down?' She leaned into my ear. 'I dinna want to have to rely on some men to save my skin.'

I understood the sentiment. Half-closing my eyes, I delved deep inside myself. My powers were returning but in a trickle rather than a flood. There might be enough, though I couldn't be sure. 'Possibly,' I murmured.

There was a sudden guttural grunt from one of the young Mages and I saw with alarm that his knees were buckling. From the other side of the parapet, I heard a scream from the woman he'd been lowering. The Mage's eyes rolled back into head and he collapsed with a thud.

I yanked on all the power I had and rushed to the side to look down and save the woman he'd been helping. She was already in freefall. Before I could do anything to stop her body from smashing into the sharp rocks, Laoch muttered, '*Folis.*'

The woman's body jerked and, in the nick of time, she went from certain death to floating three feet above the ground. Her face screwed up and she started to sob as the enormity of what had just happened hit her.

Laoch focused on lowering her gently. She curled into a tight ball on the ground until one of the other survivors darted towards her and helped her to stand up and stagger down the slope to join the rest.

I watched her for a moment then my attention returned to Laoch. He was the only one who'd been able to react quickly enough to save her. He didn't look at me – thanks to Aspen's nasty command, he *couldn't* look at me – but I was certain that he was aware of my gaze.

He was staring forward, a muscle ticking in his jawline. His matt-black horns coiled tightly against his head as they always did, but his dark curling hair around them was mussed and he still looked unwell. There was a taut stiffness to his body that I'd never seen before.

I moved towards him before I even realised what I was doing. It was Belle, whose fear of heights hadn't diminished her capacity for self-preservation, who reached across and pulled me back.

Angus nodded approval at her action and sent me a warning glance from his fatigue-ridden eyes. 'Alright, woman,' he said to Belle. 'It's your turn to go over the edge. I'll need some help, though.' He gestured at Laoch and Teasag.

Aspen, who was frowning at the collapsed Mage as if he were disappointed by his magical exhaustion, jerked his head upwards. 'No. They need their strength to get the three of us down.' He indicated himself and the two Mages. 'You lot are on your own.'

Teasag started waving her hands frantically. At first I thought it was silent disapproval of Aspen's command but then I saw what she was looking at. A large group of ragged Afflicted men and women was heading directly for the cluster of people waiting for us below. From our vantage point, it was obvious that the Afflicted knew exactly where they were heading.

'You have to go and help them!' I hissed. 'Now!'

Angus reacted first. He grabbed hold of Belle and jumped off the parapet with her trembling body clasped to his own. '*Folis*,' he murmured. The young Mage who was still standing scooped up his fallen companion and did the same.

I rushed towards both daemons. I reached Teasag first and shoved her over the edge before Aspen could stop me. When I glanced down, she was floating in the air and staring back up at me with both surprise and approval. She quickly lowered herself and ran towards the group of cowering people.

I darted over to Laoch – but this time Aspen blocked my way. 'Not a chance, bitch. He's staying with me.'

'I've got you, Mairi,' Andy said boldly, his tone belying the exhaustion that lined his face. 'We'll go down together.'

Aspen leaned over the edge and glared down at Teasag. 'Two can play your game,' he snarled at me. Before I could stop him, he rushed at Andy and slammed his hands into his chest, pushing him over the edge of the parapet in the same way that I'd pushed Teasag.

Andy let out a strangled yell as he fell backwards. It was all he could do to mutter enough folis magic to save himself, but his eyes remained on mine as he descended.

Aspen chuckled, drawing back my attention. 'Fucked now, ain't you, girlie?' He grinned nastily and pointed at Laoch. 'He won't save you.' He pointed at himself. 'I won't save you. So have you recovered enough magic to get yourself down? I don't think I can do it without Nicholas's help, so I don't think you can either.'

He was such a wanker. I scowled, more from annoyance than anything else. That was when a flicker of movement caught my eye. Someone was emerging from the door that led onto the battlements.

Aspen's back was to the door and, from his self-congratulatory smirk, he was oblivious to the fact that we were no longer alone. But Laoch knew. He turned and his eyes widened when he saw who was approaching.

'You might make it out of here,' Aspen beamed. 'You might not. But think of your friends. They'll be better off without you.' He patted Laoch's shoulder. 'You've brought them nothing but trouble.'

'And what,' Cadal Righ enquired, 'is the problem with trouble?'

Aspen froze. In an instant his expression was wiped clean of smug satisfaction and replaced by fear. He turned slowly and his eyes met those of Cadal Righ's.

'Trouble is what makes us better,' the red-eyed bastard murmured. 'Trouble teaches us to strive, to fight, to rise up against that which holds us down.' He strolled towards Aspen, stopped in front of him and reached out to stroke his cheek gently with one long fingernail.

My nostrils flared. Cadal Righ reeked of rot and death; in fact, the strong stench emanating from his pores was incredibly similar to the nauseating smell in the Mages' death gardens.

Aspen shuddered. Laoch and I could only look on.

Cadal Righ's pale lips curved upwards. 'You're all but empty now,' he mused. 'But you have great innate power. You will be useful to me, as your friends have been.'

Aspen's hand shot out and his fingers curled around Laoch's

bicep. '*Belz fit*.' His body juddered and I let out a squeak. He was drawing on Laoch's own magic and taking it for himself.

Cadal Righ's eyes narrowed. '*Ins veil*.'

Laoch was thrown to one side. He sailed through the air and landed with a heavy thump several metres away. He groaned in pain and I flinched.

Cadal Righ, it appeared, was only getting started. 'I have no use for daemons,' he murmured to Aspen. 'It's you I want.'

Aspen's nostrils flared. 'Nicholas! Defend me!' His voice was quaking.

Despite his obvious pain, Laoch heaved himself up to his feet and hobbled towards Cadal Righ.

'Attack the bastard!' Aspen screeched.

And, while Laoch lunged for Cadal Righ, Aspen leapt backwards and fell from the battlements down to the rocks below.

Cadal Righ's muttered another incantation and swatted Laoch away as if he were nothing more than a pesky fly. Laoch tumbled backwards and his body collided with mine. As he crashed into me, his elbow slammed into my chest and then I too was falling, away from Cadal Righ and away from the only man I'd ever loved.

Harsh air spun past me as I fell. My stomach rose to my mouth, and the shock and cold caused tears to stream unbidden from my eyes. I was dimly aware of my arms and legs flailing desperately as the ground rushed up to meet me. There was no time to react; there was no time to do anything other than squeeze my eyes shut.

But then there was nothing.

I opened one eye, then another. I hadn't hit the ground and I wasn't dead; instead, I was suspended in the air as tendrils of someone's magic spun around me and lowered me to safety.

I let out a choked cry. I didn't want to be here. I didn't want to be safe – not while Laoch remained above me with only the murderous form of Cadal Righ for company. 'No,' I whispered. 'No.'

'I've got you, Mairi!' Andy said. 'It's okay, I've got you!' His hands reached for me, helping me to plant my feet on the ground and remain upright. I didn't look at him. I could only crane my neck upwards. I couldn't see Laoch anywhere, only Cadal Righ's sunken features staring down.

The air trembled with more magic and I saw a bolt of blue lightning fly after the fleeing figure of Aspen. He twisted left and narrowly avoided it. Even from down here, with the whistling wind in my ears, I heard Cadal Righ's frustrated curse.

The air trembled again and Andy gave a strangled squawk. His hand let go of me as he collapsed from the force of Cadal Righ's second spell which had bolted straight for him.

Shite. *Shite.*

I wasted no more time. I reached for Andy, his unconscious form a dead weight in my arms as I gathered him up and hung his limp body over my shoulder. Then I ran down the same narrow path that Aspen had taken, zigzagging to avoid further magic attacks. None came.

I panted and heaved and did everything I could to get away. Only when I was sure that Cadal Righ wouldn't try another attack did I pause long enough to send a single message. *I love you, Laoch. I will come for you.*

CHAPTER

FOUR

There wasn't time to catch my breath. As soon as I reached the group of frightened people, two of them rushed towards me to take Andy's heavy, motionless body and relieve me of his weight. Angus and the sole Mage who remained conscious leaned towards each other and chanted the same words, their twin voices becoming one.

Belle snatched at me, pulling me towards the road. I stumbled with her while behind us the stone building where everyone had been cowering collapsed, creating a barrier between us and the approaching Afflicted.

Aspen, who had already taken up position at the front of the group, curled his lip. 'That won't last long. They'll smash through your pathetic attempt at a blockade in minutes.'

I could no longer help myself. I ran at him, my fists curled, swung a punch then kicked. He raised his hands to defend himself before headbutting me. We both fell backwards. I felt the warm dribble of blood sneak down from my forehead but I ignored both it and the throb of pain.

I scrambled up to attack Aspen again. 'You took Laoch's magic! You left him defenceless and abandoned him up there!'

This time, before my fists could connect with Aspen's face, the young Mage reached for me and pulled me back.

'Listen, bitch,' he hissed. 'I know you've got problems. We've all got problems. But this is not the time. We need to work together to get away from here. These people need us.' He waved his hand at the white-faced, wide-eyed group. 'And when your powers return properly, they'll need you too.'

I hawked up a ball of phlegm and prepared to spit in his face, then my shoulders slumped and I swallowed it back. He was right. A fucking Mage was right. Another tear rolled down my cheek as I shook him off. 'Fine,' I snapped. 'He'll keep. But I won't forget.'

A nasty bruise was already forming on Aspen's forehead but it didn't prevent him from smiling coldly. 'The daemon,' he said slowly. 'It's not merely that you're allied together. You care for him.' He tilted his head. 'Do you *love* him?'

There was an enough of a sneer to his voice that I almost threw caution to the wind and went for him again. Instead, I wrapped my arms around my body and looked away. 'I already know that love is an emotion you could never understand,' I said.

Aspen snorted. 'Love makes you weak. As you have just proved.'

The young Mage opened his mouth again but Angus stepped up instead. 'It's alright, Marcus, I've got this.' He looked at Aspen. 'Speak again and I will kill you, regardless of the circumstances and regardless of the consequences.'

'Go on then, old man. I'd like to see you try,' Aspen scoffed.

Belle pulled back her shoulders and marched between us. 'Enough!' she roared. 'Andy is half-dead. That other Mage is half-dead. The rest of us are on the verge of being attacked yet again by the Afflicted. All of youse need to shut the fuck up. We have tae get out of here!'

Nobody said anything as she glared at us. 'Tha's more like it! Now, come on!' She marched off, away from the castle and towards Princes Street. The others glanced at Aspen and at me, then took off after her. And they were right; Belle was making the only sensible move. A second later, the rest of us joined them.

~

Everyone was tired and everyone was struggling; it was likely little more than adrenaline that was keeping us moving after all that had happened at the castle. We managed to maintain a steady but agonising jog until we reached Princes Street and turned left, away from whatever dangers lay behind us.

Soon more people joined us, ducking out from their hiding places in the fervent belief that there might be safety in numbers. The Afflicted weren't only at Edinburgh Castle; they were charging through the empty streets in small groups. The only saving grace was that they all seemed to be pulled towards the castle and Cadal Righ, so when we moved quickly enough we could get out of their path and avoid them. The larger our group grew, however, the harder that would become – and it didn't help that the first streaks of sunset were appearing in the sky. We all knew by now that daylight was no longer an obstacle for the Afflicted but that didn't mean we wanted to be caught out here in the dark.

We didn't have a destination in mind; we were running aimlessly away from the castle to put as much distance between ourselves and Cadal Righ and his disease-ridden allies as possible. That wasn't a plan and it only solved our immediate problems.

I did my best not to think of Laoch and what might be happening to him. Imagination could be a terrible, soul-sapping thing. I couldn't help him right now, but I could do something to help our growing brigade of desperate survivors. I sucked my bottom lip and put on an extra spurt of speed to reach the front of the group.

Belle was still in front, her shoulders back, her head held high and her gaze zipping from side to side as the shadows lengthened and she checked for impending danger. She didn't glance at me when I reached her side, but she did stretch out for a brief moment and grab my hand. She squeezed it tightly before quickly letting go as if she were afraid someone would notice.

'Neither of us know this city,' I said quietly. 'We don't know where to go. We don't know what we're doing and it's getting dark.'

She grunted. 'I'm well fucking aware o' that, Mairi.'

'We need to stop, allow everyone to rest and re-group. We need to come up with a plan. We can't continue like this.'

She waved a hand at the towering buildings and narrow streets. 'An' where do you suggest we go? Hmm? We're surrounded by city. If we stop anywhere here, we'll be sitting ducks. We'll nae even make it tae sunrise.'

'I know a place,' a voice said.

I twisted in surprise. Belle continued to scan the street ahead but her brow creased as she silently acknowledged the young Mage. He was carrying his unconscious friend on his back, but that didn't seem to stop him from moving quickly. I gave him a wary nod. 'Where?'

'There's a cemetery not far from here. It's surrounded by high walls on three sides so we won't be taken unawares, but staying outside will prevent us from getting trapped. It's a good spot. It'll be quiet and as safe as anywhere else, at least for a few hours.'

'A cemetery? You want us to hang out wi' the deid?' Belle's

voice was rising. 'As if we dinna have enough problems already?'

'The dead won't try and kill us,' I pointed out. 'Or eat us.'

'Aye.' Her voice took on a sarcastic edge. 'An' there'll be plenty of handy graves for us to bury our own deid when the Afflicted come for us again.'

'It's as good a place as any,' the young Mage insisted.

'What reason do we have to trust you?'

His response was immediate. 'Because I don't want to die any more than you do.'

For a moment neither Belle nor I said anything. 'What's your name?' I asked finally. 'Marcus?' He nodded. 'And him?' I nodded towards the slumped body on his back.

'Arthur.' He shot me a baleful look. 'And our friend who died back at the castle was Kenneth.'

I wasn't convinced Kenneth was dead, though I didn't say so. He might as well be dead at this point. I could only pray the same wasn't true of Laoch. 'What about Lord Aspen? He's your superior. Shouldn't you wait for him to make decisions about where to go?'

Marcus stared at me. 'The cemetery is the best option.'

'Belle?' I asked.

'Aye.' She sniffed. 'Alright then.' And with that, it was decided.

We let Marcus take the lead. I wasn't convinced of the merits of allowing a Mage to herd us through the streets of Edinburgh but he knew the way and, at least on the surface, he appeared more sensible and less self-centred than Aspen.

If Aspen realised what was happening, he didn't show it. Whenever I glanced back to check on him, he was trotting alongside Teasag and murmuring to any of the people close to him who would listen. I didn't know whether it was poison or merely complaint that he was pouring into their ears, but

Angus had positioned himself beside Aspen and was listening to every word. For all his ornery posturing, I trusted Angus. That had to count for something.

Once the sun dipped behind the buildings and the sky really started to darken, fewer people sneaked out of their homes and workplaces to join us. There were probably a good number of Edinburgh folk who had no clue yet about what had happened. I envied their ignorance, temporary though it would be.

The darker it became, the more anxious everyone became. We were forced to veer away several times to avoid incoming clusters of the Afflicted so our journey took far longer than it should have done.

I was starting to think that Marcus had invented this supposed cemetery of temporary sanctuary or was deliberately leading us on a wild-goose chase, when he suddenly raised his arm and pointed. 'There,' he said. 'It's right there.'

Peering through the gloom, I finally spotted large wrought-iron gates and high stone walls. The cemetery was larger than I'd expected and looked to be as good a spot as any to rest up. I exhaled a long breath of air. I was exhausted and emotional and that wouldn't help me if I suddenly had to produce any magic. But the well of power inside me was filling up and finally returning, and I was in as healthy a state as anyone else.

I motioned to Marcus and Belle to stop and hold back the rest of our large group, then stepped forward to check that the cemetery was safe for us to enter.

As soon as I walked through the gates, I felt the subtle shift in atmosphere. It was wholly unexpected and, whether the traumatic emotions of the day had finally caught up to me or it was something to do with the place itself, my eyes pricked with tears. At the City Chambers in Glasgow and in Edinburgh Castle, the Mages took the corpses they robbed of magic and buried them in their indoor gardens. Those gardens looked beautiful but contained a rotten heart; by contrast, this cemetery was a place of absolute peace. It really did feel like somewhere we could rest.

'Well,' Aspen drawled from behind me, 'isn't that just like a woman to cry? Tears won't help us, you know.' He snorted. 'You really are the weaker sex.'

I knew he was baiting me and at any other time I might have risen to his taunts. Instead I walked away from him and examined each corner of the cemetery until I was satisfied the place was free of lurking Afflicted or other hidden dangers.

By the time I reached the far corner and was checking the last spot behind a grandiose vault that seemed to house several generations of the same family, Aspen was calling to the others. 'You can come in now. I've made sure it's safe for you all.'

Eejit.

I walked back down the path as streams of people entered. Marcus lay his friend, Arthur, gently down on top of a grassy mound and began checking him over. Two women and a man who had been carrying Andy, did the same to him. I strode over and knelt down by his side.

'He's breathing,' one of the women said. 'But he's affy peelywally.'

I placed my hand against Andy's forehead. His skin was warm but not worryingly so; with sleep, he'd likely recover. All the same, I stood up and headed for some of the graves where I'd spotted errant nettles and struggling echinacea. We couldn't risk a fire, but if I could find a way of warming some water and steeping the plants for several minutes, the concoction might help Andy's recovery. There would probably be enough left over to help Arthur as well, together with anyone else who needed medicinal sustenance.

'I'm going to require some decent rest if I'm to protect you all from what's to come,' Aspen declared loudly. He gestured imperiously at a group of young men, some of whom were wearing the livery of the castle guards. 'You lot will keep watch. Position yourselves around the walls and keep an eye out for anyone approaching. If I find that any of you fall asleep, I'll have your left eye removed as punishment.'

His threat was too specific to not be genuine and I stared at him in disbelief.

'It's cold,' Aspen continued, 'and I need something warm to wear. So do the other Mages.' He waved a hand and I realised that we'd been joined by half a dozen of the black-cloaked bastards during our journey, as well as Marcus and Arthur. 'Those of you who are wearing warm coats, good jumpers or have quality boots on your feet need to hand them over now.'

No matter what was going on out there on the streets of Edinburgh or at the castle, the people here were still afraid of the Mages. Several of them immediately started to shrug out of their coats or look down questioningly at their feet.

'Stop that!' My voice was louder than I'd intended and shocked even me. Angus sent me a warning glance, not because I was gainsaying Aspen's command but because we needed to avoid drawing attention our way. There were Afflicted people out there.

I cleared my throat and spoke at a normal level. 'Nobody is to hand over their own clothing or food unless they choose to do so willingly. Nobody has to hand over anything to a Mage. They have magic and they are perfectly capable of warming themselves without your help. And we will use volunteers to keep watch at staggered intervals. This is a democracy.'

Aspen maintained a genial tone; he even half-smiled. 'A democracy will get these people killed. Someone has to provide proper leadership. Mages have both the power and the experience. And, as the most senior Mage, I am leader by default.'

'I can't believe that in the face of certain doom and the annihilation of this city, you people are having a stramash aboot who gets to be in charge,' Belle muttered. 'Screw the lot o' youse. I'm off to get some shut eye.' She whirled around, plonked herself down against a slightly askew gravestone and closed her eyes.

'We'll keep watch,' said one of the guardsmen. He looked at me and then Aspen. 'Because we choose to do so.'

I sighed. Fine. Aspen smiled smugly. Then my gaze landed on Teasag, who was standing beside him with her arms crossed over her chest and her expression stony. 'You promised to release the daemons from your enslavement once we were free from the castle,' I said. 'Let her go.'

'All in good time.'

I stood my ground. 'Is a Mage's word not trustworthy anymore?' I asked loudly. 'Because if we can't trust anything you say then—'

Aspen interrupted me. 'I'm far more trustworthy than any woman could be.' Even the guardsmen rolled their eyes at that.

'I tell you what,' he continued. 'I'll free one of them to prove to you that I am a man of my word.' He smirked. 'Far be it for me to stand in the way of true love. Nicholas, you are free. Dead. But free.' He glanced at me. 'Happy now?' He laughed to himself.

Laoch wasn't dead. I refused to believe that, and I wouldn't give Aspen the satisfaction of seeing how much his gibe stabbed at me. 'You promised to free both of them.'

'One will have to do for now.' He sniffed.

Teasag's expression betrayed nothing.

Killing the Glaswegian Ascendant had freed Laoch. Killing Aspen would free Teasag – and it would solve a number of my immediate problems. I stepped up to Aspen, eyed him up and down and considered it.

He knew exactly what I was thinking. He raised his hands

and displayed the blue flickers of magic around his fingers. 'I'm feeling quite recovered,' he said. 'I'm almost back to full capacity and I rather suspect these good people might have need of my magic in the near future. They'll likely need yours too.' He pursed his lips. 'Such as it is.'

He nudged Teasag. 'They'll need hers as well. If I release her, she'll vanish back to her homeland and we'll be another warrior down. We can't afford that, not now. I'll release her when we're completely safe.'

He wasn't ever going to release her and we all knew it. And he was right, bastard that he was: we did need his powers.

We were at an impasse but I wasn't done negotiating yet. 'In that case,' I said, 'you must allow her to use her voice again so that she can warn us of approaching danger. And you need to allow her freedom of movement so she can offer help to whoever needs it.'

Aspen's eyes narrowed but he gave an expansive shrug. 'Very well. I am, after all, a kind master.' He turned to Teasag and murmured the appropriate words.

It would do for now. I met her eyes, hoping that she understood I would ensure her freedom before long. Teasag simply turned away and gazed towards the castle, which was shrouded in darkness. I knew what she was thinking; I was thinking it too.

'Get some sleep, lass,' Angus said to me quietly. 'If you rest, the others will too. We will need our energy tomorrow.'

I looked up at the castle. *Laoch? Are you there?*

Of course there was no response. Even if he were conscious, we were too far away to communicate telepathically. I sighed and then I nodded at Angus.

CHAPTER
FIVE

There were close to two hundred of us in the cemetery that night, but I was reasonably certain that the only two people who slept well were Angus and Belle. They were certainly attempting to outdo each other in the snoring stakes.

I got up several times to make my herbal drink for Andy and Arthur, as well as to check on the guards and look up at the darkened outline of the castle. I must have fallen asleep at some point, however, because by the time dawn arrived and I opened my eyes, there was a painful crick in my neck.

An enormous black-eyed raven was perched atop the statue of a weeping angel opposite me. Old fears getting the better of me, I bolted upright. The raven tilted its head and cawed softly then started to preen its feathers. I watched its every move.

Aspen groaned and also sat up. The bird flapped over to him, landed on his shoulder and dipped its beak to his ear. He stroked its head and murmured something. The bird took off and soared into the lightening sky. Aspen stood up, dusted himself down and opened his mouth to speak.

I wasn't the only one watching him. Almost everyone else

was awake and looking at him. I didn't need to check their expressions to know that they were filled with hope. Most of them wanted to hear him say that the Mages were on their way to save us.

'Good people,' he intoned in a manner that made my eyes roll, 'you are fortunate that I am here. I have only now been able to confirm that, despite the horrific events that have occurred in Edinburgh during the last twenty-four hours, Glasgow remains safe. We will depart on foot. Once we reach the city limits, we will be joined by a flock of ravens who will alert us to any trouble and keep us safe during our journey. The Glasgow Mages are already preparing for our appearance. We will regroup there, then make plans to regain Edinburgh. This time next week, all this will be little more than a bad memory.'

I hadn't pegged Aspen as an optimist. I wondered if he believed his own words.

'With this many people,' a low voice said next to me, 'and the others that will join us as we flee, it will take two days to reach Glasgow on foot. That's another night out in the open. It will be risky, and we can't assume that Cadal Righ will remain here in Edinburgh. He said he wanted Scotland. All of it. That doesn't bode well.'

I turned to Andy and examined his pale face and drawn features. 'How are you feeling?' I asked. 'Are you alright?'

He rubbed a hand across his forehead. 'I feel like I've been hit by a shire horse,' he admitted. 'But on the whole, I'm not too bad.' He grimaced. 'I don't think Cadal Righ was trying to kill me.'

'He needs you alive in order to take your magic from you.'

Andy started. 'Take my magic?'

I nodded. 'I think that's what he's doing.' I described what I had witnessed with Kenneth. 'When my magic was taken before the last round of the Ascendancy Challenge, it was only a temporary thing. With Cadal Righ, I don't believe it is temporary. I think he takes away magic then turns his victims into the Afflicted.' I gave Andy a long look. 'A lot of Mages were left inside that castle. A lot of them didn't get out.'

'You mean Cadal Righ could already be a hundred times stronger today than he was yesterday?'

My mouth flattened into a grim line. 'Pretty much.' I tilted my head from side to side to stretch my neck. That was when I realised Aspen was glaring at me.

'You disagree, woman? You think we should stay here and fight? Because these people will die if that happens. I hold their lives in far greater regard. We need to help them now and fight back later.'

He truly was skilled in the art of propaganda. I'd only found my voice a few weeks ago and I hadn't progressed to lying convincingly. I sincerely hoped I never would.

I knew beyond a shadow of a doubt that Lord Arsehole Aspen would sacrifice every single one of these people if it meant that he would survive. If he couldn't do a deal with Cadal Righ, he'd eventually fight him – but he would do it when he had an army of Mages at his back. Even then, I suspected he'd lose. We all would.

I met his eyes, aware that everyone was watching me. 'I don't disagree at all. Anyone who remains in Edinburgh is taking their life into their hands. Glasgow is the nearest city so it makes sense to head there and regroup. There are old libraries, including the remains of the one in the City Chambers, that might shed some light on Cadal Righ. We need to know who we're fighting and how he's managed to command the Afflicted. We have to know our enemy.' There. I'd said it: *our* enemy. We were in this together whether I liked it or not.

'I am glad I've finally managed to persuade you to see sense,' Aspen said, as if this had been a long drawn-out argument. He looked around. 'Gather up your belongings. We leave in five minutes.'

Angus sidled up to me with Belle in tow. 'You're giving him a lot of power by letting him take charge, lass.'

'Heading to Glasgow is the right move.'

Belle sniffed. 'Aye, it is. Twister will be worried about me.'

I turned and looked at the castle silhouetted against the morning sun. If I squinted, I could see tiny shapes moving on top of the battlements. No doubt they were Afflicted souls. 'Aspen isn't our biggest worry,' I said. My fingers twisted together.

'Laoch is strong and he's a survivor. He can look after himself,' Angus said.

Not against thousands of Afflicted and Cadal Righ he couldn't. 'I'm not going to Glasgow,' I stated quietly. 'Not yet.'

Teasag, who'd been leaning against an elaborate stone monument, pushed herself away from it and joined us. 'You're going back to the castle.' It wasn't a question.

I hadn't thought it was possible for Andy to turn any paler but he did.

Belle and Angus stared at me with horror. 'The daemon is gone.' Belle's voice was flat. 'He's already deid. You cannae risk yourself for him.'

'I'm not risking myself for him,' I said. I pulled a face. 'Alright, I am. But that's not the only reason I'm going back to the castle.' I turned away from Angus and Andy and focused on Belle and Teasag. 'Do you think being ruled by Cadal Righ will be better than being ruled by the Mages?'

Belle's eyes dropped. 'I didna think it was possible for anyone to be worse than those bastards, but Cadal Righ might be.'

Teasag didn't reply. I raised my eyebrows and she gave a minute shake of her head.

'You're not going to ask our opinion?' Angus enquired.

'You're both Mages,' I said.

'I'm a traitor. So is he now.' He pointed at Andy. 'We're not Mages any longer. Not in the traditional sense.'

I ran my tongue around my teeth. 'Let me phrase it in a different way for you two. Would you rather be ruled by Aspen or by Cadal Righ?'

Andy's bottom lip jutted out. 'Aspen,' he whispered.

Angus looked reluctant but he nodded. 'Aye. As far as I can tell, Cadal Righ's plan is to Afflict every soul in Scotland.'

I gazed at them all meaningfully. 'We have to stop him. What I said to Aspen was correct – we have to know our enemy. I have a theory I want to test, so I have to go back to the castle.'

'Whit theory?' Belle asked.

'I'll let you know once I've proved it,' I said with a faint smile.

'If you go back to that castle, you will die,' Angus cautioned.

I shook my head. 'I'm pretty canny. I can do it.' I looked at Andy. 'The books you found that mentioned Cadal Righ. Where are they?'

He swallowed. 'In my room. There were a few more in the Arcane section of the library that I was planning to investigate.'

Good. 'Tell me what they are and where to find them.'

'I'll come with you. I'll show you where they are.'

'No, you can't come. I have to do this alone.' My tone brooked no argument. I forced my smile to widen. 'I survived most of the Ascendancy Challenge unscathed. I'll survive this.' And if there was anything at all left of Laoch, I'd help him to survive, too.

'You're making a mistake, lass,' Angus growled.

I straightened my shoulders. 'Probably not the last in a long line of many.'

IT TOOK LONGER than we expected to get two hundred people ready to leave. Aspen's irritation grew by the second, and I would have found it humorous if the situation hadn't been so dire. Then, before he could direct the sorry parade out, there was a strange sound from beyond the cemetery walls.

At first I couldn't work out what it was; it sounded like a muted rush of water or an unnatural wind gusting through the streets. It was Teasag who pushed her way out of the cemetery gates first to see what it was. I watched her face. She didn't look afraid but she did look sad. A moment later, I understood why.

The sound was coming from thousands upon thousands of people. None of them were speaking, none were whispering; the noise came from their shuffling feet as they made their hunched way past the cemetery. Some held children in their arms, some were coated in dried blood. Plenty of them were carrying bags, no doubt containing their most precious processions. They hadn't spent the night sleeping in a cold cemetery but they all knew they had to leave Edinburgh.

Aspen had said that Glasgow was ready to take in the people of Edinburgh. I doubted they were this ready.

I grabbed hold of one man who seemed more animated than many of the others. 'You're leaving the city?'

'Aye. We're going to Glasgow. The Afflicted are everywhere. I saw three of my neighbours turn in front of my own eyes. We have to get out of here. It seems they've quietened down now, but they'll be back. They'll come for us all if we stay here.' He nodded at me. 'You should leave too.' He glanced past me. 'Are there Mages there with you?'

'A few.'

'I never thought I'd say I was pleased to see a Mage, but I am now. Those black-cloaked wankers are all we've got.' He nodded again and moved away, obviously keen to get on his way.

Teasag looked at me over the heads of several other people. 'He won't stop at Edinburgh.'

I didn't need to ask who she was referring to. 'No, he won't.'

She pursed her lips then said, 'I love Laoch too, but stopping Cadal Righ is more important. Anyone who can command the Afflicted is already a monster of their own making. Laoch isn't more important than an entire country. None of us are.'

I knew she was right, I just didn't want to admit it. 'Take care of yourself, Teasag.'

'I will try, Mairi. Good luck to you.' She turned away to help an old man with his bags.

Marcus passed me with his friend next to him. Like Andy, Arthur had recovered enough to walk on his own, so that was something. Neither of them said anything but they both inclined their heads. A lot of the others did too, although a few people averted their eyes.

I waited till most of them had left the cemetery and joined the flood of departing refugees, then hugged Angus, Belle and Andy and murmured my goodbyes. Once they'd taken their places among the fleeing thousands, only one person remained.

I eyed Aspen. Until now, I hadn't appreciated how dishevelled he looked. He wasn't the impeccably dressed, stern Mage any more. A streak of dirt ran down his cheek, his hair was matted on one side and his cloak had several rips down it. 'I thought you'd already gone,' I said.

'Upon reflection, it seemed wise not to lead the way,' he replied. 'I have no wish to draw attention to myself if Cadal Righ comes after us.' That was probably the most honest thing he had ever said to me.

I shrugged and turned to go.

'You're going back, aren't you?' he asked.

I didn't look at him. 'Aye.'

'You're a stupid bitch. You don't have the power to beat the likes of him on your own.'

I already knew that. 'My reasons are my own.'

'The daemon is already dead.'

I paused a moment longer but I didn't say anything. Then I slipped out of the cemetery gates and started walking in the opposite direction to everyone else.

CHAPTER

SIX

It wasn't an easy return journey. I had to battle against the tide of escaping people and ignore all those who didn't recognise me and who urged me repeatedly to join them and flee. The occasional person who recognised me didn't help either. 'The saviour! The saviour of Glasgow will rescue us!'

Not today, not on my own. The hope in those voices made me feel less confident, not more. Most of these people were escaping the Afflicted; they hadn't yet realised that there was someone like Cadal Righ at their helm. They'd learn soon enough.

It was a good hour before the crowds thinned out and eventually disappeared. Anyone from the centre of Edinburgh who'd been planning to leave was already on their way. I knew that plenty of people would be determined to remain but, given that the emptier streets allowed me to see more of the destruction from yesterday, I doubted that was a wise decision.

There was more blood than I'd noticed during the previous night's escape, and there were more dead bodies lining the streets. I found myself picking through smashed glass, fallen bricks and scattered belongings far more often than I liked. I only saw a few Afflicted people, however; they were focusing on reaching the castle. They'd only attack me if I stood in their way.

Although I had a plan for once I was inside Edinburgh Castle, I hadn't given much thought to how I would gain entry. Magic was the obvious choice, especially now I was almost back at full strength, but if the Mages could sense magic then Cadal Righ would certainly be able to do the same. There had to be a smarter way to get inside.

When I spotted a group of snuffling, grunting Afflicted coming up the street behind me, I knew what I could do – even if I wasn't sure it would work.

I saw a house with its front door hanging open and I darted inside. I paid no attention to the chaos of strewn dishes and smashed glass; instead I grabbed the first clothes I saw that were lying in a clump at the foot of the stairs.

Snatching them up, I went towards the back. Good: there was a garden and at this time of year it would contain few plants and a lot of mud. I shook out the blouse and selected a long skirt, then ripped the fabric along several of the seams. In the garden I rubbed the clothes in a pile of dirt, shrugged out of my own clothing and substituted it with the now damp, smelly and very dirty attire.

My skin crawled, not because of the state of the clothes but because I'd stolen them from some poor soul who had lived here and was quite possibly already dead or Afflicted. I couldn't waste time on my emotions, however. I grabbed more handfuls of dirt and rubbed it into my cheeks and hair before hunching my shoulders and hastily leaving the house without a backward glance.

My disguise wouldn't pass muster if I were up close to any of the Afflicted, and it was possible that I'd end up infected if I touched them or spent too much time in their company, but it was a risk worth taking. I hoped that from a distance I resembled them enough to sneak by. The rotting mud smelled so bad that my scent wouldn't give me away and I looked grubby enough. It was the best I could do for now.

The large group of Afflicted who had been behind me were now ahead, following the road towards Princes Street before it curved up to the castle. Copying their shuffling gait, I fell in behind them, taking care to leave a decent distance between us. A few of them looked around, some deeper instinct telling them that they were being followed, but I tried not to react. When their mad eyes slid over me and they turned away again, I exhaled. This might actually work.

It was harder than I'd expected to maintain a slumped posture and limping stumble. By the time I started up the hill, my back was aching and I longed to stretch out my limbs, but I kept up the façade. Appearing Afflicted was more important than my discomfort. I had to get inside that damned castle, and not just for Laoch's sake. I had to test my theory. If I were right, it could prove vital.

I limped upwards, doing everything I could not to appear alert. I kept my head down and avoided scanning the castle rooftops for any indication of what was happening inside. I'd find out soon enough. My stomach churned with anxiety but I plodded on. I didn't look at the bloodstains at my feet or the odd dismembered limb or sightless corpse. My focus had to be on saving the living; mourning the dead could wait.

The grunting mutters of the Afflicted in front of me rose in intensity. They were becoming more and more excited as they reached the castle's main gate. I added my own occasional snuffles and moans, regardless of how alien the sounds were to me.

When the road finally curved around to the worn stone steps leading up to the Royal Mile and the castle itself, I bit back a gasp. There were Afflicted people everywhere and suddenly I was questioning my plan. It would be a damned miracle if I made it out of here without becoming infected.

I slowed my steps and waited for a gap in the crowds so I could move forward without veering too close to any Afflicted souls. As soon as I saw my chance, I sped up the steps until the castle's gate was in sight. I held my breath, as if avoiding inhaling the same air could keep me safe from Affliction, and hurried beneath the stone arch into the castle.

It was less than a day since I'd left the place but a great deal had already changed. In the first main courtyard, there were still the remnants of the Ascendancy Challenge where Mage had been pitted against Mage in a magic-less fight to determine who was the strongest and who should lead Glasgow. Timber was strewn around the cobbles, doubtless from the stands that had housed the audience members. The roped-off arena had vanished and in its place were groups of motionless Afflicted men and women.

At first I wondered if they were dead but when I saw their chests falling and rising, I realised they were merely sleeping. The fact that they were resting outside in broad daylight was a testament to how much things had changed. They weren't even trying to shield themselves from the sun's rays.

I picked my way through the bodies, neither moving quickly nor pausing. My feet faltered when I saw several familiar faces amongst the slumbering Afflicted. How many people had been infected during the last twelve hours? Maybe we all were truly doomed.

A group of whooping Afflicted men ran past me deeper into the castle. Moving slowly, I shook off my fear and followed them. They skipped and lurched towards the open space where Mage Kenneth had been attacked, although there was no sign of him now.

I looked around. A large ornate chair had been dragged out, probably from one of the grander reception rooms, and placed in the centre of the courtyard. It lay empty for now, so there was no telling where Cadal Righ was. I averted my gaze from the blood trickling down its green-leather upholstery and glanced at a small leather-bound book sitting precariously on one of the arms. Hmm.

There were too many Afflicted close by and it would look suspicious if I darted forward and scooped up the book, but I felt certain it was important. This had to be Cadal Righ's chair and that meant it was probably Cadal Righ's book.

I shook my head. Laoch first, everything else later. I turned away and edged to my left. I would start at the topmost battlements where I'd last seen Laoch. It made the most sense.

There were far more of the Afflicted outside than inside the castle. Once I walked into the building towards the staircase that led upwards, I felt I could breathe properly again. The air was foul but it smelled sweeter than any Afflicted person ever could.

Less concerned now that I'd be noticed, I started to jog. I climbed the staircase, nauseous with dread and hope. My heart rate quickened and I could hear the rush of blood in my ears.

I'm coming, Laoch. I'm coming.

Eleven steps. Ten. Nine. Unable to stop myself, I bounded up the rest three at a time, burst through the doorway and onto the battlement. My gaze immediately snapped to where I'd last seen Laoch after Cadal Righ had blasted him with magic.

He wasn't there. Nobody was there.

A tiny moan escaped my mouth. It had been too much to expect that he'd still be there but that didn't alleviate my disappointment. My body trembled and my legs quaked as if they were about to give way. No. I clenched my jaw and steadied myself. I couldn't be weak. Laoch's absence here didn't mean that he was dead; I wouldn't believe that until I saw his corpse with my own eyes. Besides, I had other tasks to fulfil. An entire country needed help.

I scanned the empty battlements, making absolutely sure that nobody was here, then I turned on my heel and headed back down, checking every room as I went. There was always a chance that Laoch had sneaked inside one of them to hide and heal. But, other than more dozing Afflicted bodies, there was nobody to be seen.

From the destruction in the rooms, it was clear that we'd made the right decision to leave the castle when we did. Every room had been ransacked in the intervening hours and we wouldn't have survived if we'd remained. The only saving grace was that the rampage had come to a natural end; other than those Afflicted people who were arriving through the castle gates, this was the satiated, calm aftermath.

I decided to pick my way through the rest of the castle and take advantage of the relative peace to search as many buildings and rooms as I could. I recalled what Andy had told me: the Mages' quarters and his room were in another building towards the western edge of the castle walls. I'd go there first and find the books that referenced Cadal Righ. With any luck, I'd find Laoch along the way.

I was halfway down the winding staircase when I heard a thump followed by the sound of running feet. I froze immediately. The sounds had come from below, somewhere along the narrow first-floor corridor. I tilted my head and listened. There was a guttural shriek of joy, followed by the sound of banging that did nothing to decrease my tension. I hissed under my breath and headed for the source of the noise.

As soon as I reached the landing and glanced to my right, I saw an Afflicted woman. She wasn't newly infected; her clothes were hanging in rags and she had clearly been Afflicted for some time. She was also on the trail of something – or someone. She was thumping repeatedly on a closed door, attempting to get into the room. That could only mean somebody was hiding in there, but it had been empty when I'd checked it minutes earlier.

There were still people inside this castle who were not infected. Or dead. There were still people who needed help, so I didn't spend time thinking about it. I marched towards the woman. She was so intent on her quarry that she didn't notice my approach until I was only a few metres from her. Then she paused, her pockmarked face swinging slowly in my direction.

At first, my disguise seemed to fool her but her gaze was too direct for it to mislead her for long. A second later, her reddened eyes widened as she recognised me for what I was. Her thin mouth with its cracked lips spread into a wide smile, revealing yellowing, decaying teeth. Before I could do anything, she sprang towards me.

I couldn't allow myself to use magic yet, not unless I absolutely had to, and I couldn't risk drawing the attention of other Afflicted people who might be sleeping in nearby rooms. If they awakened and came after me, I'd be screwed.

I exhaled a rush of fearful air, then I turned and ran.

The woman came after me. I heard her heaving breaths and her thundering footsteps as I sprinted back to the staircase and darted up it once again. I knew the battlements were empty. They were the only place I could go, though I dare not move too quickly. If I put too much distance between me and the woman, she might wake her friends to help; if she thought she could have me all to herself, maybe she'd work alone.

I held back until I felt her hands and her claw-like fingernails snatch at my grubby blouse, then I pulled away again.

It only took seconds to return to the chill air of the battlements though it felt far longer. I escaped through the doorway and ran to the spot where Laoch had fallen. As soon as I reached it, I spun and watched the woman lunge for me, her expression a mask of rage and hunger.

I leapt away in the heartbeat before she grabbed me. She howled in frustration but at least the wind whipped away the sound. I backtracked, keeping her in view until she attacked me again. Again, I dodged her long-armed reach but this time I didn't dart away. I twisted, moving quickly until I was directly behind her.

Without allowing myself to think about what I was doing, I grabbed a hank of her hair with one hand and the back of her head with the other, then smashed her forehead down onto the stone at our feet. She gurgled and went limp.

I breathed out. That had been easier than I'd expected. But battling one of the Afflicted was different to battling thousands of them.

Fighting my natural revulsion, I knelt down to press my fingers against her skin and check for a pulse. It was there; she was still breathing.

'Is she deid?'

I started and whipped around. A young girl was standing in the doorway less than ten metres from me and the fallen woman. My jaw dropped.

'I said,' the girl repeated with considerable impatience, 'is she deid?'

I blinked and recovered. 'No. She'll be alright.'

The girl scowled. 'Put her over the edge. She'll fall down onto the rocks and split her heid open. She willnae come back after that.'

'I won't do that.'

'Why no'?'

'It's not her fault she's Afflicted.' I glanced at the woman's slack, ravaged face. 'There will be someone out there who loves her desperately. Before she became infected, she had friends and family and dreams and desires. She doesn't deserve to die because she's ill.'

The girl cocked her head. 'She'd kill us, given half the chance.'

'It doesn't matter.'

'Tell me that again when all your family is dead or Afflicted. The less of them there are, the better.' There was no malice or bitterness in her voice. She sounded matter of fact, which was somehow more heart-wrenching than if she'd displayed emotion.

I looked her over. She couldn't be more than thirteen years old. She wasn't wearing the uniform of a castle servant, so I doubted she had worked here. She didn't appear injured or afraid. This girl, I decided, was something of an enigma.

'Why are you looking at me like that? Like I'm some kind o' bug?'

I cleared my throat. 'I'm surprised to see you here, that's all. Were you hiding downstairs? Were you behind the door that she was banging on?'

'Aye.' Her face screwed up. 'Are you that woman? Mairi? The one fae Glasgow?'

'Aye.'

She sniffed. 'I thought you'd be taller.' She looked me up and down. 'You look Afflicted – but you're not.' There was an odd note of certainty in her voice.

Not yet. I shook my head.

'You reek like they do.'

A faint smile crossed my mouth. 'What's your name?'

The girl looked at me suspiciously. 'Why do you want tae know?'

'You know my name.'

'So?'

I frowned. Before I could say anything else, something underneath the girl's blouse bulged. The bulge started to move from down by her stomach, past her chest and up towards her neck. A moment later, a tiny questing pink nose framed by long whiskers appeared.

I couldn't help myself and I jumped forward. The girl immediately threw up her hands and I gasped as flickers of blue light appeared at her fingers. Her mouth opened. 'No! Don't!' I yelled. 'He'll sense it!'

She didn't lower her hands but neither did she utter any magic words. 'The red-eyed bampot? The one who looks like a deid body?'

I nodded. 'His name is Cadal Righ.'

'I ain't afraid of no Mage.'

'He's more than a Mage.' I forced my hands to drop loosely by my sides, desperately trying to show her that I wasn't a threat. 'You've got magic.'

'Aye, well, so do you.' Her lip curled. 'You're no' the only female in Scotland with power, you ken.'

I couldn't help smiling. 'The mouse.' I nodded at the tiny head poking out of her blouse. 'You found him here?'

'He's no' vermin. He's smart. You cannae kill him.'

'I don't want to kill him. His name is Mungo. He's from Glasgow. He came here with me.'

Her eyes narrowed. 'He's *my* mouse. And Mungo is a stupid name.'

Aye, it was. My smile grew into a grin. 'He looks happy with you. Thank you for looking after him.'

Mungo chirruped then his head disappeared inside her blouse again. The girl seemed to relax slightly. 'You came back here for the daemon, right?'

My smile vanished.

'He kept saying your name,' she said. 'Over and over and over again.'

It was my turn to tense. 'You know where he is? Is he alright? He's not dead? He's—?'

She interrupted me. 'He's no' deid. I dunno if he's alright, but he's definitely no' deid.'

'Tell me where he is.' Desperation curled around my words.

The girl seemed almost amused. 'I'll take you to him.' She met my eyes. 'And it's Isla.'

A flash of unexpected nausea roiled in my belly. 'What?'

'My name is Isla.'

I swallowed hard. 'My best friend was called Isla.'

Her eyes narrowed. 'Was?'

'The Mages killed her.'

She sniffed. 'Aye. They do that.' She jerked her head. 'Come on, he's this way. We should be quick. The rest of those diseased fuckers will wake up soon.' She turned and trotted for the door.

CHAPTER

SEVEN

I kept my distance from Isla as we descended once more. I was wary of the contact I'd had with the Afflicted woman and concerned that I might already be Afflicted. Isla didn't appear particularly bothered and kept up a steady stream of chatter, though she was smart enough to keep her voice low.

'I didnae come here voluntarily. I saw them all heading to the castle and I heard the boom when they smashed through the walls. I was on my way home from work when it happened. I tried to run, but one of the fuckers grabbed me. He hauled me up to the castle and thew me in front of that red-eyed eejit. Whit did you call him? Cadal Righ?' She glanced at me and I nodded.

'I thought he was going tae kill me right there on the spot, but he didnae even look at me. He wasnae interested, he was more interested in a group of men who'd been dragged here.'

'Mages?'

She flicked her right hand dismissively. 'Nah. They were ordinary folk.' Then she added in a barely audible whisper, 'He killed them all.'

I shivered, quashing the vile taste of bile as it rose in my mouth.

'I managed to sneak away,' she said. 'I couldnae find a way out o' the castle without being noticed, so I hid here. That's when I met the daemon – and the mouse.'

'You've been very lucky,' I told her quietly.

She shrugged. 'Aye, I guess so. I ain't deid yet, anyway. And I feel alright, so I dinna think I'm Afflicted. I dinna think you are either.'

Before I could ask her why she thought that, she stopped abruptly. A moment later I heard the snuffles of several passing Afflicted people. We waited a few beats then she beckoned me once more and we kept moving.

Finally we reached the ground floor and headed outside. It seemed wrong somehow to allow a child to lead the way. By being here, she was putting her life in great danger. But she'd survived alone in the castle for hours and I suspected I needed her far more than she needed me.

We slipped out of the building, sneaked around the corner and managed to stay out of sight of the few Afflicted people who weren't curled up asleep. I looked around for the Mages' quarters, but my heart sank when I saw how many Afflicted were in front of them. I'd never get into Andy's room and retrieve the books he'd found; there were far too many of them for me to slip past unnoticed, even in my haphazard disguise.

The library was no longer a possibility, either; to all intents and purposes it had been destroyed. I wondered grimly if Cadal Righ had ordered its destruction in case there was information about him within its shelves. I hissed under my breath. He was evil, intelligent, and a careful planner; that was going to cause problems.

Staying as quiet as possible, we hurried through the open areas. Eventually Isla stopped and pointed silently towards a nearby building. Suddenly I realised that it was the same one where my room had been; this was the one spot within the castle that I knew well because I'd wandered through it both as a human and as a mouse.

Isla placed her finger on her lips, indicating unnecessarily for me to stay quiet. I was fairly certain that she thought she was dealing with an idiot. She pointed upwards towards a tiny narrow window, and I held my breath. That had been my room, I was sure of it. Laoch must have found his way back there after he was attacked.

I waved my hands, trying to tell Isla that I knew how to get to him and that she should stay here and hide so as not to risk herself further. She either pretended not to understand my gestures or simply ignored them because she leaned her head towards the doorway, listened for a moment and then ducked inside. I had no choice but to follow her.

The door to the now-deceased Edinburgh Ascendant's study lay ajar and there were flickering of shadows of movement beyond it. Isla and I tiptoed past. We stepped over the slumbering figures of three Afflicted, who appeared to have fallen asleep in the middle of the hallway, and edged towards the staircase before climbing steadily upwards.

When Isla emerged at the first floor and moved to the right, I knew I hadn't been mistaken. Laoch was in the room we'd shared when we first arrived at the castle, before he'd been enslaved by the Mages for a second time. My heart started to hammer against my ribcage. Isla had said he was alive but my fear for him was becoming uncontrollable. Despite the potential danger, I picked up speed and moved past her to the door. I twisted the doorknob and entered.

It was him. He was there.

Laoch lay curled up on the narrow bed, his back turned to me. I could hear his shallow gasps so I knew he was alive, even if he was struggling to breathe. I gave a small cry and darted towards him, dimly aware that behind me Isla was closing the door to mute the sound.

'Laoch!' I threw myself down beside him. 'Laoch!'

He moaned slightly. I bent over him and felt his forehead. He didn't have a temperature, although his skin felt clammy to the touch. His eyes were half-closed but, when I brushed away a lock of his hair, he opened them fully and gazed at me. Their bright, emerald depths were clouded with pain. 'Mairi.'

'I'm here.'

Confused, he blinked slowly and stared at my grubby disguise, then he sat up and reached for me. The sudden movement didn't do him any favours and he immediately turned an alarming shade of green.

'He'd better not puke,' Isla said darkly. 'I can deal with a lot o' shite but I cannae deal with puke.'

'I told you to get out of here,' Laoch croaked. 'It's not safe for you in this castle.'

'I tried, except an Afflicted eejit saw me and I had to hide. An' then your girlfriend showed up.' She shrugged and shot me an irritated look. 'She also tried to take my mouse away.'

'I didn't try to take him,' I began.

Laoch's mouth curved up. 'Mungo seems to have a taste for magic,' he wheezed. 'He finds it wherever he goes.'

'You know she has power?' I asked.

'*She* has a name,' Isla muttered while Laoch jerked his head in assent.

'And *she*,' I said, 'needs to get out of here. We all do. We can swap stories once we're safe.' My fingertips brushed against his throat and his wrists, which were bare now that the cruel slave cuffs were gone. 'Aspen thought you were dead so he freed you as a joke. The joke's on him now. Let's go.'

'Mairi.' His gaze continued to reflect his pain. 'I can't. I don't

have the strength. I can't tiptoe past hundreds of the Afflicted –
I'm not capable of it.'

'You can.' I glared at him. 'You will.'

'In a day or two, maybe, but you can't wait that long. It's too
risky. You shouldn't have come back here. Leave me and I'll get
out of here later and join you.'

As if. 'I'm not leaving you.'

'You have to.' He swallowed. 'I'm a liability. As soon as
Aspen caught me, I became nothing but a danger to you. You're
better off without me.'

'It was my fault he caught you.'

'No.' He shook his head. 'It was mine and—'

'Fucking hell!' Both of us turned to look at Isla. Her hands
were on her hips and she was glaring at us with almost comical
fury. 'You sound like bairns. "It's my fault".' She altered her
voice to a squeaky tone. '"No, darling, it's my fault."' She threw
up her hands. 'Who gives a fuck? Let's just go.'

Isla, it appeared, was a mini-Belle in the making. 'She's
right.'

'Mairi.' Laoch's eyes implored me. 'I won't make it twenty
steps.'

I sucked on my bottom lip. 'We can use Mungo.'

'I don't have the energy for that kind of spell.'

'I do. My magic has returned.'

'If you use any magic, Cadal Righ will sense it and come
running.'

I flashed him a quick smile. 'Actually,' I murmured, 'I'm kind
of hoping that he does.'

I washed my face in the small basin and ran my fingers through
my hair to shake out the worst of the dirt. To test my theory

properly, I couldn't look Afflicted; I had to appear normal. It helped that some of my original clothes remained in the room. I quickly got changed, relieved to peel off the dirty clothing I'd stolen earlier.

'You understand what to do?' I said to Isla as she carefully withdrew the little mouse from his hiding place.

'I'm no' stupid. You only had to explain it once. You don't have to keep checking on me.'

'If Cadal Righ sees you,' I said. 'Or if any of the Afflicted grab hold of you again—'

'They won't. I willnae allow that to happen again.' At my look, she snorted. 'I willnae.'

'If I don't join you at the battlements within fifteen minutes, you have to leave by yourself. Use *folis* to get you down.'

'Dinna fash yourself. You'll be lucky if I wait that long.'

Laoch growled but we both ignored him.

'Will it hurt him?' Isla asked. 'Will it hurt my mouse?'

'No. But if I don't join you, you'll have to wait until Laoch recovers his strength and can release himself. It might take a while.'

She considered and then nodded. 'Alright.'

I drew in a deep breath. 'Ready?'

'Aye.'

'No.' Laoch glared. 'This is a terrible idea. There must be another way.'

'The risk is worth the reward,' I said.

'No, it's not.'

'You're not in any position to disagree.' I injected a light-hearted note into my voice though I was genuinely terrified. Then, before that terror could get the better of me, I reached inside myself for my magic and hummed, focusing not on myself but on Laoch.

'Mairi,' he said, sounding strained. 'Don't.'

Too late. *Belsh za tum.*

The air throbbed with power and the little room lit up for a second. Isla squeaked, her emotions getting the better of her. I flinched against the bright light and closed my eyes. When I opened them again, Laoch had gone.

Isla stared down at Mungo curled up in her hands. 'Did it work?' she asked in wonder.

I looked at the mouse. His head turned towards me and he stuck out his tongue. 'Aye,' I said. 'Now go. *Run.*'

Isla nodded and darted out of the door at high speed. I crossed my fingers as I sat on the bed, stroked the indentation left by Laoch's body, and waited.

It didn't take long. I heard Cadal Righ approaching before I saw him. 'I smell Mage!'

I stood up slowly and backed into a corner of the room, pressing my back against the cold, stone wall and dipping my shoulders to appear as small and unthreatening as possible. I'd told Laoch the truth: the risk I was taking was indeed more than worth the potential reward. But that didn't mean I wasn't terrified.

I wrapped my arms around my body. A beat later, the door burst open and the man himself appeared. A tiny whimper escaped my lips that wasn't entirely feigned.

Cadal Righ stalked in. 'Where is he? Where is the Mage?' His red eyes landed on me but he didn't pause. Instead he spun in a circle before marching to the bed and flipping it on its side. 'Somebody used magic in here!' he roared. 'Where are they?'

I kept my mouth pinned shut.

'*Brasha za!* Reveal yourself!' The air shivered with his magic. It felt wrong, in the same way that the death gardens belonging to the Mages felt wrong. There was a rottenness at the core of his power that made my skin crawl. I held my breath and waited.

'Nobody's hidden themselves through magic, so the bastard must have run,' he muttered to himself. He stalked towards me and grabbed hold of my upper arms. 'You! Where did the Mage go? Who performed magic in here?'

I recoiled at his touch but his grip was strong. Using every ounce of courage I had left, I raised my eyes to his. There was a cold hard quality to Cadal Righ's gaze. Even when they were performing their most vicious deeds, the worst of the Mages possessed some form of emotion, but his eyes looked dead.

I lifted my hands awkwardly and motioned to my mouth, using the same gestures I'd been forced to use for most of my life. *I can't speak.* My hands fluttered and I prayed this would work. *I'm mute.*

He stared at me, his pinched white face more like that of a bleached skull than a living human. 'Then show me,' he snarled. 'Show me which way the Mage went. I want to know who dares to use magic in *my* castle without *my* permission.'

I didn't respond immediately. Cadal Righ's bony fingers tightened. 'You look familiar,' he said. 'Have I seen you before?' The chill in my bones deepened. When I still didn't reply, he hissed a curse. 'Stupid woman.'

He released his grip. Using the tip of his index finger, he trailed his long fingernail down my cheek, scraping my skin. 'You're not one of mine yet, but you soon will be. Stay here long enough and you will become like my other children. Do not worry. Once that happens, you won't be afraid like this again.'

His pale lips tightened and tilted upwards into what I assumed was supposed to be a smile. 'Now tell me, darling. Which way did the Mage go?'

This time I answered. Enough time had passed for Isla to get to the battlements by now. She'd be safe and so would Laoch. With shaking hands, I raised my arm and pointed. There were more than enough rooms and draughty hallways to keep

Cadal Righ busy for several minutes, even with powerful magic to aid his search.

'Good girl,' he cooed. He stroked my cheek once more. 'Good girl. Come and see me once you're Afflicted.' He smirked. 'If you can remember.' He marched out of the tiny room.

The dark pressure caused by his presence vanished immediately and I sagged with blessed relief as I expelled the breath I'd been holding. That had been much harder and more terrifying than I'd expected – but it had worked.

I allowed myself a tiny smile of self-congratulation. I had been right: Cadal Righ had no interest in – and no expectations of – anyone female. His focus was on the Mages and he had no idea that someone of my gender could perform magic.

When we'd escaped the battlements, he hadn't looked at me. He'd attacked Andy and tried to attack Aspen but I'd been beneath his notice. He couldn't even remember seeing me there. Neither had he been interested in Isla. That intelligence could prove vital.

I nodded, satisfied, then quickly took off in the opposite direction.

I stayed light on my feet. There was no point in disguising myself now that Cadal Righ had seen me, but as long as I kept out of the path of the Afflicted I reckoned I could get out of the castle without too much trouble. Moving fast was key.

I darted down the hallway and the familiar winding flight of stairs, bypassed the Ascendant's study and jogged outside to the first courtyard. I passed more clumps of sleeping Afflicted men and women. My gaze was fixed on the building that led up to the topmost battlements where Isla was waiting. Then I hesitated and twisted back.

I stepped over a drooling, dreadlocked woman and stretched my hand out to the empty chair in the middle of the courtyard. Grabbing hold of the small leather-bound book that had been left there, I stuffed it inside my blouse for safety. Then I put my head down and sprinted.

I saw Isla as soon as I went through the final door. She was standing at the very edge of the battlements, her eyes wide and fearful. I hadn't been sure that she would still be there – in her position, I might have already gone. That girl was far braver than most men I knew.

'You took your time!' she called, using irritation to mask her fear.

'I'm sorry,' I said. 'We can go now.'

She stared at me. 'Was it worth it?'

I couldn't shake the grin from my face. 'More than worth it. We have an advantage that Cadal Righ doesn't know about.'

And that could mean everything.

CHAPTER

EIGHT

Rather than test Isla's powers under such strained circumstances, I dug deep and used my own magic to lower her down from the battlements. She didn't complain; in fact, she took Mungo out of his hiding place as she descended and allowed the wee mouse – and, more importantly, Laoch inside him – to see that I was safe.

Once her feet were flat on the rocky ground beneath the castle walls she started to run, veering away from the collapsed building that blocked the road to the right until she was waiting for me around the corner. She was merely a hair's breadth from where the people had cowered yesterday when I'd taken to my heels. This time my escape was less stressful, and this time I wasn't planning to return.

I stepped forward until my toes were over the edge of the parapet. I glanced around to double-check that the way was clear and I wasn't about to be ambushed by any approaching Afflicted. That was when I heard the grunt behind me.

At first I thought Cadal Righ had realised his mistake and come to stop my descent, in the same way he'd appeared behind Aspen. Dread rippled through my veins as I turned.

There was a solitary figure behind me – but it wasn't Cadal Righ. I swallowed hard and stared at the shuffling Afflicted man. He wasn't wearing a black cloak – he'd lost that long before Cadal Righ entered Edinburgh Castle – and he looked far worse than he had the last time I'd seen him. His skin and large patches of his hair were coated in dried blood and there were several welts and wounds across his face and bare arms. I noted, also, that he'd lost one of his boots.

'Hello, Noah,' I said softly.

He lifted his head and gazed at me. His red-rimmed eyes possessed the unfocused, glazed look of the Afflicted but, I realised, not the cold deadness of Cadal Righ's eyes. He snuffled and a dribble of drool dripped uninterrupted down his chin. He flapped his hands uselessly. 'He,' he groaned. 'Is. Here.'

'Aye,' I said. 'He is.' I turned away again. It was time to go.

'He Is Here.'

We'd been through this. I glanced down at the distant figure of Isla. I had to catch her up. My magic was holding Laoch in place and I couldn't afford to drain all my power. The sooner I reached them and released him from Mungo, the safer we'd all be.

Noah coughed, then whispered a single word. 'Help.'

I spun back, my eyes seeking his. For the briefest moment, I glimpsed lucidity in their chocolate-brown depths. I stared at him and he stared at me, then his hands started to flutter again.

Shite. Buggering shite.

'I have a feeling that I'm definitely going to regret this,' I muttered to myself. I reached for my magic and directed it towards Noah's helpless figure. '*Folis.*'

He rose into the air and floated several feet above the stone battlements. I directed him over the edge and let him hang there. For a second, I considered letting him drop – it might be a kindness. Then I shook my head and directed the same magic towards myself. A moment later, both Noah and I were floating downwards.

I landed upright and braced my knees for the gentle impact; Noah, however, collapsed as soon as his feet touched the ground and let out a howl. Aye, this was definitely a mistake. I straightened up and looked at him. Perhaps I should leave him here after all. But then he lifted his head and I was sure I recognised another flicker of sentient consciousness.

He wouldn't have been the first Afflicted to maintain some semblance of his former self; back in Glasgow, I had encountered another Afflicted man who had been aware enough to help me. Something indefinable tugged at me. For reasons I couldn't articulate, I felt that Noah still had an important part to play.

I sighed deeply. 'Come on then.'

He heaved himself upright. As I started to trot further down the hill to where Isla, Mungo and Laoch were waiting, Noah followed.

'He cannae come.' Isla was adamant.

Noah hung back from us, as if some part of him understood that he risked our health if he drew too close, but he didn't try to return to the castle and the supposed protection of Cadal Righ.

I understood her concerns — of course I did. 'We need to understand what's happening with the Afflicted,' I reasoned. 'We can't do that without examining them. If he follows us, we shouldn't stop him.'

Isla snorted. 'If he follows us, we should kill him.' She reached into her pocket and pulled out Mungo. 'Go on then.' She jerked her head at the little mouse. 'Do your thing. If you're going to let that freaky bastard trail after you, I ain't sticking around. Me an' my mouse will go our own way.'

I frowned. 'You can't do that. You'll be safer with us.'

She looked at Noah. 'You reckon?'

'I'll keep him away from you.'

Isla spat on the ground in disgust. 'Are you planning on no' sleeping, then?'

'We'll work something out.' I was unsure why I was trying to persuade her when I despised Noah with every atom of my soul. 'He's keyed into Cadal Righ because of what he is. Something tells me we can use that.'

Isla rolled her eyes, though she did stop arguing.

I reached out and gently stroked Mungo's head, then I hummed and concentrated on the magic for releasing Laoch. There was a flash of light and the air crackled. A moment later he appeared, curled into a ball between Isla and me. Mungo squeaked and scurried back inside Isla's pocket.

Laoch stood up slowly and stretched out his limbs. His face was as fatigued as it had been before, and he retained the same sickly pallor, but his gaze was warier.

He didn't look at Noah, but he did meet my eyes. 'I agree that we need to examine the Afflicted to see what's changed now that Cadal Righ is here,' he managed in a croaky voice. 'But there are any number of them we can use, both here and back in Glasgow. We don't need *him*.'

'Actually, I think we do,' I said. 'You remember when Noah was infected?' Laoch nodded. 'The Afflicted who attacked him killed the carriage driver.'

'So?'

'They didn't kill Noah. They didn't kill the one with magic. Cadal Righ is draining the Mages' power and taking it for himself. There is a reason for that. We need a Mage who's

Afflicted if we're to understand what's happening. Also, I think there's something of the original Noah still in there.'

'You know that's not a good thing, right?' Laoch asked softly.

I grimaced as Isla's eyes widened in horror. 'Wait,' she said. 'That bastard isn't just Afflicted? He's a fucking Mage as well?' She started to back away. Her expression conveyed pure hatred as she stared at Noah.

'It'll be hard enough getting out of Edinburgh,' Laoch said. 'I'm barely at a quarter strength. Dragging him along won't make our lives any easier.'

All my logic screamed that they were right, but the way Noah had looked at me up on the battlements and his pleas for help wouldn't leave me. Besides, I was genuinely convinced that there were secrets locked inside his diseased mind that could help us.

I looked at Isla. 'You mentioned earlier that you had a sense I wasn't Afflicted, even though I've been close to dozens of them. Tell me more about that.'

She shifted from foot to foot, suddenly looking every inch a young teenager. 'I dunno.' She shrugged and looked down. 'If I concentrate, sometimes I see things inside people. I try not to – it's usually better not to know what a person is. I don't use magic unless I have to. It's safer that way.'

I took her hands and squeezed them gently. 'What do you see inside me?'

Isla's head dropped further. 'Dunno.'

'Take a look,' I urged. 'Open yourself up to the magic and look properly.'

She exhaled loudly and pulled her hands away, raised her head and stared into my face. I felt the thrum of power surround her. 'You're not Afflicted,' she said flatly after a moment or two.

It was Laoch's turn to suck in a sharp breath. 'How can you tell?' he asked. 'What can you see?'

Isla spoke with obvious reluctance. 'When someone is Afflicted, I can see it inside them.' She paused as she searched for the right words. 'No. Not *see* it exactly, not with my eyes. It's more like a sense. I sense the rottenness inside them. It starts out slowly. Right here.' She touched the centre of her chest. 'Then it spreads up to their head.' She tapped her temple. 'And then everywhere else. I can't explain it properly. It's just what I see.'

Despite his exhaustion and obvious illness, Laoch straightened and his voice changed. 'How long?' he asked. 'How long have you been able to do this?'

'Since my baby brother was infected, then my ma and my pa. I saw it growing inside them until there was nothing of the real them left.' She glared at both of us. 'There. Are you happy now?'

A wave of empathy rushed through me. 'I'm sorry.'

She folded her arms across her chest; it was clear that the last thing she wanted was platitudes. I understood that. Isla had been through far more than any teenager should have to deal with.

I didn't want to push her any further, but I had to. 'And Laoch? What do you see inside him?'

Isla's bottom lip jutted out. 'He's not Afflicted.'

'And Noah?'

She didn't look at him. 'He's Afflicted. You don't need me to fucking tell you that.'

'Isla.' She glared at me. 'Look at him. Look properly. Tell me what you see.' I hesitated. 'Please.'

She sighed but reluctantly stared at Noah again. He flinched under her gaze and started to moan softly. Isla's brow furrowed then suddenly she gasped.

'What?' I asked. 'What is it?'

'He's Afflicted,' she said. 'He's definitely Afflicted.'

Laoch growled. 'But?'

Isla touched her forehead with the tips of her fingers. 'There's a part in here that's clear. It's normal.' She squinted at Noah. 'I've never seen that before. Maybe it's because he's a Mage.'

Maybe. I tamped down my surge of hope. Until we knew more, I couldn't allow myself to have high expectations. 'We have to bring him with us,' I said.

Laoch bared his teeth but he no longer disagreed aloud.

'Cadal Righ doesn't know that there are still women who can do magic,' I said. 'That's what I was testing back there at the castle. That knowledge is important. Maybe he also isn't aware that the Affliction doesn't completely take hold of every person. *We* didn't know it until a moment ago.'

I touched the small book hidden inside my blouse. 'The more we know that Cadal Righ doesn't, the better position we'll be in to defeat him. We have to get to Glasgow and meet the others. Maybe they'll have discovered more. We're not dead yet.' I didn't turn my head. 'Even Noah isn't dead yet.'

'Do you want to save him?' Laoch asked quietly.

'Not him,' I answered honestly. 'But I do want to save everyone else.'

Isla and Laoch exchanged looks. 'I suppose we'd better get the fuck to Glasgow then,' Isla muttered. She sniffed. 'Which way is it?'

I grinned and pointed. 'It's over there. Can you walk, Laoch?'

'For an hour or two. I'll need to rest soon, though.'

'I know a place,' I said. I took a few steps then checked over my shoulder. Noah also took a few steps but he maintained a distance between us. 'He'll keep away from us.'

Laoch's voice echoed in my head. *You can't be sure of that. He might attack us at any moment. I understand your reasoning, Mairi, but this remains a terrible idea.*

I know. I tugged at my tangled curls. *But we need every shred of advantage we can muster.*

He sighed. *You're the boss.* He paused. *Thank you.*

For what?

You came back for me. You shouldn't have done that. But thank you.

I love you, Laoch. I'll always come back for you, just as you came back for me.

He offered me a crooked smile. *I love you too.*

I leaned forward and allowed my mouth to brush against his.

'What the fuck are you doing?' Isla screeched. 'The world has ended and you two are smoorikin! Stop that!'

I touched Laoch's rough cheek and glanced at Noah whose gaze was swinging in every direction but ours. Aye. It was time to go.

CHAPTER

NINE

There was no snoring in the high-walled cemetery that night, although my rest was as fitful and unsatisfactory as it had been the night before. At least on this occasion I had Laoch's warm body pressed against mine. His chest rose and fell with soothing regularity. He was recovering and, despite everything else that was occurring, that made my spirits soar.

Although I'd encouraged Isla to sleep on my other side for warmth and protection, she had declined with a hasty snort and taken up a lonely position beneath the cracked slabs of an old family vault. Every time I opened my eyes during the night she was awake, the glint of moonlight reflecting in her restless gaze.

I couldn't blame her for not being able to sleep properly. Noah remained close to us, though he didn't sit or lie down; instead he shuffled around the cemetery in unceasing circles. Occasionally he muttered to himself, but I couldn't make out his words and I was unwilling to expel any magic to listen more closely. I might need every ounce of my power to get us safely to Glasgow.

As soon as the first streaks of dawn lit up the sky, I felt relief rather than trepidation. The faster we got out of Edinburgh the better I'd feel, even if I suspected the journey to Glasgow would be perilous.

I wasn't the only one in a rush to get going. I'd barely stretched my limbs when Isla got to her feet, brushed the dirt from her clothing and cleared her throat. I nodded at her and shook Laoch gently. His eyes opened with a momentary cloud of confusion that subsided as soon as he saw me. The sudden warmth that flared in his gaze relaxed me.

I helped him to his feet. 'How are you feeling?' I asked quietly.

He smiled, although it was obvious that he was still in pain. 'Better,' he said. He flexed his fingers. 'I have far more energy than yesterday. And power. I can protect you if need be.'

Isla expelled a cold, derisive chuckle. 'She doesnae need your protection. You need hers.'

Laoch didn't disagree. 'Aye,' he said. 'You're right.' He looked to his left and his smile disappeared when he registered that Noah was still with us. 'If he follows us, that's one thing,' he growled. 'But you're not to risk yourself for him.' His green eyes fell on me. 'You're not to risk yourself for any of us – and certainly not him.'

I touched his hand. 'No fear on that count.'

I ran my hands through my hair and edged towards the cemetery gates to peer out at the empty street. Unlike yesterday morning, there was nobody there. Anyone who wanted to leave Edinburgh seemed to have done so already.

Our bedraggled trio didn't speak; we didn't need to. With silent resolve, we fell into line and trudged away from the cemetery towards the edge of the city. At first it seemed that Noah wasn't going to follow us, but I heard his shuffling footsteps behind us when we reached the first crossroads and turned to our right.

I didn't look around or ask him why he felt the need to remain with us rather than cling to Cadal Righ. Although I was convinced that something about Noah's Affliction could help us, I had to focus on the more important task of getting to Glasgow in one piece. For now, it was the only goal.

As we walked past broken shop fronts and discarded luggage, the steady pounding of our feet and the gentle whistling of the wind were the only sounds. Laoch drew in a sharp breath when the misshapen black lumps in a nearby gutter turned out not to be pieces of strewn clothing but the fallen bodies of dead ravens. Isla, however, marched past them without a second glance.

Curiously, I glanced over my shoulder and watched Noah approach the feathered corpses and kneel down. At first I thought he was stroking them and mourning their death, but a moment later I realised he was actually choosing one to eat. Without a moment's hesitation, he yanked off the feathers and chomped down on the cold flesh. My stomach churned and I looked away. I was also feeling pangs of hunger but it would be a long day in hell before I resorted to eating anything like that.

Eventually, the battered shops gave way to houses. The streets were as deathly quiet as the ones that we'd already passed through. The only time our journey was interrupted was when a stray dog trotted down a side street towards us. As soon as it raised its head and caught sight of us, it whipped around and moved in the opposite direction. It seemed that even the animals were learning that it was wise to stay out of sight.

Thanks to our quick pace, we left the last of the buildings behind after about three hours of walking. I paused as we marched out of Edinburgh and glanced back at the castle, which continued to stand tall over the city. Black smoke was rising from one section, but otherwise it seemed quiet. I wasn't sure whether that was a good or bad thing.

Laoch reached for my hand and squeezed it tight. I pulled away my gaze. I couldn't say that I'd enjoyed my trip to Edinburgh, or that I was anything but delighted to be leaving.

Once the last buildings were behind us, all three of us relaxed slightly. Isla started to chatter, filling the earlier strained silence with random titbits about her old life and questions about Glasgow. I did my best to answer her and Laoch chimed in from time to time. Under any other circumstances, an onlooker might have been forgiven for thinking we were out for an enjoyable hike.

By noon, the sky had darkened and icy rain was starting to fall. Even with a mild drizzle, it wouldn't take long for us to be drenched. We didn't have suitable clothing to protect against the weather – and sooner or later we'd need sustenance to keep us going.

When we saw a small farmhouse on the horizon, we needed no encouragement to alter our course slightly and head towards it. Noah also seemed to snuffle agreement.

We clambered over a fence and trudged through muddy puddles beside a large field until we reached the house. It was sturdy, with solid stone walls and a well-maintained thatched roof. There was a small coal shed to one side and what appeared to be a barn some distance away. The farmhouse door, neatly painted dark blue, lay slightly ajar.

I paused and listened carefully. There weren't any signs of life, so I knocked on the wooden door frame, waited for a beat then entered.

Isla turned to Noah and admonished him sternly. 'You fucker. You stay oot here. Got that?'

If Noah understood, he didn't reply – though he didn't attempt to enter the house. He hunkered down next to the kitchen window where the overhanging thatch protected him from the worst of the rain. Laoch nodded in satisfaction, then he and Isla followed me inside.

Unless some people fleeing Edinburgh had stopped here along the way, it appeared that whoever lived here had left in a hurry or was a very messy pup. I glanced around the kitchen, with its open cupboards and ransacked shelves, and checked the sitting room. The soot-blackened logs in the hearth were cold to the touch. The place seemed safe.

Laoch headed for the cupboard under the stairs and found a number of coats, while Isla and I searched the kitchen for food. She chortled with pleasure when she found a small basket of wrinkled apples. I retrieved some cooked meat that smelled alright from the pantry, and some slightly stale bread. It felt like a veritable feast.

'We can take the apples with us,' I said decisively. 'We'll use the bread and meat to make a sandwich to eat here before we head out again.'

Isla, whose cheeks were already filled with apple, glanced at me. 'It's too dreich outside. Can we no' wait here until the rain stops?'

This was Scotland. The rain might not stop for a week. 'It's best if we keep going. We need to get to Glasgow as quickly as we can.'

She pulled a face. Laoch walked into the kitchen and handed her a coat. 'Here,' he said. 'It's too big but it'll keep you mostly dry. Try it on.'

Isla swallowed her mouthful of apple and shrugged on the coat. It had obviously been made for a far larger person and she was swamped by the fabric. I stifled a smile while Mungo poked his head out and sniffed delicately.

'I look like an eejit,' Isla muttered.

I took a second coat from Laoch and started to put it on. I'd only got one arm inside it when there was a loud thump from somewhere in the house. All three of us froze.

The floorboards above our heads creaked, then somebody started to descend the stairs.

I held my breath as I prepared for various scenarios. If it was the owner of the house, I'd apologise and ask for forgiveness. Given the circumstances, they'd hopefully understand. I'd also urge them to come with us to Glasgow. If it was somebody taking shelter, I'd do the same. And if it was someone Afflicted, the best thing we could do was leave as quickly as possible.

I tensed as the footsteps grew closer. Laoch stepped next to me and indicated to Isla to get behind us. The creaks became heavier, then the owner of the footsteps turned the corner, stopped dead, and stared at us.

It was a young lad, perhaps sixteen or seventeen years old judging by his youthful features. Despite his youth, his body was muscular and I had little doubt that he worked on this farm. Perhaps it belonged to his parents.

My face relaxed into a smile, but I felt Laoch tense even more by my side. That was when I realised the lad was holding a knife.

'I thought you'd all gone,' he said. 'I thought you'd all left by now.' He raised the knife. 'You'll go now.' His eyes narrowed in a show of anger but it didn't take a genius to realise that it was a mask to cover his fear. Unfortunately for us, fear could be as dangerous – if not more – than fury.

As I put up my hands to indicate that I was unarmed, my borrowed coat slid to the floor. Nobody spared it a second glance. I nudged Laoch and he also lifted his hands.

'We thought this house had been abandoned.' I kept my voice reassuringly low. 'We only came in to see if we could find food and something to wear to shield us against the rain. We're heading to—'

'Glasgow.' He spat. 'Aye. I know.' He brandished the knife shakily in the air as if he were as afraid of it as he was of us. 'Go on then. Go to Glasgow. Fuck off out of here.'

I ignored his trembling command. 'Are you on your own? You should come with us.'

'I'm staying here.'

'It's not safe here on your own,' I persisted. 'Where are your parents?'

A spasm of agony crossed his face. 'They're no' here. Now get out!' He waved the knife again and raised his voice to a squeaky shout. It was loud enough for the sound to carry outside because there was a sudden howl from Noah.

The boy stiffened, his eyes darting from side to side. 'No' another one.' His shoulders sagged. 'There's no space left for any more.'

Laoch stepped forward. 'What do you mean?'

The boy's bottom lip jutted out. 'The barn,' he whispered. 'They put them in the barn when they came past.'

'Can you show us?' I asked.

His eyes slid from Laoch to me and back again. 'What are you?' he asked, paying no attention to my anxious question. 'You're no' human.'

'I'm a daemon,' Laoch answered. 'And I won't hurt you. Can you show us the barn?'

The boy's eyes slid from side to side again. 'You dinnae want to see whit's in there.'

'What's your name?' I asked.

He gave me a distrustful look. 'John.'

I very much doubted his name was John, but it would do for now. 'Please, John,' I said. 'Show us what's in there.'

His shoulders sagged. He held onto the knife tightly with his right hand; with his left he reached into his pocket and pulled out a key. 'Here,' he said. 'See for yourself.' He tossed it onto the floor. Laoch bent down and picked it up.

'Mairi.' Isla tugged at my elbow.

'Wait a minute.' I wanted to see what was in the barn first. I had an idea of what it might contain but I needed to see it with my own eyes.

Laoch and I sidled past John-not-John. Isla nipped out of the door in front of us, seemingly desperate not to spend another second inside the farmhouse. As soon as we were outside, the boy closed the door. We all heard him bolt it shut.

'He's Afflicted,' Isla hissed. 'It's not reached his brain yet but it's in his chest. I could see it.'

I clenched my jaw. 'You're sure?'

She nodded mutely and I winced. Shite. For all his posturing, John was still a child.

'Come on.' Laoch's voice was full of grim foreboding. He walked past Noah, who was cowering by the coal shed and sending frightened looks towards the farmhouse door. Isla and I followed.

We heard them long before we reached the barn. The rain had masked the sound before – or perhaps we simply hadn't wanted to hear it – but now we heard the grunts and the groans from eighty feet away.

'Stay here, Isla,' I ordered.

'I want to see too.'

I glared at her. 'Stay here.' Her face twisted but she did as I said.

Laoch and I edged forward towards the large wooden structure. Once we reached the large door, I glanced at the key in Laoch's hand. 'I'm going out on a limb here,' I said, 'but I don't think we should open that door.'

His mouth flattened. 'I'm going to agree with you.'

We abandoned the door and walked around the building.

There were no windows to peer through, but halfway along the barn's length I found a small hole about two feet off the ground. It wasn't much larger than my fist but it fitted my purpose. I crouched down and peered through it. When I saw what was inside, I exhaled sharply.

'Afflicted?' Laoch asked.

I swallowed hard. 'Hundreds of them.' Men, women, children; diseased people of all shapes, sizes and backgrounds were locked in there. It was a nightmare.

Laoch bent down next to me and looked through the hole, then bared his teeth and moved away. 'They must be from Edinburgh,' he said.

I felt ill. 'People who were escaping but who were already infected. Or,' I added darkly, 'they weren't Afflicted but looked ill, so they were dumped inside here with the rest.'

'If they weren't Afflicted before, they will be now.'

I met his eyes. 'There were plenty of Mages among the thousands who left. They could have found a different way that didn't mean imprisoning all these people.' Not that they'd be imprisoned for long.

I kicked at the barn wall. It was holding for now, but any concerted effort by the Afflicted inside would free them in moments. It wouldn't be long before they were rampaging through the countryside.

'The numbers of the Afflicted have been kept down for decades,' Laoch said. 'All that's changed now. Some people are infected more easily than others. Some, like that poor boy back there, can sustain an Affliction for hours, perhaps days, before it consumes them.' He shook his head. 'All those heading to Glasgow...' His voice trailed off.

I realised what he was saying. 'If Glasgow lets them in, its endangering its own citizens.'

'And if Glasgow doesn't let them in,' Laoch said, 'they'll

probably end up like this sooner or later and cause us much greater problems.'

'Is this his plan?' I asked. 'Is this what Cadal Righ wants? To rule over a diseased and dying country?'

'I guess we'll find out. Sooner or later.' He looked over his shoulder. 'I was wrong earlier. Bringing Noah along was a good idea. If there's any way we can find answers, even if it's a long shot, we have to try.'

I nodded. Aye – but would the Mages let us? I sighed. 'John is alone.' I jerked my head towards the barn. 'Do you think his parents are in there?'

Laoch looked unhappy. 'Probably.'

'We should take him with us. Afflicted or not, he can't stay here. Between us, we can control him when he turns fully. Maybe he'll be like Noah,' I said hopefully. 'Maybe he'll still be able to control part of himself too.'

From deep within the barn, there was an agonising howl followed by some vicious snarls. Laoch bent again and peered through the hole.

'What's happening?' I asked.

'They're attacking each other.' He glanced at me. 'I think Noah will prove the exception to the rule.'

My gaze dropped.

I THUMPED ON THE DOOR. 'JOHN!' I called. 'Come out! Come with us to Glasgow!' He didn't answer. I tried again. 'John!'

'We have to leave him,' Isla said. 'He's Afflicted. We cannae pick up every one of those diseased bastards. They'll only make things worse for everyone else – *he*'ll only make things worse. We need to leave him.'

If we were taking Noah with us, we could take John-not-John. I banged on the door again. 'We can help you!'

'No, we can't,' Isla said.

'Mairi.' It was Laoch. 'She's right. I accept there might be reasons for allowing Noah to remain with us, outlandish as they seem, and I understand that he's acting differently to other Afflicted we've come across. Isla has confirmed that. But we're still endangering more than ourselves by bringing him along. If we bring this lad too, that risk will increase.'

A strange growl emitted from somewhere deep inside my chest. 'If we leave him, we're no better than they are. If he doesn't come with us, I might as well admit that I'm the same as them!'

'The same as who? The Mages?' Laoch blinked. 'Mairi, you're not like them.'

I gestured at the closed door. 'We're leaving that boy – that child – here for the greater good? What if we do find a way to help the Afflicted through Noah?'

'And what if we don't? John will only infect more people.' Laoch's voice was gentle but there was steel there too. 'Frankly, it's a miracle that the three of us remain disease free.' He paused. 'At least for now.'

I stared at him desperately. 'This is how it started, Laoch! This is where everything went wrong the first time around. And now it's happening again on a far greater scale.'

His brow furrowed. 'What do you mean?'

I drew in a ragged breath as the impotent frustration inside me continued to build. 'When the Affliction started, the male Mages got rid of all the female Mages for the greater good, to protect the people.' My voice rose. 'And we all know how that ended up. If I leave that boy here, I'm the same as them. Where's the line? How many people have to be sacrificed?'

There was an edge of hysteria to every word. I couldn't stop myself.

Laoch's green eyes were calm and so was his voice. 'Mairi, you can't help that boy now. None of us can. Frankly, the safest thing for *him* is to leave him here and work on finding a way out of all this. We help him by finding a way to stop Cadal Righ. I know it doesn't feel right, but it's all we've got.'

Tears pricked at my eyeballs but I held them back furiously. 'The Mages have spent generations trying to find a way to end the Affliction. All their power and all their numbers, and they've not achieved anything.'

'You have to admit that they didn't have much motivation before. Maybe things will be different now. And,' he added, 'now there's you.'

'I'm only one person,' I whispered, although as soon as I said the words, I knew they weren't true. I had lots of people on my side.

Isla clicked her tongue and pushed past me. She knocked on the door and started to yell. 'Oi! You're already Afflicted. You'll end up like those poor eejits in the barn, maybe tomorrow or the day after. We cannae help you now. But this woman here is Mairi. She saved Glasgow.'

'I didn't save Glasgow,' I began.

Isla ignored me. 'We'll do everything we can to help you and all those like you, but it's safest if you stay here for now.'

The boy hesitated. When his voice finally drifted through the closed door, there was an edge of uncertainty despite his brave words. 'I know what's happening to me. I can feel it. Whoever she is, she cannae help me now. Nobody can. Get on your way and leave me be.'

My stomach twisted but Isla shrugged. 'See?' she said to me. 'He understands. Let's go.'

It wasn't right.

'If you become Afflicted, what should we do with you?' she asked me. 'Lock you up or let you tag along till you infect us all?'

I didn't answer; I didn't have to.

'Well, then.' She pointed to herself. 'Same for me.' She pointed to Laoch. 'Same for him.' She nodded at the farmhouse. 'Same for all of us. It doesnae make you like the Mages.' The corner of her mouth crooked up. 'Nay yet, anyway.'

Noah let out a long, rattling groan. Defeated, my body sagged. I bit my lip and then I nodded. Tragically, we had no other choice.

CHAPTER

TEN

The lighter mood from earlier had given way to doom and gloom that was matched by the continuing bad weather. Isla and Laoch had managed to keep hold of the coats they'd taken from the farmhouse and several times Laoch tried to force me to take his – and several times I refused. I wasn't playing the martyr; he was still recovering from what had happened at the castle. Other than the small wounds and bruises I'd received during the Ascendancy Challenge, I felt fine. Wet, shivery and cold but otherwise fine.

We trudged on through puddles and mud and driving, icy rain. Noah shuffled twenty metres or so behind us. There was nothing we could do but put our heads down and keep going. I thought briefly of my old umbrella that Laoch had taken from me the first time we'd met and how scared I'd been of him. I was still scared, that much was true, but I certainly wasn't scared *of* him. These days I only felt scared *for* him. And for Scotland.

'Is there no' a spell we can use to stay dry?' Isla asked, as we reached the crest of a small hill and were confronted by more soggy fields, waterlogged roads and dark clouds.

I couldn't think of any, and I didn't think it was a good idea to waste energy on that sort of spell. 'Magic isn't an infinite resource. We might need our powers later. Given a choice between staying alive and staying dry, I know which I'd prefer.'

'Given a choice between getting pneumonia now,' Isla began, 'and maybe not dying later, I know which *I'd* prefer.'

She had a point. We could conserve our magical energy and waste all our physical power as a result. I considered then glanced at Laoch. 'Do you have anything?'

'No spells that will work.'

I started to shrug then I thought of something. '*Vaz* creates an invisible barrier.'

'Against magic,' Laoch said. 'Not rain.'

'But if we combined *vaz* with *belz*, the word for "cover", we might be able to fashion something that'd work.'

Isla halted in mid-step and stared at me. 'You can combine words?' she asked. 'To make new spells?'

'I can't,' Laoch told her. 'The Mages can't.'

'But can *she*?' Isla persisted.

'I did it once before,' I said. During the Ascendancy Challenge, I'd created an armour out of water by mixing two different spells. If I could do it then, perhaps I could do it now. If I controlled how much power I used, I could retain enough magic to use in an emergency. I exhaled and started to reach inside myself.

'Wait,' Isla said. 'Can I try first?'

There was no harm in it. I wiped several droplets of rain of my face. 'Knock yourself out.'

She inhaled, drawing a long breath of air into her lungs, and I sensed her magic coalescing. 'I dinnae have a lot of power, I dinnae use it very often because...' Because if she did, the Mages would find her. I nodded my understanding. She clenched her fists and muttered. '*Vaz belz*.'

The air snapped. The rain continued to fall. 'It was worth a try,' I said.

'Wait. Let me try again.' She squeezed her eyes shut. Strain was etched on her face. '*Vaz belz.*'

'Don't worry about it, Isla,' I said. 'It's not—'

Laoch interrupted. 'She's done it.' Marvelling, he held out his hands. 'It worked.'

I tilted my face upwards then I gasped. Although the rain continued to fall around us, it was no longer falling *on* us.

Isla's expression was triumphant. 'I did it!' She stamped her feet in delight, splashing into a nearby puddle and sending muddy water flying in all directions. 'I did it! I did it!'

I grinned. 'Well done!' As I took several steps forward, the magical protection followed me. 'Bloody well done, Isla.'

She dropped into a curtsey, her cheeks flushing red. 'Thank you.' Then she added in a quiet voice that maybe I wasn't meant to hear, 'That means a lot coming from you.'

I looked at Noah, who had stopped. While Isla's spell didn't stretch to cover his body as well as ours, there was an odd expression on his face as if part of him understood what had just happened but couldn't quite comprehend it.

I glanced again at Laoch. 'You're certain that you can't do this?' I asked. 'You definitely can't combine two spells, even when you're working at full strength?'

'Definitely not.' His eyes met mine. 'And I know the Mages can't either.'

'But if I can and Isla can, and the one thing we have in common is that we're both female, do you think...' My voice trailed off. I was unable to say out loud what I was thinking.

'I do think, Mairi. I very much do think.'

'Think what?' Isla asked. Her brow furrowed then cleared as she realised. 'Oh. Only women can do this? Only women can mix magic?'

'It's a strong possibility.' Cadal Righ's dead looking eyes flashed into my head. 'Cadal Righ doesn't know women can still do magic. He won't know anyone has this ability.'

Laoch's voice echoed in my head. *Don't get your hopes up*, he warned. *We don't know what we have yet.*

He was right. It wasn't much in our pitiful arsenal against Cadal Righ. But it was something.

ALTHOUGH MY THOUGHTS inevitably trailed back to John alone in his farmhouse waiting for his Affliction to set in, our journey became much easier. Without the constant rain, we moved faster and we made good time, even though we wouldn't reach Glasgow before nightfall.

I had no desire to knock on the doors of any other seemingly abandoned farmhouses, but continuing our journey during the inky blackness of night would be unwise. We didn't know the area well and there could be any manner of beasties crawling around as well as the Afflicted.

As soon as the rain cleared, sunset coloured the sky, shooting trails of pink and purple through the dissipating clouds. I couldn't admire its beauty; all I felt was my tension ratcheting up again. It didn't help that Noah, who until now had given little more than the occasional grunt, started to howl and screech as if he were in pain.

'We can't keep walking through the night,' I said. 'We have to find shelter and continue on to Glasgow as soon as it's daylight.'

Laoch was in full agreement and nodded but Isla, emboldened by her earlier magical success, clearly wanted to argue. 'We can get there. It cannae be more than another ten miles. If we keep walking...'

'If we keep walking, we might lose our way in the dark or run into something we can't cope with. We've done well so far, but that doesn't mean we can fight something bigger than us. We each have magic but there's only three of us. We don't know what will come out once the sun goes down.'

She cracked her knuckles. 'I can take whatever comes.'

I didn't want to burst her bubble of confidence but we couldn't take unnecessary risks, not right now. 'We have to stop.' My tone brooked no argument.

It helped that the air was filled by a distant roar from somewhere to the east as soon as I finished speaking. Isla started and her eyes widened. She swung her head from side to side and twisted her fingers together. 'Aye, well, if youse two are tired, maybe we could take a break overnight.'

I smiled faintly. 'Maybe under those trees?' I suggested. 'We can't risk a fire but the branches will provide some cover.'

Laoch started to nod then paused. 'Wait,' he said. 'I recognise this place. Isn't that the hill where you were attacked on the way to Edinburgh? Where Noah became infected?'

I looked around. No wonder Noah was howling. There was no longer any sign of either the broken carriage or of the dead beithir that the Mages had conjured forth in a bid to test my powers, but it looked like the same place. That meant there was a hidden cave a few hundred feet away, beyond the nearby copse of trees. Last time, the cave had been inhabited by three of the Afflicted – the very Afflicted who had attacked and killed our carriage driver before knocking out and infecting Noah. Although they might still be there, I had to admit that sheltering in a cave seemed like our best option.

'It's dangerous to leave the road,' I mused. There was another roar from the east; it sounded louder this time. 'But,' I added, 'we should check out the cave and see if it's still occupied. Those Afflicted people might still be there, but it's worth checking.'

'Agreed.' As the shadows lengthened, Laoch's expression was becoming particularly grim. 'There are unsavoury creatures to be found in the countryside at night time.'

'The two of you should stay here,' I cautioned. 'I'll go ahead to the cave.'

Laoch growled, 'You're not going alone.'

'Someone has to stay and look after Isla.'

Isla snorted. 'Isla can look after herself.'

They weren't making this easy. 'Fine.' I rolled my eyes. 'We'll go together. But both of you will hold back once the cave is in view. I'm the only one who's been inside, it so it makes sense that I'm the one who checks it out. If the Afflicted are still there, we'll need to come up with another plan.'

Noah howled once more. I gritted my teeth. 'He needs to stay quiet.'

'My pleasure,' Laoch said. He flicked his hand forward and blue flames twitched at the ends of his fingers. '*Vair al.*'

Noah's howling stopped immediately and Laoch sighed with immense satisfaction. 'You cannot imagine how much I've always wanted to do that to a Mage,' he murmured.

Actually, I probably could.

I smiled then we all headed into the trees. It was darker in the tiny wood than I remembered. I picked my way through the under-growth, taking care to listen out for any sounds of approaching trouble. Angus had taught me a new spell when we'd been here before and now I licked my lips and tried it. I hummed softly. *Tinza.*

The sounds altered. I could hear the rattle of Noah's breath from behind us, the steady beat of Laoch's heart and the faster thump of Isla's pulse as she pretended not to be frightened. There were rustles from earth-dwelling creatures and soft coos from birds settling down to sleep, but there was nothing unnatural and nothing that sounded like the Afflicted trio.

'What the fuck is that?' Isla's screech broke through the other noises, whining painfully in my ears as a result of the spell. I winced and cut off my magic before turning to see what had made her cry. Oh.

'Bones,' I muttered. 'Nothing to worry about.' The carriage driver's corpse had been picked clean of all its flesh. 'Wheesht. We don't want to draw attention to ourselves.'

'Sorry.' She grimaced and lowered her voice. 'I've seen plenty of deid bodies before but I've never seen any like that. They usually have faces.'

'Don't fash yourself. It's fine.' I squeezed her arm while Mungo, who must have been snoozing throughout our journey, poked his head out before nuzzling at her skin.

Isla expelled the air in her lungs. 'No problem. S'all good. Fine and dandy. Braw and bonnie. Happy days.'

I squeezed her arm again. I kept forgetting how very young she was. Her bravery was immense, especially given the circumstances, but it was clear that she'd found it easier to be brave on familiar ground in Edinburgh than in this strange rural landscape. None of us were used to travelling, not even within our own country.

I motioned to her and Laoch to stay where they were. Before Laoch could argue, I projected silently, *She's too scared. Stay here with her and I'll check the cave. I won't risk it if the Afflicted are there.*

Last time I let you out of my sight, we both almost died.

I licked my lips. *There were Mages then. This will be easier.*

Laoch managed a telepathic snort. *Famous last words, Mairi.*

You're still not at full strength. I've got this. I smiled at him. Before he could disagree further, I left them and tiptoed forward.

The path leading to the cave was reasonably easy to find. The Afflicted had left a trail so it didn't take me long to pick my way forward. My nostrils itched as the faint smell of their rot filled the air. I wasn't sure if it was misplaced optimism but the reek seemed to be stale. I plunged ahead, hoping I was right.

A moment later, the dark maw of the cave itself came into sight – and there were no signs of life, Afflicted or otherwise. All the same, I hung back for several moments. When nothing changed, I knelt down and scrabbled in the dirt until I found a sharp stone. I squinted, then threw it. It thudded into the jagged cave wall, creating a quiet echo. Still nothing stirred.

It wouldn't be long until darkness overtook us so I willed my feet closer to the cave. Before I'd taken another three steps, something crashed through the trees from behind me. I spun, a hum already on my lips. A second later, Noah burst through undergrowth with Isla and Laoch hot on his heels. I motioned urgently for them to stay back but Noah loped past me on heavy, stumbling feet, and ran straight into the cave.

'I'll follow him,' Laoch said.

No. 'I'll do it.'

'Mairi—'

I ignored him and strode after Noah through the dark cave entrance. The smell inside was far stronger, considerably worse than I remembered. I held my breath and edged forward. All I could hear was my own heartbeat and Noah's ragged gasps. I hummed once. *Altus Ish Moy.*

Light flared and illuminated the cavern. I blinked rapidly to clear my vision so I could take a good look inside. Other than Noah and me, the cave was empty. I wet my dry lips and edged around. There were the same nauseating clumps of dirt and faeces and gnawed bones, but I sensed that none of them were fresh.

I bent over, sniffed carefully then stood up. I was as certain as I could be that the three Afflicted who'd been living here had left the cave, probably drawn towards Edinburgh and Cadal Righ's siren call. Satisfied, I turned my attention to Noah.

Huh. He was on his knees facing the massive rune that had been etched crudely into the cave wall. He rocked back and forth, silent tears streaming from his red-rimmed eyes. I watched him for a long moment until Laoch voice called anxiously into the cave, 'Mairi?'

'I'm fine. There's nothing else here. The Afflicted have gone.'

Laoch strode in, his gaze falling on Noah.

'Well, apart from him, of course,' I said.

Laoch squinted. 'What's he doing?'

I pursed my lips. 'Mourning? Praying?' I shrugged. 'Honestly, I have no idea.'

'He's crying.' Laoch smiled. 'Good.'

I searched inside myself for any dregs of sympathy for Noah and his current situation. It wasn't easy. Eventually, I gave up.

Isla hovered at the cave's entrance. 'It honks in there.' She pinched her nose. 'We're not seriously sleeping here tonight? The stench alone will make me want to Afflict myself.'

'If we stay at the entrance, we'll get the fresh air from outside and some cover. It's better than hiding underneath a tree,' I said.

Her lip curled. 'If you say so.'

'I'll take first watch,' I said. 'The two of you should get some rest while you can.'

Mairi, you don't need to look after me. I'll stand guard. You need to sleep as well.

I do need to look after you, Laoch, because I need you to be well. I'll wake you up after a few hours and you can take a turn. I gave him a long look. *Alright?*

He sighed. *You'll have to keep an eye on Noah, too. He still might turn on us.*

No fear on that score, I returned.

I made myself comfortable with my back against the cave wall by the entrance, while Laoch and Isla curled up. From there, I could see both the dark woods outside and Noah inside. I was tired, but I knew I was too keyed up from the high emotions of the day to sleep yet. And I hadn't lied to Laoch; nearly losing him at the castle had made me painfully aware of how much I relied on his presence. He was recovering from his ordeal but he wasn't at his full strength yet. I'd need him to be one hundred percent when we got to Glasgow. I suspected we had a long fight ahead of us as well as behind us.

I spent a good hour scanning the dark trees and listening for signs of trouble. Whatever creature had been roaring as the sun went down seemed to have gone elsewhere to hunt. Even Noah finally quieted and curled up into a tiny, foetal-like ball at the foot of the rune.

Eventually, I relaxed enough to delve inside my blouse and pull out the little leather-bound book I'd grabbed from Cadal Righ's bloody, makeshift throne. It was time to find out why he'd been reading it.

I stroked the soft leather cover. It looked old. I held my breath and opened it to the first page.

CHAPTER
ELEVEN

It was some time after midnight, when the moon hung in the velvet-black sky like a benevolent, glowing orb and the stars twinkled down as if nothing at all in the world could ever be the matter, that I realised Laoch had woken and was looking at me. I put the book down and returned his gaze. Isla remained fast asleep next to him, so rather than speak aloud, I projected my thoughts. *How long have you been awake?*

A slow, easy smile lit his face. *Long enough. I like watching you.*

I blinked, then I peered at him and registered the warm glint in his eyes. *You're feeling better.*

I am indeed. His smile vanished momentarily. *So you don't need to keep babying me. I should be your protector, not the other way around.*

I raised an eyebrow. *You don't want to be babied?*

No.

I shuffled towards him. With gentle, questing fingertips, I reached up and stroked his hair. *So you don't want me to do this?* I asked.

No.

I allowed my hand to drop until my fingers grazed his cheekbone. I scraped the base of my thumb along the length of his not-inconsiderable stubble. *Or this?*

His breath caught. *No.*

I moved my head until we were nose to nose, dipped my mouth forward and kissed him on the lips. *And you wouldn't want me to do this.* My hand stroked downwards, drawing a trail across his collarbone, down his chest and towards his groin. *And you definitely wouldn't want me to do this.*

Laoch groaned aloud. *Mairi.*

My mouth curved into a smile before I sent a reluctant look in Isla's direction. She was still asleep but she wouldn't remain that way for long if we kept this up. I pulled back out of temptation's way. *Thank you,* I projected.

He looked at me quizzically.

For yesterday with that boy, John – or whatever his name was. I wish we could have done something for him but you were right to encourage me to leave him. And thank you for being with me. I hesitated. *Most of all, thank you for still being alive. I don't know what I would have done if you'd died in Edinburgh.*

Laoch's expression softened. *You'd survive. You'd fight. You'd keep going because that's who you are. I love you, Mairi, and I know you love me too. But your existence and your will to do what is right for Scotland is not dependent on me. Make sure you remember that.*

I pushed down the sudden well of sadness. *This fight is bigger than both of us.*

Aye. It is.

He reached across and pulled a stray twig from one of my curls. *You know, it doesn't smell as bad once you've been here for a while. I no longer feel like I'm going to vomit every time I breathe in.*

Every small win counts.

He nodded. *You should get some sleep. If we're to have more small wins tomorrow, you'll need some rest. Has there been any disturbance?*

Not from out there.

And in here? From Noah?

He's been quiet, too. I bit my lip then picked up the little book and passed it to him. *I found this when I was escaping from the castle. I think Cadal Righ was reading it.*

Laoch frowned and turned it over in his hands. *What is it?*

Some kind of diary, I think. I swallowed. *It was written by a female Mage.*

His eyes shot to mine. *It's old, then?*

Yes. The woman who wrote it knew him. She knew Cadal Righ. She was there with him before. It's important.

I'll read it.

I breathed out. Good. I brushed my lips against his and lay down next to him to get some sleep.

I woke up with a start when something hit me on the side of my head. Springing up, ready to take on whatever was attacking us, I blinked away sleep and tensed. Then I saw the apple by my feet and registered Isla's smirk.

'Sorry,' she said, not sounding apologetic in the least.

I rubbed my eyes. It wasn't light yet, but I had the sense that morning was approaching. 'I can think of better ways to be woken up,' I grunted, glaring at her angrily.

Her face fell and I instantly felt guilty. I hastily pasted on a smile to reassure her. I didn't want to have apples thrown at me while I slept but this wasn't the time to make Isla feel bad. There was enough of that in the world.

I stretched out and scooped up the fallen fruit up, rubbing it on my sleeve before taking a bite. I glanced at Laoch, who turned the last page of the book before snapping it shut. He raised his eyes to me and seemed surprised that I was awake. 'You're up.'

He must have been too absorbed in the diary to pay attention to what Isla was doing. 'Aye.'

Before I could ask his opinion of the book Isla danced in front of me, shifting her weight from foot to foot and placing her hands on her hips. 'Well?' she demanded. 'Let's get our shit together and get out of here! We need to get moving.'

'It's still dark.'

'It'll be light soon. We need to go.'

I was beginning to suspect that Isla was far more nervous of the countryside than she was letting on. 'When the sun rises, we'll set off,' I said firmly.

'But—'

'It won't be long.'

She huffed loudly and flounced down to a sitting position.

I gazed into the interior gloom of the cave to check on Noah. He was in the same position in front of the huge rune as he had been all night. 'Did he sleep?' I asked Laoch.

'No. Not as far as I could tell.'

'Did you read the whole book?'

He jerked his head in wary assent and tapped the cover. 'If it's true—'

'You think it isn't?'

He sighed and pushed back his hair. 'I believed every word.'

'Either Cadal Righ has been carrying that diary with him for more than a hundred years or he found it in the castle. If he did find it there, it's hard to believe that nobody else has read it.'

'It was written by a woman.'

I looked at him. Laoch's mouth twisted. 'I've never seen nor heard of any Mage, not even the likes of Angus, giving credence to anything written by a woman. There was a section of female-led writing in the library at the City Chambers in Glasgow. It was left untouched the entire time I was there.'

'You're saying this book could have been in Edinburgh in plain sight for generations and nobody bothered to read it?'

'If they did read it, they'd probably have dismissed it as the foolish ramblings of an old biddy,' Laoch said.

'I like old biddies,' Isla interjected. 'Interfering elderly women always ken more than everyone else.'

I smiled at her; I had no doubt that she was right. I looked again at Noah.

'Who wrote it then?' Isla asked. 'Who was she?'

I didn't take my eyes from Noah. 'A female Mage.'

'A *what?*'

Laoch explained. 'Before the Afflicted started to appear, there were as many female Mages as male ones. If this diary is to be believed, they were more powerful than the men. A female Mage called Elspeth Calder wrote the book. She mentions Cadal Righ, who was apparently christened Malcolm Finch. The Mages have never had one overall ruler but he tried to become that person.

'In his bid to become overlord, he killed several people who disagreed with him. Eventually a group of female Mages brought him down and captured him. When he was questioned, he told them that he was changing his name to Cadal Righ. He swore vengeance against all the Mages, told them the entire country would regret their actions and that their children would die horribly of disease – then he declared himself king. The Mages laughed in his face. Cadal Righ was a joke – a joke who vanished the night before his execution and was never heard of again.'

Isla stared at him with her mouth open. 'This happened when?'

'More than a hundred years ago.'

'So Cadal Righ is over a hundred years old?'

'More like a hundred-and-sixty.'

'No wonder he looks like a walking corpse,' she snorted.

Laoch didn't smile. 'Three days after he disappeared, the first of the Afflicted appeared when a baby was born to a young Mage in Edinburgh. That baby was a girl and she was Afflicted.'

'Which is either an extraordinary coincidence or Cadal Righ was responsible,' I said.

'He created the Afflicted because his ego was damaged?' Isla asked with a sniff. 'Figures. But how is he still alive?'

Laoch handed her the book. 'He probably drew power from the Afflicted to sustain himself, though it wouldn't have been easy. That's probably why he's not been seen for such a long time. He must have gone into hibernation and used the magic that sustains Affliction to keep himself going. But as the numbers of the Afflicted have swelled, so has Cadal Righ's power.'

Isla exhaled sharply. 'If magic is what keeps the Affliction going, then why do we no' just get rid of the magic?'

Noah's fingers were twitching against his legs as if he were communicating some kind of message. From time to time, his eyes lifted to mine then he hastily looked away again.

'Cadal Righ doesn't think that women have magic any more,' I said. 'He must have known what would happen when he made female Mages appear to be the source of the Affliction.' I nodded at the book. 'According to Elspeth, the females were attacked and killed one by one until almost none of them were left. Most were taken by surprise. The diary ends abruptly, suggesting that Elspeth was also taken by surprise and killed.

'Once they'd decided that female Mages were the root of the problem, the male Mages stamped them out. They acted first and didn't bother to ask questions, not then and not later. They were so focused on their own problems, they didn't stop to remember Cadal Righ and what had happened to him.'

'Fuck,' Isla breathed.

'Aye,' I said. 'Fuck.' Now Noah's legs were twitching too; he seemed unable to keep still. 'But as interesting as those details are, they're not what's important.'

'Huh?'

'You said it yourself, Isla,' Laoch told her. 'If magic is what keeps the Affliction going, then why don't we get rid of the magic? If Elspeth Calder is to be believed, she tried it – and it worked.'

'I dinna understand.'

My eyes continued to travel up and down Noah's body. 'Twice,' I said. 'Elspeth Calder pulled the magic from the body of Afflicted Mages twice. Both times, the Mages lost their magic forever and both times their Affliction was cured.'

Isla hefted the book in her hands then, without warning, she threw it at the wall. It bounced off the side and thudded to the ground. I finally ripped my gaze away from Noah to stare at her. Throwing things was becoming a nasty habit of hers. 'What did you do that for?'

'Most o' the fucking Afflicted are ordinary people! They dinna have any magic! Who cares if you can help an Afflicted Mage? What about an Afflicted cleaner? Or chimney sweep? Or bookkeeper? Elspeth Calder is a waste o' time!'

'I don't know how we help them,' I said. 'Not yet.' I pointed at Noah. 'But if we can help someone like him, we'll have done more to stop the Affliction than anyone else has in a century. It's a start. We have to try something, Isla. We have to find a way to stop Cadal Righ and his Afflicted army before there's nobody left in Scotland who is healthy. If we can understand Noah's disease, we can understand the others and maybe we can help them.'

'His disease is different! I already told you that!'

'He's all we've got,' I said. 'What else would you have me do?'

'We should leave,' she muttered, turning away. 'We should head to Glasgow now before Cadal Righ comes after us.'

'We will leave as soon as the sun rises. Until then,' I pointed to Noah's sorry figure, 'I'll try Elspeth's method. Before he was Afflicted, he was a Mage, the worst type of Mage. He was petty and cruel and ambitious. If I could have, I'd have stabbed him through the heart and watched him bleed out in George Square. Instead, I'll try and save him.'

I looked at Laoch and Isla. 'If I save him, I might learn how to save everyone else. And then bloody Noah can become the saviour of Scotland.'

Laoch's green eyes flashed. 'I despise him, everything he has ever done and everything he has ever stood for – but I'll help you try to save him, Mairi.'

'You bampots! Awa' an' bile yer heids,' Isla said. Her shoulders dropped. 'Fine. I'll help you, too.'

I smiled and turned to Noah. 'Who would have thought that the future of this country might actually lie with you after all?'

As Noah's head swivelled in my direction, an odd, satisfied expression crossed his face. A moment later, another unpleasant odour was layered on top of all the others. I frowned. 'Did he just...?'

'Oh, aye.' Isla shook her head in disgust. 'The potential saviour of Scotland just pissed himself.'

CHAPTER

TWELVE

I ate all of my apple, including the core, but still my stomach gurgled and complained at the lack of a real meal. I paid it no attention as I paced up and down in front of the cave preparing myself.

Not for the first time, I reflected on the perils of hope. The blood in my veins was fizzing with anticipation because if this worked it could change everything. It would give us a genuine head start in our bid to defeat Cadal Righ.

I had no doubt that healing the Affliction would strip of him of most of his powers. He wasn't our only problem but he was the biggest one. Returning Noah to his original self, awful as that thought was, truly felt like our best option. If this worked, we could learn how to save ourselves and our country. I couldn't bear to contemplate the alternative.

'We could wait until we get to Glasgow before you try this,' Laoch said. 'I remember what happened in Edinburgh when only part of this double spell was used against you.'

It was difficult to forget. The Mage who'd performed the spell had dropped dead afterwards from the effort, although

108

admittedly he'd temporarily removed magic from several of us rather than one person.

According to Elspeth Calder, if you controlled the power in short bursts – something at which female magic users were supposedly more adept than males – and didn't over-reach, you'd survive without any problems. We'd see. My fingers were tightly crossed. It would be amazing if this experiment didn't kill me; there again, *anything* that didn't kill me was a bonus these days.

'They'll never let Noah into the city,' I answered. 'Not now. But Elspeth did this and that means I can do it too.' I met Laoch's eyes. 'We both know what sort of chaos will be going on at the City Chambers and in the city. We need to present the Mages with a *fait accompli* to get them to listen. Only then can we use their combined knowledge to enhance what we learn with Noah and apply it to everyone else.'

My mouth tightened. The Mages had education and books and years of experience that I couldn't match. Much as it galled me to admit it, I needed their help. Scotland needed them. 'If we can show them a fully healed Noah, they'll pay attention.'

'Aye.' Laoch's expression was impassive. 'But then we'll have to deal with a fully healed Noah.'

A ghost of a smile crossed my lips. 'We can always knock him over the head with a rock if he's too much to deal with. As long as we don't kill him, it'll be alright.'

Isla's hand shot up into the air. 'I volunteer to stand behind him with a rock.'

'You,' I told her sternly, 'need to keep out of the way. I want to draw him out into the fresh air to do this. You need to stay a safe distance away.'

'There's no such thing as safe,' she returned, though she did back away towards the trees. Smart lass.

I tilted my head up at the sky. Half an hour, I reckoned, maybe less. By then the sun would be up and we could make our way safely to Glasgow. I nodded decisively. It was time. 'Noah,' I called softly into the cave. 'Noah? Come here.'

There was no answer. I glanced at Laoch. 'Have you removed the silence spell?'

'Aye.'

I licked my lips and tried again. 'Noah!'

I heard a muted groan but nothing else. It was time to try a different tactic.

'He Is Here.' I said it quietly, as if yelling out the words would somehow make them true.

It turned out that I didn't need to shout. As soon as I'd finished the sentence, Noah emitted a long, ear-piercing shriek, stumbled to his feet and lurched towards me and the cave entrance. I watched him carefully. I had to get my timing right.

When he was less than twenty feet away, I tensed my shoulders. He had to be close because it wouldn't work otherwise. Fifteen feet. Ten.

Almost there, Mairi.

As soon as I could stretch my arm out in front of me and touch Noah's chest, I hummed. *Desh mar tun desh mar.* Remove the magic and block it.

Come on, Mairi. You can do this.

My magic was tentative at first; I didn't want to flood Noah's system or destroy myself in the process. He stopped in front of me and a confused look crossed his ravaged face. He scratched his head, then performed the most Afflicted version of a shrug I'd ever seen.

My spells hadn't been enough. I hummed again and pushed out more power. *Desh mar tun desh mar.*

Noah's mild confusion started to change into something that could have been panic.

'I can see it! I can see it working!' Isla cried.

I didn't look at her, but I heard the shocked thrill in her voice. Despite her misgivings, she was as excited by the prospect that the magic was taking effect as I was.

'The rot inside him is fading at the edges. You need to do more. Throw more power into it!' she demanded.

Next to me Laoch growled, '*Don't* throw more power into it. Don't hurt yourself, Mairi.'

'I'm in control,' I gasped. 'It's alright. I've got this.' I hummed for a third time, sending more of my energy towards Noah's body. His knees buckled and he started to whimper.

I felt my own legs shake but now I didn't need Isla to tell me it was working. I could feel it happening; the vile, seeping Affliction inside Noah was fading. It was actually going to work. I was going to do it.

Draining my energy, I tugged on more magic. Noah cowered until he eventually curled into a tight ball to shield himself from me, which made it harder to target my power. When I threw out another surge, I staggered backwards.

Dimly I heard Laoch hiss then his hand gripped mine. 'Take magic from me.'

No. That was one of the Mages' tricks and I wouldn't go that far. Besides, he'd only just recovered. Taking his magic could send him straight into a relapse.

'Fucking hell, Mairi. Do it,' he ordered.

The rot was leeching from Noah bit by bit. He was so close. I gritted my teeth, clutched at Laoch's hand and pulled on his power. The resulting energy pulse that passed through me and out to Noah was like nothing I'd ever felt before; the only thing that had ever come close was an orgasm. No wonder the Mages borrowed each other's magic when they needed an extra push. The sensation was extraordinary.

Noah's body was shuddering. He uncurled himself, but his

legs and arms were shaking as if he were having a seizure. Sweat was pouring down both his face and mine and we were both shivering. But it wouldn't take much more.

'There are only a few Afflicted bits left!' Isla called. 'Just a few last snaky bits and then it's gone!'

I hummed. I wasn't sure I had enough power left, even with Laoch's help. 'I can't,' I stuttered. 'I don't think … I… Shite.'

Isla grabbed my other hand. 'Use me,' she whispered into my ear. 'Use me, too.'

I tugged magic from her. It would be enough. Hum, Mairi. Hum for all you're worth. A fraction more and then…

The roar behind us was so loud that it made the ground beneath our feet shake. The connection between Noah and me was cut as suddenly as if someone had taken a pair of glistening shears and sliced through a magical thread.

I collapsed to the ground. Isla let out an ear-piercing scream and darted towards the mouth of the cave. Laoch spun around and I turned my head. Buggering shite.

I didn't know what the monster in front of me was but I knew it was terrifying. I'd never seen anything like it – it seemed to be a strange mix of horse and man, an equine body with a male torso perched on top. It possessed a single, red, glowing eye in its forehead and, horrifically, no skin; instead it was covered from head to toe in a pulsating mass of veins of black muscle. It towered over us, rearing its forelegs in the air. When it opened its mouth to roar a second time, I saw row upon row of sharp pointed teeth.

I hummed *Ins veil,* but I'd expended too much power on Noah. All that was left was a stuttering gasp that caused the creature's eyes to flatten and its nostrils to flare. My attempt at an attack had only served to make it angrier. It shook its head and leapt towards me.

Laoch shouted, '*Meshar al*!' The air vibrated with his magic and the monster fell to the ground with a thump.

Then Laoch was grabbing my arm and hauling me away. 'It's a nuckalavee! Don't let it breathe on you. Its breath is poisonous.' He dragged me past Noah and away from the fallen beast. 'I've never seen one this far inland before. We have to get away.'

I shook him off and pulled away to get to Noah.

'Mairi!'

'We have to help him too!'

'It won't stay down for long. I don't have enough magic left to hold it, Mairi! We need to get the fuck out of here!'

My fingers scrabbled towards Noah and plucked at his arm. If I could drag him away, maybe I could scoop him up over my shoulder and we'd all escape. But the nuckalavee was already stirring, sloughing off the effects of Laoch's spell. Bloody hell, that thing was tough.

'We need him!' I yelled at Laoch. 'Help me!'

I heard him curse but then he was by my side, reaching for Noah's left arm while I heaved up his right one. The nuckalavee raised its head. I thought it had been angry before but that was nothing compared to the look in its eye now. It blinked once, then it came at us again.

'*Ins veil*!' Laoch's magical command threw the nuckalavee back several metres, but the thing was five metres long and such a short distance wouldn't protect us.

I reached inside and dredged up as much remaining magic as I could. I hummed, adding a second wave to Laoch's first. *Ins veil.* Again, the monster was thrown back. If we could keep this up until we reached the trees and then ran for it, we'd make it. Surely we had enough magic left...

At least that was what I thought until I heard the second roar. 'Mairi!' Isla screamed. 'There's another one!'

I dropped Noah and twisted around. Another nuckalavee was emerging from the far side of the cave, smaller than its terrifying companion but no less dangerous. The first nuckalavee charged at Laoch and me as the second one bolted towards Isla. A tiny desperate hum escaped my lips. *Vaz.*

The creature heading for Isla smacked into an invisible wall – which immediately started to give way. It would last mere seconds. Isla was mouthing words, desperately trying to conjure up enough magic to help herself, but her panic was too great. Too much emotion stifled effective magic use, and Isla had reached her limit.

'Laoch...' I muttered in warning.

'Get Isla,' he said. 'I'll hold off the nuckalavees for as long as I can.'

'What about Noah?'

He didn't look at me. 'We have to leave him, Mairi. I'm sorry.'

Fuck. Me too. Frustration gnawed at me, but I spun away to Isla's side. 'Come on! We have to go now!'

'You dinnae need to tell me twice. I told you we should have left for Glasgow already.' Despite her complaint, she ran with me.

I turned my head and watched Laoch bellow a final spell. Both nuckalavees were thrown backwards; the larger one hit a tree, while the smaller one tumbled to the ground.

Laoch sprinted towards us, his jet-black hair streaming behind him. The larger nuckalavee was already on its feet again and I screamed at Laoch to hurry up. He reached Isla and me as it sprang forward.

It stopped next to Noah's body and opened its jaws. Noah's head jerked. 'Wh – what's happening?' As clarity returned to his recovered mind, he raised his arms to ward off the creature. 'What...?'

The nucklavee grabbed Noah's arm with its sharp teeth. Blood sprayed everywhere, arcing into the air and splattering on the ground at Noah's feet. Then Laoch was pulling me away and we were running into the trees and away from the cave as fast as we possibly could.

THIRTEEN

We ran and ran and ran. None of us looked back. I heard a roar from one of the nuckalavees, but they didn't seem to be coming after us. Noah was probably more than enough to satisfy them for now. All the same, we kept moving at a fast pace for a good two miles through uneven terrain, spiky bushes and thorny trees.

By the time we reached the main road we were covered in scratches, but we kept on running for another ten minutes. The nuckalavees had appeared so suddenly that I knew we had to put as much distance between us and them as possible.

We'd probably have sprinted all the way to Glasgow if Isla hadn't stumbled when her toe snagged in a tiny pothole. Laoch caught her before she planted her face on the ground, but it was clear she was running on empty. After the attempt to save Noah, the nuckalavee attack and our subsequent escape, it felt like I was too.

We stopped. Laoch and I scanned the horizon for signs that anything – nuckalavee or otherwise – was coming after us, but there was nothing. The road, the fields, the hills and the nearby woods seemed clear.

Isla had wrapped her arms around her body and huge, silent tears were streaming down her face. I went over to her and opened my mouth to ask if she wanted a hug. Before I could speak, she flew into my arms and buried her head in my shoulder. Her whole body was trembling.

I looked at Laoch. 'Those things came out of nowhere.'

He nodded grimly. 'I've only seen one of those bastards before, and that was in a rural spot far up north by the sea. All I can think is that they've sensed what's going on with Cadal Righ and the Afflicted, and they've come to join the fray. Perhaps his foul magic is drawing them in – or maybe it was nothing more than bad luck. Either way, we have to be on our guard. There might be more of them.'

Isla let out a tiny whimper and I stroked her hair. 'It's alright. It's not far to Glasgow now. They won't dare come near the city.' I met Laoch's eyes. *Will they?*

His response was dark. *I certainly hope not.*

We could have put up a better defence if we'd not already used up so much magic on Noah. I paused. *It worked, you know. At the end. Noah was aware and conscious and ... unAfflicted.*

I know.

But without him with us as proof, the Mages will never believe that's possible.

Laoch ran a hand through his hair. *You'll make them believe,* he answered simply.

I ground my teeth in frustration. *I don't have the gift of the gab, Laoch. I don't possess a silver tongue. Until a couple of months ago, I couldn't even speak. I don't have the powers of persuasion that others do.*

He offered me a crooked smile. *You've not been paying attention. You're far more eloquent than you give yourself credit for. Isla doesn't know that you used to be mute – I doubt it has ever occurred to her. Don't let your past get in the way of your future.*

That was easier said than done, but I nodded and looked down at Isla. 'It's okay,' I soothed. 'We're safe now.'

'Safe?' She didn't try disguise her adolescent derision. 'We're not safe. We'll never be safe.'

I hadn't heard her sound this defeated before and her tone stabbed at my heart. 'I know things are bad but look at what we've already been through. Look at what we've survived! It's more than a lot of other people have managed. We won't give up, not ever. If we give up, there's nothing left for the likes of John back at that farmhouse. There's nothing left for those thousands of people who left Edinburgh to march to Glasgow. This is our country and we'll fight for it.'

See? Laoch said silently. *You can speak eloquently enough to persuade anyone to your cause.*

'Aye,' Isla replied, her disbelief visible on her face as well as in her voice. 'And when you beat Cadal Righ, cure every Afflicted person in the country, tame the creepy horse things that don't have any skin and get to parade around the streets of Glasgow with a triumphant smile on your face, the Mages will pitch up again and hang you by the neck until you're dead because you're annoying them.'

You were saying? I asked Laoch.

He stifled a smile. *Teenagers are a different breed. I'd rather have her like that than in tears.*

Me too. I gave Isla a long look. 'One problem at a time,' I said. I looked down the road. 'Right now we have to get to Glasgow. Let's focus on that and worry about everything else later.'

She folded her arms. 'At least that bastard Mage is dead. Serves him right.'

I pinned my mouth shut. It wasn't in me to express sadness that Noah was gone, but I wished it could have been otherwise – for all our sakes.

WE DIDN'T STOP AGAIN. We continued towards Glasgow, placing one foot in front of another, plodding through the puddles and twists and turns of the road. At least the skies remained clear and there was no longer any rain; it wasn't much of a silver lining but at that point I'd have taken anything.

Eventually, after a few hours of miserable walking, we turned a corner and the familiar skyline of Glasgow appeared. My spirits lifted immediately. This city had been my entire world for most of my life. Despite all the heartache it had brought me, it was my home and it was good to be back.

I scanned the rooftops, noting the lack of rising smoke or devastated buildings. Glasgow was still standing, untouched, and that counted for more than I dared to admit to myself.

'What's all that shite?' Isla asked, her hard façade replacing her earlier vulnerability, as if she could wipe away the terror of the past few days by acting tough. Perhaps she could; perhaps I should try it, too.

I followed her gaze then I frowned. Good question. What *was* all that shite?

It was Laoch who worked it out and answered for both of us. 'Tents,' he said grimly. 'Lots of tents.'

I'd been too distracted by the skyline. The massive jumble of low, drab structures almost surrounded the city limits. Even from this distance, the makeshift city looked enormous. With nausea rippling through my belly, I wondered if anyone had been allowed to enter through the city gates. The walls around Glasgow, which the Mages had commissioned decades ago to keep out the Afflicted roaming the countryside, were too high for any non-magical person to climb over. These days, the gates were the only way in or out of the city.

Were there Mages sleeping under canvas and living

without running water, or had Aspen and his cronies been admitted? I shook my head. There was no point voicing that question; I already knew the answer. 'If Cadal Righ marches on Glasgow, those people will be the first to be slaughtered,' I said.

Laoch's mouth twisted. 'Aye. But can anyone risk letting them into Glasgow when many of them might be Afflicted? Would you?'

I wasn't sure I knew the answer to that. I sighed. 'How many people do you think are there?'

'Thousands,' Isla answered. She reached into her pocket and drew out Mungo. 'This is Glasgow,' she told him. 'This is where everyone is going to be fucked. Including us.'

Mungo seemed unfazed. Squeaking contentedly, he nuzzled Isla's thumb. I felt a brief stab of irrational jealousy before chiding myself and returning my attention to the tents.

We were in the last throes of winter, so it had to be freezing down there. So much for the warm Glaswegian welcome that Aspen had advertised. I curled my fingers into tight fists, until my fingernails bit into the soft flesh of my palms, then I swallowed hard and straightened my back. 'Come on,' I said. 'Let's see for ourselves what's going on.'

Instead of walking abreast as we had done for most of our journey, Laoch and Isla fell into step behind me. I scowled; I knew what they were doing and why, and I didn't like it. 'No,' I snapped. 'Enough. Walk beside me.'

'You're the star of the show, Mairi,' Laoch said. 'The saviour of Glasgow. You need to take the lead.'

'We are equals.' My voice hardened. 'I'm not a Mage. I'm not your leader. And, frankly, I don't believe I've saved a single soul yet.'

'You saved me,' he replied.

'And me,' Isla said. 'I suppose.'

I glared at them and Isla smirked. 'Aye, well, I could have saved myself without your help.'

Laoch stayed silent. I cleared my throat. 'And you,' I said to him, 'saved me more times and in more ways than I can count. You also gave me my voice.'

He started. 'No, I didn't.'

'You did, whether it was deliberate or otherwise.' I gestured either side of me. 'Now both of you get up here next to me. No airs and graces. No matter how people react, we're not conquering heroes. I didn't win the Ascendancy Challenge.'

'Nobody won the Ascendancy Challenge,' Laoch muttered.

'And,' I continued, ignoring him, 'the whole country is in a worse place now than it was when we left Glasgow two weeks ago. Let's see what's going on with the tents and inside the city, then go to the City Chambers to speak to the Mages. That's our first priority.'

Isla raised an eyebrow.

'What?' I asked.

'You said you weren't our leader but that sounded like you were leading to me.' She shrugged. 'Jus' saying.'

I stared at her then, because I had nothing else to say, I turned to the front. 'Come on,' I repeated. 'Let's go.' This time, they returned to my side without a word.

Although it had seemed quite a distance to the edge of the city, we reached the first line of tents within the hour. I expected to hear a considerable hubbub but there was little activity and even less chatter. The first people we saw were withdrawn, barely raising their heads to glance at us as we approached.

It was no wonder they were shell-shocked; everything they had ever known had been upended in hours. The people of Scotland had always lived on a knife-edge, subject to the vagaries and whims of the Mages, but this was something different. Neither was the situation helped by the state of their temporary accommodation.

When Isla had pointed out the tents, I'd assumed that at the very least they'd be made of canvas scrummaged together from Glasgow's stores and supplies. That certainly wasn't the case with the first ones we saw, which had been strung up with little more than old bed sheets and precarious poles. There wasn't a single makeshift shelter that would withstand even a mild bout of bad weather. Some tents had small hearths set up nearby but they were all either cold and empty, or displaying little more than a few embers and emitting barely any warmth. Fires required fuel; while they were plenty of trees and woods nearby, venturing into them could be perilous indeed.

And yet it wasn't all bad. As we picked our way along a muddy path between rows of haphazard shelters, I saw a family with two young children beckon an elderly man and encourage him to join them for something to eat. Groups of women were going from person to person, taking down names and details of missing family members. A teenage lad was carving a set of crutches for his new neighbour who seemed to have broken his leg.

The deeper we got, the more we saw. While the voices remained muted and the mood was mostly sombre, there were occasional barks of laughter and deep-throated chuckles. No matter how dire a situation, people retained a sense of humour. In fact, the worse things became, the stronger the community spirit. This was what we were fighting for, not the Mages or a vague idea of a Scotland that didn't exist but each other.

It wasn't long before we came across the very epitome of fighting spirit; it just wasn't the sort of fighting spirit I wanted to see.

There were clearings between the clusters of shelters, presumably places where people could congregate. It was astonishing that such forethought had gone into the rapid growth of this refugee city, given that none of it had been here three days earlier. These little clearings were already being used to extraordinary effect.

'Listen up!' yelled a young man in the centre of one of the larger ones. He was wearing a strange collection of clothing – a multi-coloured shawl, patched trousers and a feathered cap. There were a few tired-looking people in front of him, including one older woman who, judging by her exasperated expression and similarity in features, was his mother.

'We need to seize this opportunity and leave here. We should have stayed in Edinburgh! We can speak to this new king and make a deal with him. He can have the Mages and we can have our country back!'

One or two of the watching people gave ragged murmurs of agreement; one or two turned away in disgust.

'The writing is on the wall, people! There is a new world order and anyone who doesn't embrace it will die in this place!'

'Aye, well, you can go ahead and become Afflicted if you want,' somebody shouted. 'I'd rather keep hold of my faculties.'

The young man fixed on him. 'Maybe becoming Afflicted is what we all should do. Maybe they're happier.' He sniffed. 'Are you happy right now? Because I'm not.' He raised his eyes and his gaze fell on Laoch. Both startled and dismayed, he swallowed hard and drew back his shoulders. 'A daemon!' he shouted. 'Look! There's a daemon!'

Shite. 'We should go,' I muttered.

'Are you here to spy on us for the Mages?' the lad bellowed. 'Because you can go back to them and tell them that their rule is ending!'

His shout didn't have the effect he'd hoped for. Instead of agreeing with him, several people turned to Laoch, desperation filling their faces. 'Help us! We need to be allowed into the city! We cannae stay oot here!'

Laoch raised his hands and attempted to call for peace. 'I'm not with the Mages,' he began.

The young man who'd been speaking snarled, 'All daemons are with the Mages.'

'I'm not,' Laoch said. 'Not anymore.'

'How's that possible?'

Laoch pointed at me. 'She freed me.' Technically that wasn't true, but it was too late to explain. People were already turning to look at me. I registered the dawning epiphany from at least half of them as they worked out who I was.

'Mairi.' The murmur rose through the small crowd. 'You're Mairi.'

More shite. I hadn't wanted to be recognised this early on but I couldn't run away now, so I stepped forward and lifted my chin. The murmur fell away and everyone stared at me, waiting to hear what I had to say.

I don't know what it was. It wasn't the pressure of the last few days catching up with me and it wasn't the optimistic anticipation reflected in the watching eyes. Neither was I scared, not of these people. And yet for some reason when I searched for the words to address them, I came up short. My mouth opened and no sound came out. My hands fluttered and I felt the familiar weight of expectation that I should speak when I could not.

Panic clawed at my throat and my cheeks reddened. I saw the expectant gazes turn to confusion, disappointment, even disgust. I flailed for the sounds, for *anything* to come out of my mouth other than stuttering breaths.

'Can she no' fucking speak?'

Isla whirled towards the young man. 'Of course she can! But she doesnae have the verbal diarrhoea that a bampot like you seems tae possess! She thinks about what she's going tae say. And when she speaks, you're gonna want tae listen! So wheesht!'

'Aye,' the man's mother said. 'Wheesht, Dougie.' She gazed at me with desperate hope as if I could give her all the answers.

Laoch slipped his hand into mine and gently squeezed my fingers. The warm pressure of his hand was enough.

'Cadal Righ is not the solution to the Mages,' I said, beyond grateful that my voice was finally ringing out loud and clear. 'And if anyone thinks that becoming Afflicted is a good idea, then you haven't been paying attention. We have to work together, defeat Cadal Righ and reclaim our country from everyone who wants to rule over us without our say so.'

An older woman interrupted. 'Right now, all I want to work on is getting a proper roof over my head and real food into my belly. Are you going to help us with that?'

'I'm going to try. You need to be patient.'

'Patient? We'll die if we stay oot here! If the Affliction doesnae get us, then hypothermia will.'

I could sense panic growing. 'Listen to yourselves.' I injected as much cheery joy into my voice as I could. Several brows furrowed. 'This is the sort of energy we need to win against Cadal Righ. We won't beat him back or deal with the Mages by *letting* things happen. We have to *make* them happen.'

I looked at Dougie, the young man who'd given the impassioned speech. 'Your ideas might be misplaced, but your energy is not. Let's harness that and *fight* for survival. I will get into the city and I will talk the Mages. We'll find a way to get all of you inside the city walls where you'll be safer.'

Nobody cheered, nobody was daft enough to think that one speech would provide salvation, but I saw renewed optimism and the glint of determination in more than one eye. It was enough for now, although these people would need concrete help soon.

Dougie, apparently still stinging from his mother's rebuke and a scolding from a teenager, spat on the ground. 'You're just a woman. You dinnae ken anything and you have no power.'

Before I could respond, the air snapped with magic. My eyes narrowed and I glanced at Isla, but it wasn't coming from her. It wasn't coming from Laoch either. It was Dougie's mother who had sparks of blue glittering at her fingertips. '*Belzac.*'

Dougie frowned. A half-second later, he screeched and frantically slapped at the tiny flames that had appeared from nowhere around the edges of his shawl. He yanked it off his shoulders, threw it on the ground and stamped out the flames, then stared at his mother.

'Women ken plenty,' she said clearly, 'and we have plenty of power. So you watch your mouth, you wee eejit.'

Dougie's face was white. 'You can do magic? *You?*'

'I'm no' just your mother, Douglas. I'm a person in my own right, too.' She pointed at the singed scarf. 'Now pick that up and go and fetch some water fae the river. I've got a thirst on.'

I half-expected Dougie to refuse, but he was so stunned by his mother's revelation that he obeyed her order and staggered away. As soon as he'd gone, a few people came up to me.

'I dinna ken if you can help us,' another young man said. 'But you're willing to try. Sometimes that's enough.'

'God speed, Mairi,' an old woman told me. 'You give that Cadal Righ what for!'

I smiled faintly at the well-wishers. Sooner or later, they would need far more than mere words and promises. I glanced at Laoch and Isla, then I sidled over to Dougie's mother.

'I shouldnae have done that,' she muttered.

'Why not?' I asked.

She snorted. 'You dinnae need to ask that question.'

'I don't see any Mages around.'

She shook her head. 'Word will get back to them. And when Cadal Righ is dealt with, they'll come for me. They always find out, sooner or later.' She dropped her head. 'It's not as if I have a lot of magic or knowledge. That's the only damned spell I can use.'

'Then you showed great bravery in using it.' I licked my lips. 'What's your name?'

'Maggie.'

'I need you, Maggie,' I said.

Her head snapped up. 'What? Why?'

I looked at Laoch and he nodded. 'Tell her,' he said.

I drew in a breath. 'Cadal Righ doesn't know that women can use magic.'

Maggie's eyes clouded with puzzlement. 'So?

'We think he's the reason the Afflicted started, and the reason why women with power have had to hide for so long.' I frowned. 'Well, he's not the only reason for that part, but he started it.'

'I don't follow.'

'The important thing is that we know something he doesn't so we have an advantage over him. Women can still do magic.' I gestured at her. 'Lots of them have power.'

'It's no' much of an advantage.'

'It is,' I said confidently. 'If we use it properly. I need you to find as many women as you can who have power like you. It doesn't matter if it's only a little bit or if they don't know any spells. Just put the word out and gather as many women as you can.'

'I can do that,' she said. 'But why?'

It was Laoch who answered her, his eyes glittering as he read my mind. 'Because then we'll have an army.'

CHAPTER

FOURTEEN

We moved through the other tents with greater purpose. There was a skip to Isla's step, my shoulders were pulled back and Laoch maintained a small smile on his face.

'Can I be a general in the new army?' Isla asked.

'Honorary general,' I replied.

'What does that mean?'

'It means that you'll provide support from the rear by staying out of any fights.'

She frowned at this and a sly look came into her eyes. I'd have to keep an eye on her before she went after Cadal Righ and challenged him to a duel. But I knew that if enough women possessed her spirit, our odds of success would increase enormously.

I was beyond glad that her earlier sense of defeat had vanished, and I resolved to be more like her. There came a time when everyone hit the rock bottom chasm of depression; it was climbing your way out of that chasm that counted.

We turned a corner, avoiding a cluster of people leaning against each other for warmth and comfort, and the main city

128

gates came into view. My body tensed when I saw the hundreds of people clamouring to get in past the guards whose numbers had increased tenfold from their usual cohort.

The guards weren't the only ones keeping watch: dozens of sharp-eyed ravens were lining the walls and circling the air. The Mages at the City Chambers were clearly terrified of what their own people might do.

I motioned to Laoch and Isla and we stopped, taking a moment or two to watch the hubbub. I wasn't convinced that appealing to the guards' better nature to let us in would get us anywhere. Although I knew from Edinburgh that some of the ordinary men who worked for the Mages were sympathetic, plenty weren't. The Mages would have selected the most loyal for this most important of duties.

'Even Queen Mairi the Magnificent isn't getting into Glasgow through these gates,' a familiar voice remarked.

I turned my head and experienced a surge of joy as I saw Angus. I dropped Laoch's hand, rushed towards him and grabbed him in a huge hug. He remained stock still for a moment and then reciprocated, wrapping his arms around me. 'It's good to see you too, lass.'

'I'm glad that you're alright,' I mumbled into his chest. 'Where's Belle?'

'Around here somewhere. I'm sure she'll show up soon. That woman is like a bad penny.'

'And Andy?'

'He went off with Aspen and the others. They were allowed through. Aspen dragged the female daemon along with him.'

I felt a surge of dismay for Teasag. I hoped for all our sakes that Andy hadn't defected and was merely playing nice with the other Mages so he could retrieve the books at the City Chambers and find out more about Cadal Righ.

I wasn't surprised that the Mages had gained admittance to

Glasgow when nobody else had. Privilege knew no boundaries where the Mages were concerned, even with the risk of potential Affliction to contend with.

I released Angus and stepped back. He eyed Laoch then stuck out his hand. 'You're not dead then. That's good.'

Laoch didn't shake his hand and I couldn't blame him. Angus was on our side but he had been a Mage for a long time. There was a lot to forgive, especially for Laoch. 'You weren't allowed inside with the other Mages?' he asked instead.

Angus examined his own outstretched hand for a moment before dropping it with a shrug. I doubted he'd lose any sleep over Laoch's attitude; Angus wasn't the type. 'I might be a Mage, and we might be facing the biggest threat our country has ever seen, but I'm still a dirty traitor.' He winked cheerfully.

Isla stared at him in horror. 'You're a Mage?' She swung her eyes towards me. 'What is wrong with you?' she whispered. 'Your boyfriend is a daemon, you tried to save that Afflicted Mage bastard, and now you have another mate who's a fucking Mage, too? I thought you were one of the good guys.'

Angus raised his bushy white eyebrows. 'Who is this sweet cherub?'

'Fuck you,' Isla snarled.

'This is Isla,' I said. 'She came with us from Edinburgh.'

'Uh-huh.' Angus watched her as if she were a wild animal. 'And what's this about an Afflicted Mage bastard?'

'It was Noah,' I said quietly. I explained in as few words as I could.

'Lass,' Angus said when I'd finished, 'nobody will believe you. I don't believe you – and I don't believe you're capable of lying.'

'We have to *make* the Mages believe me,' I said. I crossed my arms over my chest. 'This is how we win.'

He pursed his lips dubiously. 'This is not the magical solution you think it is. You've got nothing.' He waved at the empty space behind me. 'Literally.'

'We've got more than we did before,' I returned. 'Besides, how about you? How was your journey here?' My jaw tightened. 'Lock a bunch of people inside any barns along the way, did you?'

Guilt coloured his pale eyes. 'You found that place, did you?'

'Aye.' Laoch glowered.

Angus tutted. 'You do realise I'm the same as you now? I have no more voice than you do. I couldn't have done anything even if I'd wanted to.'

'Did you try to help them? How could you be sure they were all Afflicted?' Laoch demanded.

A growl of anger rumbled in Angus's chest. 'Listen, laddie. Have you seen what's happening here? People are terrified. There's a containment area over to the west where anyone is dumped who's remotely suspected of Affliction. At the rate we're going, it'll only be a matter of time before everyone here is Afflicted too. Nobody is saying it but everybody knows it. We're fucked. We can't tell who's infected until it's too late, and more and more cases are appearing by the hour. You can't do what you did with Noah to everyone. There's no way out of this, lass.'

Isla barged past me. 'I can tell.'

'Tell what?' Angus said, looking at her as if she were mad.

'I can tell who is Afflicted.'

'No, you can't.'

I ground my teeth. 'Yes, she can.'

His mouth dropped open.

'But she can't do it for hundreds of thousands of people,' Laoch said.

'I could try,' Isla protested.

It wasn't feasible. She was one thirteen-year-old girl against thousands. 'Can we all take a minute to allow cooler heads to prevail?' I said. 'Before anything else, I need to get into Glasgow and speak to the Mages. Is there a way to sneak in?'

Several expressions flitted across Angus's face. Eventually he sighed and tugged at his beard. 'Why do you think, Queen Mairi, that I'm here with all this chaotic shite in front of me?' He gestured to the people who were still pushing forward and shouting at the guards, begging to be allowed in. 'I knew this was what you'd want, although I also know it's a pointless venture. I don't suppose there's any use in persuading you otherwise?'

'Nope,' I said. 'None.'

He sighed. 'I thought not. Well, I can tell you that you're not getting in through these gates. There's no chance.'

'But?' I questioned.

Angus sighed again. 'Wait.'

'For what?'

He turned his head. 'Her.'

I followed his gaze. When I saw what he was looking at, I smiled. Belle had appeared and she was shoving her way through the mass of people, her sharp elbows creating a path for herself.

'Oot the way, you bampots!' she screeched. A man wearing tattered clothing raised his hand to smack her. Before he could strike, she spat in his face and shoved him out of her way.

'Who's that?' Isla asked, her eyes wide with admiration.

'My old boss,' I said.

'She's amazing.'

'She's horrific,' I retorted. Isla glanced at me and I grinned. 'It's true.'

Belle bustled her way past the last of the people. 'The facilities out here are shocking,' she declared. 'Do you ken how difficult it is to pee at the best of times when you're wearing skirts like this?' she shouted at the impassive guards, pointing down at her heavy clothes which were in a sorry state. They were splattered with mud and they smelled awful. In fact, her whole body reeked of sewage.

Her mouth turned down in disgust and she met my eyes. 'You finally got here, then. You took your time.' She looked at Laoch. 'And the horned bastard, too. Back from the deid.'

'Hello, Belle,' he said. 'It's good to see you too.'

There was a time I'd never have believed I'd say it but, aye, it was good to see Belle. Given her stench, though, I didn't hug her as I'd hugged Angus.

'Hi.' Isla beamed at her with a glint of hero worship in her youthful face. 'I'm Isla.' She curtsied. 'It's an honour to meet you.'

'Well,' Belle said, 'it's about time somebody around here treated me with some respect. I'm Belle. You can call me ma'am – or lady. It's up to you.'

'Belle,' I warned.

'Whit?' she asked, the very picture of innocence. 'Is there a problem?'

I rolled my eyes while Angus cleared his throat. 'Well, woman?'

'Well, whit?' She pouted at him. 'Whit's your problem?'

He tapped his feet. Belle glared then huffed loudly. 'Patience is a virtue, you ken.' She lowered her voice. 'It's guarded. No' on this side but on the other. I think it'll be alright, though. There's no' many o' them. We can do it. It'll be grim but it'll be worth it tae see ma Twister again. He'll no' be the same without me. He cannae manage on his own.'

I resisted the temptation to grab her shoulders and shake her to get a clearer explanation. 'You have a way into the city?'

Belle's eyebrows snapped together. 'Wheesht! Do you want everyone to hear?'

'Aye, Mairi,' Isla said. 'Dinnae talk so loud.'

I met Laoch's eyes, which were brimming with amusement. Yes, there was still humour to be found in this world if you looked hard enough.

Belle picked up her skirts. 'If you will all follow me,' she said primly, 'Lady Belle will save the day.'

'I'll believe that when I see it,' Angus muttered, but he looked away when Belle glared at him. 'Lead the way,' he said. 'My Lady.'

BELLE TOOK us further away than I expected. We trailed after her, leaving the main gates and their stony-faced guards far behind us. I was aware that three of the ravens followed us but I didn't look up and give them the satisfaction of seeing my wariness. I wasn't scared of them any longer. They were only birds; if they informed the Mages that I was on my way and sneaking into the city to speak to them, it was good that they'd be pre-warned. Nobody enjoyed it when a Mage was taken by surprise.

We passed more tents, many in a far worse condition than the ones we'd seen so far. I hissed repeatedly under my breath at the state these people were being forced to live in. We could be doing more – we *should* be doing more. And I didn't feel any better once the tents and people started to thin out; this wasn't a case of out of sight, out of mind.

Eventually Belle's steps slowed. Finally she turned and faced us, her expression filled with pride. 'Ta da!'

I glanced from side to side. Nope. I wasn't seeing it.

'Woman,' Angus growled, 'there's nothing here.'

'Man,' she returned, 'you're not looking hard enough.' She pointed downwards.

Set into the muddy ground was a large grate, presumably covering a hole leading towards the old sewers that had served the city for decades. I looked from the grate to Belle and back again. 'You want us to go down there?' I asked faintly.

'It's perfectly safe.'

'You said that it was guarded,' Laoch reminded her

'On the other side,' Belle snapped. 'No' here.' She pointed down at her stained and reeking skirts. 'You dinnae think I actually got in this state by having a pee, do you?'

'My dear woman, we wouldn't dare to think anything at all about your good self,' Angus told her

Belle harrumphed but I paid their byplay little attention. 'How do you know about this?' I asked.

'Twister an' me used it to transport tartan to other cities. If the Mages didnae ken that we were taking tartan out of Glasgow, then they couldnae tax us for it.'

I was even more astonished. 'You used to wander through the sewers carrying loads of tartan?'

Belle scrunched up her face. 'You eejit. Are you mad? Of course I didnae, other people did that. We paid them to do it. More than they deserved.'

'I never knew that.'

'It was before your time.' Her eyes shifted away from me. 'Our main transporter got caught so we stopped.'

It was Isla who asked the question. 'What happened to him?'

Belle simply wrapped a hand around her neck in answer.

Angus winced. 'Aye,' he said. 'I remember that.'

'Hardly an executable offence,' I said.

He raised his pale eyes. 'What is an executable offence, lass? The prevailing wisdom of the Mages has always been to stamp out any form of dissent or lawbreaking with as much might and power as possible, otherwise anything might happen. The whole city might rise up against us and,' he paused, 'imagine what things would be like if that happened.'

Aye. Imagine. I sighed. This wasn't the time for such conversations. If the grate at my feet took us into Glasgow then it was good enough for me.

I tied up my hair, tucked the bottoms of my trouser legs into my boots and looked around. A raven suddenly screeched overhead and I glanced up, watching as it flapped away from the city rather than towards it. Several other large black-feathered birds followed it. My mouth went dry. While it was a bonus for us that the birds had decided to venture elsewhere, I was concerned about their sudden flight. Was Cadal Righ already marching this way?

I shivered and looked at the grate again. We had to get a move on. Laoch knelt down, lifted the heavy iron and peered down into the dark hole. From somewhere in the folds of Isla's clothing, I heard Mungo squeak.

'Rats?' I asked Belle.

'It's a fecking sewer. Whit do you think?'

Aye, alright. It was a stupid question. 'Lead the way then,' I said.

Belle bared her teeth. 'My pleasure.'

We watched her lower herself with surprising ease and disappear quickly into the stinking blackness. I looked up repeatedly, checking to see if anybody was paying us attention, but the closest group of tents faced away from us and there wasn't a soul nearby. For all that the stench was eye-watering, this was the perfect entry point. So far, anyway.

Angus went next, grumbling the whole time. He was followed by Isla, who appeared far more excited than put off, then it was my turn. I glanced at Laoch who offered me a reassuring smile. I held my breath, nodded at him and headed down.

It ran deeper than I thought it would. There were rusting iron rungs affixed to the side that felt sturdy enough and eased my climb, but they were cold and slimy to touch. I couldn't help wondering what other creatures lived down here besides rats. It was wiser not to think about it but it was hard not to after our encounter with the nuckalavees.

My feet finally splashed onto solid ground. A hand reached out of the darkness and grabbed hold of me. 'Are you alright, Isla?' I asked.

Her voice answered immediately. 'Hunky dory, Mairi.'

That made one of us, then. I craned my neck up at the small circle of daylight above my head. Laoch had somehow managed to pull the grate back into position and was clambering down towards me in a far more sure-footed fashion than I had managed.

'It's no' easy in the dark.' Belle's words drifted towards me. 'But it's no' bad.'

'I have a spell for that,' Angus said cheerfully. '*Altus ish—*'

I interrupted him. 'Stop!'

'Is there a problem, my Queen?'

'Angus,' I warned, 'don't call me that.'

'The only joy I have these days, other than climbing through sewers and almost dying multiple times, is finding out what irritates people and overdoing it to the point that they want to kill me,' he said. I heard the amusement in his voice. 'Don't spoil my fun, lass. And why would you not want some light? This journey will be hard enough without pitch darkness to contend with.'

Sometimes ignorance could be bliss and we might prefer not to see what was nearby, but that wasn't why I'd stopped him. I spoke more quietly. 'Listen.'

We all quietened. It took a moment or two, but then I heard again what had given me pause. There were sounds of scratching from another tunnel not too far away. A moment later, there was a muffled snort.

'That's not a rat,' Laoch whispered.

'Some of the Afflicted?' Belle asked. 'Trapped doon here?'

Possibly – or it could be something worse. 'Whatever it is,' I said, 'let's not draw its attention by blasting this place with magic so we can see where to put our feet.'

'On balance, that's a good plan,' Angus said. 'I vote we get moving. Now.'

'Ten minutes of walking,' Belle told us. 'I promise.'

There was another snort, louder this time. Without further discussion, we started to move.

FIFTEEN

It might have only been a ten-minute trudge but it felt far longer. The chink of light from the grate disappeared and we were forced to feel our way along the tunnel, one hand on the shoulder of the person in front. I kept a tight grip on Isla and enjoyed the reassuring weight of Laoch's hand on me.

It was a far from pleasant trek, and I marvelled that Belle had found her way through on her own. At least whatever had made the snuffling snorts didn't come any closer. It was about time we had some good luck.

We moved on in silence, not stopping until Belle murmured from the front. 'There's an exit here. When I was here an hour ago, there were a few guards nearby so I didn't climb out.'

'I'll deal with them,' Laoch said. He dropped his hand from my shoulder and squeezed past. 'The rest of you stay until I tell you it's safe to come out.'

I bit back my immediate reaction and refrained from telling him that he should hold back and keep himself safe. Laoch was at full strength, powerful, more than capable – and I suspected he needed to prove that to himself as well as to us.

After a few minutes his voice called down, telling us it was safe to ascend. We climbed up one by one and emerged blinking into the daylight. When it was my turn, I swung around and my gaze immediately fell on the two liveried guards standing to one side. They were both conscious, neither was bleeding and neither were tied up. Instead, Laoch was chatting to them, tilting his head as he listened grimly to what they had to say. I glanced at the others.

'Well,' Angus remarked, patting his stained clothes with a wry grimace, 'if I wasn't a dirty traitor before, I certainly am now.'

We were all dirty now. I sent him a faint smile then edged over to Laoch.

'There's a permanent curfew in place,' one of the guards was saying. 'Everyone is supposed to stay in their homes. Anyone out on the streets is to be punished.' There was no need to ask what the punishment was; I could see it in his face.

There was a sudden dull thud from a nearby street, like a door slamming shut. Both of the guards jumped and their hands immediately strayed to the weapons at their belts. 'It's no' our own people we have to worry about,' the guard said in a shaky voice. 'No' the ones in here or the ones out there from Edinburgh. It's the fucking Afflicted. They're everywhere. They're out during the day as much as at night, and they don't have any qualms about attacking anyone they see. We've lost a dozen men in the last three days from my troop alone. If they're no' dead then they're Afflicted themselves now.'

'What are the Mages doing?' Laoch asked.

Both guards snorted derisively. 'Nothing,' the first one answered. 'They're hiding away in the City Chambers and refusing to come out. Every so often some more Mages come from the cities up north, but as soon as they arrive they go into the Chambers and they dinnae come out again. They're leaving us to keep the peace.' He shook his head, disgust plainly written all across his weathered face. He met my eyes. 'You're Mairi, right?'

I nodded; denying my identity seemed pointless. 'I'm Keith,' he said. He pointed at his colleague. 'This is Alan.'

I tried not to look too surprised. This had to be the first time any Glaswegian guard had ever introduced himself to me. It was certainly the first time I'd learned any of their first names.

'I didnae think I'd see you in Glasgow again,' Keith said. 'No' alive, anyway. I didnae think I'd ever be *pleased* to see you.' He offered a bow. 'But I'm glad now. We need someone with fire in their belly. We need someone who's going to do something before we end up like Edinburgh did.'

Both guards were looking at me hopefully, which was worse than if they'd tried to kill us the moment we'd clambered out of the sewer. One person alone couldn't do anything against Cadal Righ and the Afflicted – surely they knew that.

'There are plenty of your people at the city walls and gates doing everything they can to stop people from getting in,' I said.

The guards exchanged glances. I was oddly heartened by the flicker of guilt that passed between them. 'There's even more o' the Afflicted out there than in here. If we let all those people in, it'll be days – not weeks – before Glasgow turns fully Afflicted. If we let them in, we'll all die.'

'If you don't let them in, they'll die quickly but you'll still die too. It'll just be a wee while afterwards,' Laoch said. His tone was matter of fact. That was more disturbing than if he'd sounded accusatory or angry.

The second guard, Alan, flinched. 'What are you going to do?' he asked me. 'Do you have a plan?'

I couldn't lie. 'The situation is bleak but I've got a few ideas. And we've learned a few things that might be useful.'

Alan swallowed. 'Is it … is it … is it true that the new king skinned the Edinburgh Ascendant with a single word?'

Again, I told the truth. 'Pretty much.'

'I have family in Edinburgh,' he whispered. 'I don't know where they are now. They might be right outside the gates, or they might already be dead.' His eyes looked haunted. 'Or worse.'

Keith clapped him on the back in a weak show of reassurance. 'The daemon said that none of youse are Afflicted. How can you be sure of that? Sometimes people don't turn until days after they've had contact.'

'We have someone who can sense Affliction before it manifests physically.'

Keith's eyes widened. 'Who?'

I wouldn't have named Isla, but she pushed herself forward and lifted her chin. 'Me.'

He stared at her. 'You're just a girl.'

'Aye, I am just a girl. I'm just a girl who can tell you that—'

I realised what she was about to say and shot my hand out, indicating that she should be quiet.

'Tell me what?' Keith asked. Alan leaned forward, his body tense.

'You have it.' She pointed at Keith. 'You dinnae.' She nodded at Alan. 'No' yet anyway.'

Alan sprang backwards, putting as much distance between himself and Keith as possible. Given how much time they'd spent together, if he wasn't Afflicted by now he'd probably be fine but that didn't seem to matter to him. 'This morning,' he breathed. 'When that Afflicted woman came at you—'

'No.' Keith started to shake. 'No, no, no, no, no, no.' His hands tightened into fists and he stepped towards Isla. I immediately blocked his path. He might be sympathetic towards us but he was still one of the Mages' guards and now he had every reason to throw caution to the wind. 'You're lying.'

'I'm not lying. I'm sorry.' Isla didn't sound apologetic in the slightest. 'It's already in your heart and it's spreading out to the rest of your body. You've probably got a day left. Maybe more.'

'You bitch! You – you – you—'

Isla's expression told me that she was telling the truth and not simply stirring the pot. I sighed and tried to forestall any real threat of violence. 'It's not her fault. Don't shoot the messenger. And it's not your fault either – you didn't choose this. Be thankful you've got time to say goodbye to your family but don't get too close to them. You don't want to infect them too.'

Keith paled at the thought and backed away. 'What should I do? Where should I go?' Panic lit his every word but, as I looked into his eyes, I realised he'd been waiting for this. He'd expected it. That was why he'd believed Isla so readily, even though he had no real cause to trust her.

Heading to the containment area outside the city made the most sense, but Keith had to decide for himself. Now he knew what was happening, he could decide in the same way that young John had decided. Freedom to choose his own fate under the constraints that had been forced upon him was all that we could give him.

A single tear rolled down his face. 'I'm going to die.'

I drew in a breath. 'Eventually. We're all going to die eventually. Affliction isn't a death sentence.' It was worse, but he didn't need me to say that.

'I should kill myself.' It was more of a vague mumble than a definite statement but it chilled me. I shook my head sharply then reached out and grabbed Keith's hands.

'Mairi,' Laoch warned.

'I've been in close contact with plenty of the Afflicted and been alright. It's fine.'

I squeezed Keith's fingers. 'We're working on a way to stop

this disease and cure the Affliction. It's not over for you yet – it's not over for anyone.'

He choked back a sob. 'Aye. Aye.' He met my eyes. 'You promise? That you'll keep searching for a way? That you'll do whatever you can?'

'I promise, Keith.'

He withdrew and pulled his hands to his chest. 'You shouldn't have touched me like that.' He glanced at Alan. 'I'm sorry. You've been a good mate and I should have been kinder.' He took several steps backwards. 'I'm going now. I cannae stay here. I have to get away.' His body jerked and he looked at me. 'Before I go, I know where your friends are, the ones from the church.'

I tensed. He was talking about the Gowk, Twister, Ailsa, Fee and the others. It felt like a lifetime since I'd last seen them. Belle started forward before suddenly remembering Keith was Afflicted. She stopped. 'Where are they?' she demanded. 'Where? Where is my husband?'

'Over in the East End. We were trying to catch up to them for days and then all this happened.' His shoulders drooped. 'I think they're at the old brewery. If they're not there, they're somewhere close by.' He bowed his head. A second later, he was running away in the opposite direction.

Belle whirled away from us. We didn't need to ask where she was heading. 'I'm going now!'

Goddamnit. 'Wait!' I yelled. 'Belle, hold your horses and wait! It's not safe!' She paid me no attention. She was already trotting away. 'She's going to get herself killed,' I muttered. I looked at Laoch. 'Can you take Isla and go with her? Make sure they're safe?'

His green eyes narrowed. 'What will you do?'

I only looked at him.

No, Mairi. Not alone. I'm going with you.

I'll take Angus. I won't be alone.

I am not leaving you to confront the Mages without me.

I smiled sadly. *Aspen knows I love you and he'll use that against us. He'll hurt you to get at me. Besides, right now he doesn't know you're still alive. We're all against Cadal Righ, but the Mages are still our enemy too. We have to be careful. You're my trump card.* I tried to lighten the mood. *The sexiest trump card anyone's ever had.*

When Laoch's expression didn't soften, I added, *I'm not telling you to do this. I'm not asking you to do this. I'm only suggesting it's the best course of action. Then, if anything goes wrong, you can storm in like the hero you are.*

He folded his arms across his chest. *And save the damsel in distress?*

Who will fall at your feet and sob prettily into a perfect white-linen handkerchief at your appearance.

Laoch rolled his eyes but I saw a glint of amusement in his eyes. *I will hold you to that.*

I'll count on it. I leaned across and kissed him.

He motioned to Isla, who frowned but seemed to understand. Together they ran after Belle. I watched Laoch turn his head to glance back at me several times.

Angus cleared his throat pointedly. 'As I do not possess the gift of telepathy,' he said, 'why don't you tell me what's going on?'

'You already know.' I smoothed down my clothes. There were several damp, discoloured patches that had doubtless come from the sewer. I dreaded to imagine what manner of icky liquid had caused the stains.

'You're going to the City Chambers.' His voice was flat.

'Aye.'

'And you expect me to come with you.'

I didn't flinch from his gaze. 'Angus, you know how the Mages work. They'll be more likely to listen to you than to me.'

'I'm not sure if you've been paying attention or not, Queen Mairi, but they hate me.'

I didn't deny it. 'They will still listen to you before they'll listen to me.'

Angus raised his eyes heavenward. 'Spending time with you is going to get me killed.'

That was something else I didn't deny. I shrugged. 'We all die,' I said echoing what I'd said to Keith. 'Eventually.'

'Why isn't Tall-Dark-and-Horny coming with us?'

I frowned. Angus blinked innocently. 'What? He's tall, he's dark and he's got horns.' He crossed his arms and drummed his fingers against his forearm. 'Why does he get a free pass?'

'We might need him to rescue us,' I told him simply. 'Don't mention him to the Mages. It's better if they believe he's dead.'

Angus clicked his tongue. 'You're going to get me killed,' he muttered again. 'And that lad is going to get you killed.'

I looked him in the eye. 'Frankly, it's a miracle we're not dead already.'

He didn't disagree. From the side, a small, thready voice filled the air. 'What do I do?'

I looked at Alan. In all honesty, I'd forgotten he was still there and I felt faintly guilty. When I'd been mute, people had done that to me all the time. 'That's up to you,' I said. 'You could stay here, join your colleagues at the gates, or go home. Your decisions are your own.'

He bit his bottom lip. For a moment, rather than looking like the fully grown man that he was, he seemed like a young boy waiting for direction from his parents. He inhaled. 'Can I – can I come with you?'

I hadn't expected that. 'Why?' I was genuinely curious.

He answered without missing a beat. 'You're the only person who seems to have a plan.'

It wasn't much of a plan. 'I won't stop you from joining us, but I can't guarantee your safety.'

Alan gave me a sad smile. 'Nobody can.'

SIXTEEN

Despite the obvious apathy on the part of guards like Alan and Keith who hadn't been posted to the city's perimeter, it was obvious that the people of Glasgow were heeding the Mages' edict to remain indoors.

In truth, it was the smart thing to do. We didn't see any of the Afflicted during our short journey to the City Chambers but we certainly passed plenty of evidence of their increased numbers and activity. Even the air smelled Afflicted; there was a faint rotten tinge sweeping through the cold, empty streets that was no less foul than the reek we'd experienced in the sewers. I was genuinely glad when the City Chambers finally came into sight, and I couldn't remember that ever happening before.

The last time I'd seen the dark, imposing building where the Glasgow Mages resided, one section had been destroyed leaving little more than rubble in its wake and there was evidence of the many fires that had been lit when ordinary people had attacked it. I had assumed that even though the fires had long since been extinguished, the building would look much the same, so I was astonished to see that wasn't the case. Scaffolding was already in place to support the rebuilding that was underway. There were no builders on display; the events of the last few days would have forced them to abandon the site. Even so, I gaped. The Mages worked fast when they needed to.

'They had people working here day and night until Wednesday,' Alan said. 'I think they brought in every builder, joiner and handyman in the city.'

Angus pursed his mouth. 'I don't know why you look surprised, lass. Rebuilding will have started when the smoke was still rising. The Glasgow Mages lost both face and respect when they were attacked. They have to show that they are still the power centre of this country.'

'Not any longer.'

His mouth tightened further. 'I'm not convinced my former colleagues will realise that yet.'

I sent him a sideways look. If the Mages were in denial about what had happened in Edinburgh, we might all be screwed. 'Let's hope that they do,' I said quietly.

We approached the front of the building with tentative steps. The doors were resolutely closed and there were no signs of life. 'Maybe we should try one of the back doors,' Alan said nervously

I shook my head. My days of sneaking into Mage-held buildings were over; I wanted them to know I was here. Given all that had occurred, I believed I'd earned that right. I tilted back my head and spotted a single raven glaring down at me with glittering black eyes. 'Tell them that I'm coming,' I called up to it,

It squawked loudly but didn't move.

'You know it doesn't work like that with the ravens. It's more complicated than giving them a verbal cue,' Angus said.

Whatever. I didn't care all that much. I gave the bird a mock salute designed to be rebellious rather than cowed, then I marched up the steps and banged my fist against the Mages' door.

I hadn't expected anybody to answer, so I couldn't stop myself from looking surprised when the ornate doors swung open and the unfamiliar face of a woman peered out at me. 'I am here to see the Mages,' I declared.

She stared at me as if I were stark raving mad. 'You've lost the plot, lass. Are you soft in the heid? The masters aren't at your beck and call. And you're not supposed to be out on the streets. Everyone is to remain inside.' She glanced at Alan and registered his guard's uniform. 'You're letting a woman speak for you? Whit are you doing here?' Her gaze turned to Angus. 'An' who the fuck are you?'

Angus drew back his shoulders and seemed to grow in stature by at least half a metre. His eyes flashed imperiously and he looked at the poor woman as if she were nothing more than a cockroach beneath his booted feet. 'I am Mage Angus.' His voice trembled with so much unspent power that I turned to him in genuine astonishment. 'My father was a Mage and my grandfather before him. I have been part of this city for longer than you can dream of.'

As he glared at her, she shrank into herself. 'And this,' he gestured at me with a sweep of his hand, 'is Queen Mairi, the saviour of Glasgow. You *will* step back. We *will* gain entrance.'

The woman was shaking and blinking at Angus with horrified fear. Within a heartbeat, she'd gone from stern door keeper with a heart of granite to a terrified servant who only wanted to escape this encounter with all her limbs intact. Whoever she was and wherever she'd come from, the Mages had certainly done more than enough to keep her in her place. The terror she was suddenly exhibiting was far too great for it to be anything other than borne out of personal experience.

'It's alright,' I began. 'We are coming inside to speak to the other Mages. We won't hurt you.'

'We *might* hurt you,' Angus growled.

I turned to him, fury flaring in my eyes. 'Enough!'

He stopped, then his body relaxed and he hung his head. 'My apologies, my Queen.'

The woman gawked at him. 'Come in,' she said in a hasty whisper. 'You can wait in the hallway. I'll go and fetch the masters.' She held the door open and the three of us marched through, then she slammed it shut and scuttled away at high speed.

Alan was backing away from Angus with his own version of wide-eyed fear. I glared at the old Mage. 'Was that necessary?'

He grinned. 'It worked a treat!'

'Angus...'

'Stop fashing, lass! I presented myself as a powerful and scary Mage who defers to *you*. I've just increased your power with one simple conversation.' He wagged his finger. 'It's exactly the same tactic as rebuilding this place within days. It's all about appearances.'

I gritted my teeth. 'It's bullying. Anyway, who is that woman? I've never seen her before.'

It was Alan who answered, directing his words at me instead of Angus. In fact, I doubted he'd ever be able to look Angus in the eye again. Unbelievable. 'The Mages from the northern cities brought their servants with them. There wasn't anyone left in Glasgow who could be trusted.'

The woman had called them masters rather than Mages; perhaps that was a northern convention. I opened my mouth to ask Alan more, but before I could I heard approaching footsteps followed by Aspen's familiar – and unwelcome – visage.

He was trailed by a dozen other Mages, none of whom I recognised. Although they were of different ages, shapes and sizes, they all retained the same expression of disgust mixed with studied disdain. It was uncanny.

'Well, well, well,' Aspen boomed. 'You made it back from the castle after all. Did you find poor liberated Nicholas?'

I didn't answer, though I did allow a flash of genuine hatred to cross my face. Hopefully that would give Aspen all the answer he needed.

'We need to talk,' I said. I was impressed that I managed to keep the snarl out of my voice. 'I have important information about Cadal Righ and the Afflicted that can help us all.'

The only indication that Aspen was taken aback was a faint tightening around his eyes. He looked me up and down and sniffed. 'Have you been living in a sewer? Both you and the traitor smell like a toilet.'

'We had to get into the city somehow.'

Aspen recoiled. 'You might be infected. You might have brought the Affliction to our door.'

'The Affliction is already at your door,' I said. 'It's knocking to get in, and sooner or later it will break your damned door down. And we're not Afflicted.'

'You can't know that for certain.'

'Actually,' Angus said cheerfully, 'we can.'

Several of the other Mages jerked with shock. Good. 'As I said,' I told them, 'we have important information.'

Aspen shrugged, but a cunning, curious expression flitted across his face. 'Then by all means come through and regale us with your discoveries.' He waved a hand. 'Just keep your distance. Affliction or not, that smell is horrendous.' He swept away from us with a dramatic flourish.

I rolled my eyes but I followed with Alan and Angus at my heels.

Aspen led us into the huge dining room, which was crammed with silent and watchful Mages. I already knew two-thirds of them from my time here as their servant. The others had to be from Perth, Dundee, Aberdeen and Inverness.

I glanced at the unfamiliar faces seated near the top of the table, suspecting from their purple robes that they were the Ascendants from those cities. I ought to have been pleased that all of Scotland's Mages were taking the fall of Edinburgh as seriously as it deserved, but I couldn't fail to notice the array of food in front of them. They seemed to be feasting while everyone outside was dying.

I was pleased when a good number of the seated Mages pinched their noses and stopped eating. If the reek that emanated from Angus and me was enough to put them off their food, that made me happy. Something had to stop their gluttony.

Aspen took his position at the head of the table, seating himself on the grand oak chair that had once belonged to the Glasgow Ascendant. I wondered if the others were granting him the position of de facto leader, and if Aspen was concerned that would lead to him being next in Cadal Righ's sights. I decided I didn't care.

Aspen addressed the Mages. 'As I am sure most of you have surmised, this is Mairi. She is the one who murdered the Glasgow Ascendant. We did everything we could to extend the hand of friendship to her. We invited her to participate in the Ascendancy Challenge for leadership of this great city, even though she's a mere woman and is responsible both for the death of our own esteemed colleague and the wanton chaos that ensued. Do not expect to see any gratitude from her for our forbearance. She is stubborn, vicious and entirely disrespectful.'

Hmm. Actually, I agreed with him on all three of those points – and I was proud of them, too. But I wasn't here to play the role of upstart revolutionary, and I wasn't here to antagonise the Mages. Not this time. I had to get them to listen to me and we had to work together.

Angus nudged me. 'Andy's not here,' he murmured in my ear.

I scanned the seated Mages. Shite. He was right. I hoped the young Mage was alright. Teasag was also conspicuous by her absence. I crossed my fingers tightly for their continued well-being and swallowed, trying to focus on the task in hand. This might be the most important speech I ever made and my words had never been so crucial. If ever there was a time to be thankful that I was no longer mute, this was it. I couldn't blow this chance.

'I am not here to pick a fight,' I said carefully. 'I will not pretend we are friends, even though some of you have been kinder to me than others. Neither will I pretend that we are going to be friends. We are at odds and probably always will be.' My voice sounded croaky so I cleared my throat. Several Mages smirked, more than aware of my mute past. I ignored them and continued.

'We have to put what has happened behind us, at least temporarily. The threat of Cadal Righ changes everything, and he will never be defeated unless we work together. He plans to rule Scotland and turn our citizens – *all* our citizens – into the Afflicted so he can draw power from them to maintain his control. I don't know how he managed it, but Cadal Righ has been alive for well over a hundred years.'

I held up the leather-bound diary that I'd taken back from Isla. 'There's information in here about him from a female Mage who was there at the time.'

One of the younger Mages burst out laughing and slapped his hands on the table, making his cutlery jump and jiggle. 'Well, there's your first foolish lie! There's no such thing as a female Mage!' he chortled. 'There never has been and there never will be.'

I regarded him flatly. 'You realise that the propaganda you spout so publicly, and which hardly anyone believes any more, does you no good? It is not going to help any of us. If you wish to see a demonstration of female magic, I'm more than happy to oblige.'

Aspen tutted. 'That won't be necessary. Wheesht, McAllister.'

The laughing Mage allowed himself a final giggle before shutting up. I sighed impatiently.

Alan nudged me. 'I'd like to see a demonstration,' he said.

I forced a smile in his direction. 'Later,' I promised. I tossed the diary onto the table, where it landed between a platter of sliced beef glistening with fat and a tureen of glossy gravy. 'Read it for yourselves,' I said. 'You'll see.'

One of the Mages, a middle-aged man who I remembered was called Felix, started to reach for the book.

'Stop,' Aspen ordered in a low voice that did nothing to mute his imperious tone. Felix withdrew his hand instantly. Aspen looked at me. 'This is what you have to tell us? You found an old book?'

'Oh, there's plenty more.' I glanced around, spotted an empty chair and pulled it up to the table. While the Mages gaped at me, I sat down, lifted my legs and rested my feet on the table's edge.

Angus grinned nastily. He strolled toward me, reached across and grabbed a chicken leg from a plate nearby and started eating it. I turned my head to check on Alan. He appeared horrified by our actions.

'What the bejesus do you think you're doing?' blustered one of the purple-robed Mages, pushing back his chair to get to his feet.

'Sit down, laddie,' Angus commanded through a mouthful of chicken.

'I will not! I am the Dundee Ascendant and I will not take orders from the likes of you!'

Aspen, whose expression gave little away, leaned forward with his elbows on the table and rested his chin on his linked hands. 'Let's hear what else she has to say.'

If he expected gratitude for his words, he'd be waiting a long time. At least the Dundee Ascendant sat down again, although he looked as if he'd been sucking on sour plums.

I laid out the facts without embellishment. 'The diary suggests that Cadal Righ is responsible for the Affliction. He started it by somehow infecting a pregnant female Mage. He doesn't believe that there are any women in Scotland who can wield magic anymore.' I met Aspen's hard eyes. 'But we all know that's not true. We can use that against him. We can take him by surprise.'

When none of the Mages, Aspen included, said anything, I continued. 'I came face to face with Cadal Righ in Edinburgh. He told me he plans to rule all of Scotland. He won't stop unless we do something to stop him. I have met someone who has the magic to see inside people's souls and tell whether they are Afflicted or not long before the physical symptoms manifest. If we can replicate that, we can use it to our advantage.'

'Truly?'

I nodded. 'I wouldn't lie about such a thing.'

'Where is he now?' asked another of the Ascendants.

'*She* is somewhere safe, for the time being,' I answered, without looking at him. 'But there is more, and this is what I think we need to focus on.' I licked my lips. 'I found Noah.'

Even Aspen looked startled at that. 'Lord Noah?'

I nodded. 'We left Edinburgh with him. Using information

in that diary, I combined two spells to draw the Affliction out of him.'

This time, the room didn't stay silent. It burst into a hubbub of noise and questions.

'You cured him?'

'Where is he?'

'What two spells? How is that possible?'

I didn't try to speak over the noise. If the Mages wanted answers, they'd have to be quiet first. I waited until the chatter subsided. 'The two spells were *desh tun mar* and *desh tun.*'

The room exploded again and again I waited. This time, Aspen called for silence. I had him; he wanted to hear more and that could only be a good thing.

As soon as the Mages quietened, the Dundee Ascendant spoke out. 'Combining two spells is impossible. It can't be done.'

Angus tossed down his gnawed chicken bone. 'It's not possible for men but it is possible for women. Anyone who was present during the Ascendancy Challenge knows it. Queen Mairi combined *sel ez* and *fel zor* to create an armour made out of water for herself.' He looked at Aspen. 'You know it's true.'

Aspen scratched his chin. 'It remains to be seen if only Mairi possesses this deformity,' he scoffed. 'What is more important is that those two spells together couldn't have any effect on Affliction. Using them together would only achieve one thing.' He paused until he was sure everyone was watching him. 'Those two spells would remove a Mage's magic. For good.'

I'd been expecting another explosion of sound, but this time the assembled Mages were silent as horror flitted across their faces.

I remained calm. 'Aye,' I said. 'Permanently remove the magic from an Afflicted Mage and you will permanently remove the Affliction. I strongly suspect that you would prefer that to the alternative.'

Judging from their expressions, there were plenty of Mages who disagreed with me.

'Heresy!' the Dundee Ascendant exclaimed. 'Heresy!'

Uh-huh. That man was really beginning to irritate me.

'Where is he then? Where is Lord Noah to prove these claims?' Aspen asked.

This was where things would become dicey. 'He's dead.'

Before I could explain further, Mage McAllister snorted his derision. 'Cure him of Affliction, remove his magic and kill him in the process?' He clapped his hands. 'Well done,' he said sarcastically. 'What genius.'

'It wasn't magic that killed him,' I said evenly. 'It was a nuckalavee.'

'A nuckalavee? On the road between Edinburgh and Glasgow? That's impossible. They don't venture into those parts.'

'They do when the foul magic of the likes of Cadal Righ draws them in,' Angus said

'Did you see this nuckalavee?' Aspen asked him. 'Or Lord Noah after he was supposedly cured?'

'No,' Angus replied. 'I wasn't there but—'

'Well,' Aspen interrupted, 'I think that tells us everything.'

I lowered my feet from the table and stood up. 'I understand that you have no reason to believe what I'm telling you, but I have no reason to lie. We are all at risk from Cadal Righ. You can test what I've told you. You can read the words in that diary. You can search the books here in the City Chambers for more clues about what can help us. Don't discard the only things that might save us all. Don't,' I emphasised, 'allow your prejudices or egos get in the way of our only hope of defeating Cadal Righ.'

Behind me, Alan cleared his throat. It was a timid sound but it was deliberate and deserved notice. 'You wish to say something?' I asked gently.

'You said you can remove the Affliction from a Mage,' he said, starting nervously but growing more confident with every word. 'But what if that person isn't a Mage? Can you remove it from them?'

It was telling that he was the only person in the room who asked the question. The Mages were thinking only of themselves and how the spells would affect them. Alan was thinking of Keith and the countless others who weren't lucky – or unlucky – enough to possess any magic.

He deserved the truth. 'I don't think so. Not yet. But what we have is a start. If we can learn from Mages, we have the potential to extend that knowledge to everyone.'

The hope that had flared in his face died immediately. His expression closed and I knew exactly what he was thinking. We could help Mages but we couldn't help anyone else. It was the way things had always been.

'There are hundreds of years of knowledge in the books within these walls. Somewhere there's bound to be something that can help us. This is a real chance, Alan. I promise.'

Unfortunately, my latest truth gave Aspen all the leeway he needed to squash my arguments. 'So what you've so valiantly discovered – even if it's true, which I doubt – is that you can cure Mages but not ordinary people. You can't actually help them at all. You have nothing,' he jeered.

'If we all work together,' I began, 'and build on this knowledge by—'

'*Ins veil.*' Blue flames flickered from Aspen's fingertips and my body was thrown up and back, slamming into Alan and sending us both crashing to the floor. I should have expected the attack. I'd known something like it was bound to happen, I just hadn't thought it would happen at that moment.

I growled. Aspen's spell had considerable power and I ached from its force. I staggered to my feet but half a dozen Mages were already surrounding me. When I looked across, there were more surrounding Angus.

'You've wasted enough of our time. We don't need your theories and suppositions. We already have a plan to deal with Cadal Righ and it's far smarter than anything a mere woman could come up with.' Aspen waved at the Mages. 'Take them to the garden. I'll deal with them there.'

'Aspen! You have to listen! This is the only way out!' I reached inside myself for enough magic to defend myself. There were more than a hundred Mages here, but I wasn't the quitting sort.

As I hummed the very first note, I felt the rush of air behind me and there was a flash of agonising pain at the back of my skull. Tiny lights danced in front of my eyes. I felt a surge of abrupt, debilitating nausea.

And then everything went black.

CHAPTER

SEVENTEEN

When consciousness finally returned, I felt sick. My stomach roiled, churning over and over, and I started to heave. I retched, but fortunately there was no food in my stomach for me to bring up because the gag across my mouth could have caused real problems. The Mages must have placed it there to humiliate and distress me, because it wouldn't stop me from humming and bringing forth my magic.

I fought the sense of panic, forced back the nausea and fear and opened my eyes.

It took more than a moment for my vision to adjust. I knew where I was, of course; even without Aspen's earlier words ringing in my ear, the stench of the death garden was unmistakable.

A huge butterfly with vivid red and purple markings flapped lazily past my nose and I tensed. There were plenty of insects here, and they were all over-sized like this one. Many of them were poisonous. Fortunately, the butterfly wasn't interested in me – not yet, anyway. It wandered out of my line of sight, and I started to pay more attention to my surroundings and my bindings.

I was tied tightly to the trunk of a squat palm tree by a rope that bit painfully into my flesh. Magic was also holding me back, its energy snaking around and through me, clamping me in place far more effectively than the rope. I had no knowledge of the spell but I knew the signature of the Mage who'd cast it. He was standing right in front of me with a bright smile on his face.

'You must have a thick skull,' Aspen said cheerfully. 'I didn't think you'd regain consciousness so quickly. But then you're full of surprises, aren't you, Mairi?' He strode towards me, lifted his hand and stroked my cheek. His touch was light but it wasn't tender. Aspen was touching me in the same manner he might touch a lamb before sending it to slaughter.

I suppressed a shudder then pulled forth my magic. Any spell would do. Aspen smirked and pointed to his left. I immediately released my power back into myself.

'A few of us suggested we re-use the spell that removes magic from a person,' he drawled. 'Unlike the magic that you falsely advertised in the dining room, I'm sure you'll recall that our version tends to cause problems for the caster. And we need our powers to deal with Cadal Righ. I assured my dear colleagues that you were predictable and that we could keep you muted without wasting any magic at all. It appears,' his smile grew, 'that I was right. I usually am.'

My eyes drifted from the servant woman who'd opened the door to us to Alan, and finally to Teasag. All three of them looked defeated. Alan was sporting a huge black eye, and a vicious cut on the side of his head was dribbling blood. Andy and Angus were lying on the ground. Their chests were rising but they were obviously unconscious.

'Don't worry about those two,' Aspen grinned. 'Once you're

out of the way, they'll be persuaded to return to the fold – or we'll offer them to Cadal Righ as tribute.' He shrugged. 'They're not your concern.'

He indicated the woman, Teasag and Alan. 'However, these three will be killed if I hear so much as a single note come from your bitch mouth.'

I glared at him. Alan, who had more gumption than I'd given him credit for, burst out, 'Use magic anyway! We're not important. You have to—' Aspen punched him on the side of the head. His knees buckled and he collapsed.

'Honestly,' Aspen said. 'I'd have thought better of one of our own guards. You simply can't get the staff these days.'

My eyes blazed fire and fury. I struggled against the ropes and the magical bindings even though I knew they would hold tight.

'I don't know why you're attempting to free yourself,' Aspen remarked. 'We all know what you'll say. Work together and we can beat Cadal Righ. Blah blah blah.' He sniffed. 'We don't need you to defeat Cadal Righ. We have a plan to deal with him on our own.'

The bloody eejit. Had he forgotten about all the Afflicted people by Cadal Righ's side?

Aspen laughed at my expression. 'Oh, my dear, we won't *fight* the man. We already know we won't win. We will bargain with him. It's the only way forward. He already has Edinburgh so we'll give him Glasgow, too, then we'll retreat to the north and leave him in peace. If he requires it, we'll provide tribute to him in whatever form he desires. At the end of the day, he's a man. There will be a compromise that we can reach. People will suffer but,' Aspen bared his teeth, 'not me. Not the Mages.'

He was delusional. How could he possibly think that Cadal Righ would negotiate? He had no need to because he held all the cards. Aspen knew what Cadal Righ was capable of and he was kidding himself if he thought his plan would work. The Mages would get themselves killed, and where would that leave the people of Glasgow? Or Scotland? As much as I hated the bastards, we needed the Mages' power to defend our country.

Aspen continued blithely, ' Cadal Righ has done us a favour, you know. His appearance, and the recent proliferation of the Afflicted, means that folk out there are far too concerned with him to worry about you. You can disappear without any fuss. By the time anyone realises it will be far too late.'

There was a flicker of movement from beyond the garden's glass walls. I wasn't stupid enough to look at it directly but my heart surged with sudden delight.

Aspen reached into his robes and pulled out a long, curved knife. Its blade gleamed sharply as light bounced off its lethal tip. 'It would have been nice to take my time with this but time is against us. Cadal Righ is approaching the city and Mages are already heading out to meet him. We can't fritter away our precious hours on you.'

He touched the blade's edge lightly. 'You put up a good fight, but this world is not for the likes of you. In a few years' time nobody will remember your name. It's just the way it has to be. Don't resist and I'll make it quick.'

I narrowed my eyes and Aspen evinced surprise. 'What? Would you like to say something? As a former mute, I didn't think you'd place much importance on your final words. The ways of women are a genuine mystery to me.'

He moved towards me and placed the blade at my throat. I felt its cold metal prick my skin. 'I'll allow you ten words. No more.' He tugged at my gag, pulling it away from my mouth. 'What would you like to say?'

I didn't need ten words. I only needed two. 'Behind you.'

For the briefest moment, Aspen's brow furrowed, then he realised. He spun, the first word of the spell to defend himself already on his lips, but he was too late. Laoch was three steps ahead of him.

'*Meshar al.*'

In an instant, Aspen lost control of his limbs and his body flopped, his arms and legs as much use as jelly. He collapsed to the dirt in a heap while Laoch circled around him.

Aspen croaked the words '*Kall moy*' at Laoch – but he'd already forgotten about me. No longer fearing for the lives of the servant, Alan and Teasag, I brought my own magic to the fore, humming to create an invisible wall that would protect Laoch. *Vaz.* Aspen's magic bounced uselessly off of it.

'Thanks, love,' Laoch murmured. 'But I still want a sobbing damsel in distress.'

I grinned.

'Frederica!' Aspen's voice was barely audible but that didn't mean there wasn't great power still contained within it. 'Kill him. Now.'

My grin vanished. A battle between Teasag and Laoch would be heart rending to watch. They were kinsmen, not enemies, and this could only end in disaster.

My eyes widened in fear. Alan, seeming to understand the peril, darted forward and used his trembling fingers to undo the ropes that held me in place, but even if he could undo the knots he couldn't do anything about the magic.

I hissed and tried to think, desperate to come up with something that would avoid hurting Teasag but would still protect Laoch. At the same time, we couldn't risk drawing attention to what was happening and bringing forth more Mages. None of us could fight them all.

Alan tugged at my ropes as I stared at Teasag. Then I realised something odd. Aspen had ordered her to kill Laoch and he'd even added a stern 'now' to his command, but Teasag wasn't moving.

She turned towards Laoch and tilted her head, giving him a curious look. 'You want her to play damsel in distress? *Her*?'

Laoch shrugged and my astonishment grew. 'I need something to make me feel like a big muscly daemon with incredible powers. I was promised a white hanky and pretty tears.'

Teasag folded her arms. 'Pretty tears?'

'You know,' he drawled, 'the sort that make a woman look needy and vulnerable. Not the sort that make their face turn blotchy and red.' He made a moue of melodramatic disgust.

'All these years I've known you, and I find out now this is what turns you on?'

By this point even the servant woman was staring at them with her jaw dropped.

'Look at it from my point of view,' Laoch said. 'When I first met Mairi I had to rescue her, but now she is intent on repeatedly rescuing me.' He shook his head, his inky-black curls gleaming against his matt-black horns. 'Imagine being head over in heels in love with a woman who is stronger than you in every way that counts.'

Teasag raised an eyebrow. 'The horror.'

'It's a pitiful state of affairs,' he agreed. 'Her magic can do things that mine can't. She has a strength of character that puts mine to shame. She's compassionate and considered, and she has her own nickname, "the Saviour of Glasgow". Before too long, she'll be the saviour of Scotland.' He leaned towards her. 'She's also considerably more attractive than I am.'

Despite my ridiculous position akin to that of a trussed-up chicken, I felt my cheeks glowing red.

Teasag sucked on her bottom lip. 'I see what you're saying. Your masculinity is disintegrating in front of my very eyes.'

'It's terrible,' Laoch said sombrely. Then he winked.

'I can't imagine what she sees in you.'

Laoch finally looked at me. 'Neither can I,' he said, meeting my eyes

For a moment I forgot to breathe. Alan let out a crow of delight as he managed to undo the last of the knots then glanced around in confusion. He obviously hadn't been listening to the conversation.

'Frederica!' Aspen was beginning to recover from the effects of the spell. He heaved himself up to a sitting position and pointed a long finger towards her. 'I told you to kill that bastard!'

Teasag dropped her arms, walked over to Aspen and crouched beside him. 'Haven't you worked it out yet?' She tapped the side of his head. 'Are you truly that stupid?' She reached for the metallic cuff around her neck, gently removed it and dropped it by his feet. Then she did the same with the cuffs around her wrists.

'The magic in this country has changed. The power you used to enslave me and my kind has been weakened more than enough to break through its confines. You Mages relied on corpses and foulness to boost your waning energy, and now Cadal Righ has taken that energy for himself. He's the most powerful person in this country. He won't negotiate, and all those chums of yours who are riding out to meet with him will likely die before the hour is out. Your time is over, old man.'

She stood up, raised her foot and kicked him in the head. Aspen's face slackened then he collapsed once again – and this time, as he did so, the magic that bound me vanished and I fell forward.

Laoch rushed towards me and helped me to my feet. I coughed as I gave him a wry glance. 'Thank you. Is that "damsel in distress" enough for you?'

'I've changed my mind,' he muttered, brushing a smear of dirt from my cheek. 'I don't want to witness anything like that ever again. My macho pride can take the damage. My heart cannot.'

I leaned into him. 'You daemons have a very strange sense of humour sometimes,' I said into his chest,

'I was trying to make a point,' he said. 'I'm not sure that Lord Aspen got it.'

'Isla?' I questioned. 'And Belle?'

'They're with your other friends, who appear to be hale and hearty. As soon as we found them, I left them and came here. I expected something like this would happen, so I sneaked in through the rear. That was when I sensed Teasag and the change.'

I pulled back from Laoch and looked at her. 'Is it true?' I asked. 'About the magic?'

'Seems to be,' she said. 'I felt the shift sometime yesterday but it seemed wise not to advertise that fact immediately to any of the black-cloaked wankers.'

Wise indeed, at least for my sake. I drew in a ragged breath. 'I'm glad you're free. So glad. But...'

Teaseg nodded grimly. 'I know. Believe me, Mairi. I know.'

The servant woman, whose name I didn't know and who had shown no sign of her earlier verbosity, broke away from where she'd been standing and stomped over to Aspen. She put her hands on her hips and glowered down at him. 'Why me?' She kicked him in his leg. 'Why threaten to kill me? I did nothing wrong. I did what I was told!' She sounded hurt rather than surprised. In her mind, she'd done everything right and yet she'd still been punished.

'It was probably mere convenience,' I said, attempting to be gentle.

Her mouth twisted into a snarl then she raised her foot again. 'Convenience this, you wanker!'

Before she could kick Aspen a second time, I moved to block her. 'Enough now. He's already unconscious.'

'He deserves it!'

I couldn't argue with that but that wasn't why I stopped her. 'We're better than they are. We don't have to kick them when they're down. And,' I added with heavy reluctance, 'we might still need him.'

Laoch expelled air noisily. 'There are better Mages and better men than him.'

'Aye,' I said. 'But Cadal Righ's power is beyond our ken. And if the other Mages don't realise the error of their ways soon, they're all about to be flayed alive.' I met Laoch and Teasag's eyes. 'We can't afford to lose them, much as we might want to.'

They both grimaced but neither of them disagreed.

I glanced at the servant. 'What's your name?' I asked.

Her mouth tightened and I thought for a moment that she'd refuse to tell me out of spite for not allowing her to kick Aspen. Then she clicked her tongue and sighed. 'Morag.'

'Can you stay here, Morag? Look after these two?'

Her gaze strayed to the slumped forms of Andy and Angus, neither of whom had moved. 'Aye, I suppose I can do that.'

'Alan,' I said, 'can you do something with him?' I pointed to Aspen. 'You'll have to be careful. If he regains consciousness, he might try to use magic against you.'

'I'll deal with him.' Alan drew back his shoulders and I registered a glint of pride in his eyes at being given a real task to complete. 'Don't worry.'

I swallowed and nodded. 'The three of us will have to get to the other Mages and stop them somehow. If they ride out of the city to meet Cadal Righ, they're all dead.'

Teasag frowned, her reluctance obvious. 'Aye. Alright,' she muttered.

Laoch gave me a crooked smile. 'Anything for my distressed damsel.'

I pulled out an imaginary handkerchief and dabbed at my eyes, sniffed and took off at a quick march. We didn't have any time to spare.

EIGHTEEN

We walked three abreast out of the death garden and along the familiar corridors of the City Chambers. There was a strange, desolate air to the building, as if it had already been abandoned and the Mages had been pulverised out of existence. It wasn't true, of course. Not yet.

When we reached the main area and heard the muted hum of conversation coming from the dining room, I exhaled. I expected to discover all the stupid bastards waiting for Aspen's return before they marched out to meet Cadal Righ. I truly hoped they were.

Teasag, Laoch and I walked into the room. I was prepared to be attacked by any number of furious Mages, but sixty or so pale faces only turned towards us and stared. Nobody moved.

I glanced towards the top of the table. The remaining Ascendants from the northern cities had gone and so had all of the senior Mages whose faces I knew. I frowned and addressed the others. 'Where are they?'

Not a single Mage responded. Several eyes strayed to Teasag and I knew they were registering her lack of slave adornments.

A deep rumble sounded from Laoch's chest and he stepped forward. 'Answer her.'

One shaky Mage, whom I recalled was called Philip, got to his feet. 'Did you kill Lord Aspen?' he asked, wide-eyed, looking me up and down as if expecting to see blood and brain matter staining my filthy clothes.

'No,' I snapped. 'Where have the other Mages gone?' Somebody needed to give me a straight answer in the next three seconds or I was liable to start knocking heads together.

Finally a different Mage answered. 'They've gone to speak to Cadal Righ. He's two miles from the city gates.'

Two miles. I passed a hand over my face. Bloody hell. No wonder these idiots were sitting here looking scared; they'd been left as the final defence in case anything went wrong.

They weren't doing a particularly sterling job of defending themselves so far. If they worked together there were more than enough of them to squash me, Teasag and Laoch, but they were both leaderless and rudderless. And teamwork wasn't in any Mage's nature.

'Who's in charge?' I demanded.

'Lord Aspen,' Philip told me.

For fuck's sake. 'And after him?'

His skin went an even more impossible shade of pale. Now he definitely believed I'd killed Aspen. 'Nobody,' he whispered.

'Choose someone!' I snarled. 'And then go into the city and get people ready. If Cadal Righ kills all your magic buddies, the Afflicted will swarm through those streets in minutes. You need a plan to help as many people as you can.'

From their expressions, most of them would do exactly as I said. Stranger things had happened. I ran a hand through my hair. I couldn't concern myself with these Mages now. We had to find the others and stop them.

We swept out of the City Chambers. The open courtyard in

front of the building was empty. I cursed and wondered how far the Ascendants and their cronies had gone and if we could catch up to them. Then I looked up. The single raven had been joined by a friend. They blinked down at us with their beady, glittering eyes as I stared back at them.

'Are you thinking what I'm thinking?' I asked Laoch.

'I sincerely hope not.'

Teasag followed my gaze and flinched. 'Ravens? Really?' She frowned. 'They're not like other creatures, Mairi. I know you had considerable success with mice, but this is entirely different.'

It was only one mouse but mentioning that wouldn't help my argument. 'We have to catch up to the Mages and this is the fastest way to do it.' And likely the safest. Using the ravens meant we could leave and enter Glasgow without worrying about the guards or the masses of people from Edinburgh. We could bypass them all with little more than a few flaps of our wings.

'I'll follow you anywhere,' Laoch said. 'But if there's any other way...'

'Unless you can think of anything in the next few seconds, I don't believe there is.' I met his eyes. 'Can it be done?'

'It won't be easy.'

I touched his hand gently. 'That's not what I asked.'

Laoch sighed. 'Aye. It can be done.'

'Will you come with me?'

'You don't have to ask.'

Teasag stepped away from us. 'You're crazy. Both of you.'

She was probably right. 'You should go back to your realm,' I told her. 'You deserve to be at home and to see your family again. You'll be safe there. Cadal Righ wants Scotland. He's not interested in daemons.'

'You're right, I should do that.' She sniffed. 'But this is my home too, for better or for worse.' She glanced at the City Chambers. 'I might head back in there, yell at a few dozen Mages and force them to do my bidding until you return.'

'It's your choice,' Laoch said.

Teasag smiled; it was the first genuine smile I'd witnessed from her. 'Aye,' she said. 'It is.' She eyed the ravens. 'Don't get bloody killed.'

I squeezed Laoch's hand. 'Amen.' I tilted my head and watched the ravens again. There was no time like the present to throw all caution to the wind. 'I'll take the one on the left.'

'Done.'

I licked my lips. A moment later, I hummed. *Belsh za tum.*

It wasn't the same as with Mungo. Whether his allegiance now lay with Isla or not, he hadn't resisted any attempts by another consciousness to intrude into his body. I'd go so far as to say that he hadn't minded it in the slightest – but the birds were an entirely different prospect.

As soon as the words left my mouth, I felt the raven resist. I couldn't blame it because I wouldn't have wanted anyone to do it to me, but I didn't have any choice. I pushed harder and hummed again. *Belsh za tum.*

The raven squawked, indicating its disapproval. My body shuddered with the effort but I kept on forcing the magic. Out of the corner of my eye, I saw a bead of sweat roll down Laoch's forehead. *We can do this,* I told him through gritted teeth. *We can.*

The raven's wings started to flap as it attempted to take off, to fly away from the danger we presented. It struggled to rise, though, because all its black-feathered energies were directed at fending me off and it had nothing left with which to navigate an escape. That spark of understanding gave me the final surge I needed. I drew another breath into my lungs and hummed for a third and final time. *Belsh za tum.*

The air rippled and I heard faint crackling as the magic passed through both the bird and me. Then I was blinking my eyes and gazing at the world from a very different vantage point. Below me, emboldened by my success, Laoch threw more power into his own spell. A second later, his body vanished and I knew he'd also succeeded.

I breathed out and allowed myself a moment to grow accustomed to this new body. I could feel the raven's consciousness straining against me, doing all it could to slam me out of its head, but I was there now and the bird was mine.

I stretched out my right wing and examined the feathers, feeling the strange sensation of this new appendage. Usually I didn't think of the ravens as anything other than pure black but up close the colours of each feather were glorious with threads of bright purple, shimmers of dark silver and flickers of glowing green. Amazing. I flexed the wing once more and did the same to the other side before raising one clawed foot then another. The raven's mind poked at me in irritation and I hushed it. *This is temporary. It's a one off and I won't be here for long.*

I swivelled towards Laoch, who was opening and closing his beak, testing it out. I nudged him slightly and he gave me a bird-like nod. We had to go. We had to catch up to the Mages.

'You two are cracked!' Teasag called up towards us.

Aye. But these were cracked times. I tipped the edge of one wing towards her in acknowledgment, then held my breath, fixed my gaze upwards and tensed my avian muscles. It was time to fly.

Part of me expected the take-off to prove difficult and for my subconscious to resist what was a wholly unnatural act for a human to undertake, but presumably the raven's instincts kicked in and over-rode my inclination to remain on solid ground. I rose upwards easily, extending my wings as a draft of wind hoisted me higher. Bloody hell. It was amazing.

I didn't feel cold or scared – I didn't feel anything other than pure exhilaration and joy. In my mind I whooped, and I must have projected the sounds louder than I expected because Laoch immediately did the same.

This is extraordinary! I swooped first to my right then to my left.

There was a gentle rush of air next to me as Laoch's raven form soared past me. *I know!* His response was edged with genuine glee.

He circled one way and I circled in the other direction. As we passed each other, I felt the tips of his wings brush against mine. I decided it was good to be a bird.

From somewhere deep inside I felt the raven snarl, reminding me not to get too comfortable. It was right; we were doing this for a purpose, not to perform aerial acrobatics or get our kicks.

I tilted to the left and looked down towards the ground. Although I wasn't flying particularly high, I could see most of the city. The City Chambers seemed less imposing from the air but there were other rooftops and church spires to keep a wary eye on. I didn't want to become too relaxed and fly headlong into a building because I was looking in the opposite direction.

Using an air current to gain a higher altitude, I pushed further up. Below, a trio of Afflicted people were lurching along a street, occasionally banging on closed doors and trying their luck. Nobody else was about, so they wouldn't catch any tasty prey just yet.

It was good to know that I could see an incredible amount of detail from this height. I lifted my head and looked beyond the city. I could see the makeshift tent city and, further away, the rolling hills and winding road that led to Edinburgh.

Cadal Righ was waiting somewhere out there and the foolish Mages were heading straight for him. We had to get to them before they reached him; we had to do something to make them turn back. Suddenly I felt the raven agree with me. It wanted to keep its masters safe, albeit for different reasons, but at least our goals were the same. That might make the journey easier.

I swung to my left and flicked a wing towards Laoch. *The road out of the city to Edinburgh is this way. If we follow it, it should take us to the Mages.*

Laoch responded in an instant. *Let's go.*

We picked up speed. It was extraordinarily easy to move quickly through the air. Although a lazy-looking pigeon beneath me glanced up with a definite expression of surprise, there was no need to veer out of anyone's path or be confined by man-made streets and paths. Within minutes, we reached the city gates. At this rate, we should have plenty of time to get in front of the Mages.

I flew past the walls, noting that there were yet more guards at all the gates leading into the city. People were still clamouring to get into Glasgow, yelling and shoving and pressing forward. There were also cannier folk who were moving further away from the tents and searching for more hidden routes. It was possible that some would find the sewer that Belle had taken us through.

My attention was caught by a large, isolated area on the outskirts of the encampment. It was fenced off and I felt a ripple of magic surrounding it. Hundreds, perhaps thousands, of people were inside. From this vantage point, it seemed that most of them had succumbed completely to the Affliction.

The numbers were staggering. I didn't know which Mages were using their power to maintain the magical boundary but if Cadal Righ killed them, there would be nothing more than a flimsy fence holding back those Afflicted souls. It wouldn't last seconds, and if the Afflicted got out it would be carnage. I gave an involuntary caw of dismay. We had to stop those bloody-minded fools.

I flapped my wings harder and faster, determined to pick up speed. I heard a faint squawk and, recognising it as raven, assumed it was Laoch. Then I realised that the sound had come from beneath me. I felt a surge of tension just as Laoch's voice popped into my mind, vibrating in warning. *There are more ravens. They're coming from below.*

I angled my head downwards then gave a start as the raven's mind surged against mine with sly satisfaction. There was an entire flock of its black-feathered brethren flying towards us.

I forced back my panic. As far as the ravens were concerned, both Laoch and I were the same as them. We looked the same, we smelled the same, we acted the same – or near enough. When the flock drew closer, however, I saw the grim intent in their glittering eyes and realised they were not so easily fooled. Every single one of those birds knew that something about us was wrong.

The leading raven, which was almost twice my size, let out a loud screech that was immediately echoed by its companions. With extraordinary speed it flew past and soared several metres higher than me. As I tried to see where it had gone and what it was doing, I caught a fleeting glimpse of plummeting black feathers. A moment later, the raven's curved beak slashed into my back, cutting through my feathers to pinch my flesh and draw blood. The raven inside me screamed. So did I.

Mairi! Laoch's voice bounced around my skull but I didn't have time to answer. The force of the raven's attack had knocked me sideways and I was losing momentum, falling like a brick towards the ground.

I was dimly aware of people from the tents below shielding their eyes and gazing upwards in shock. I desperately tried to right myself, flapping my wings in desperation. I only managed it in the nick of time. I swooped low over a red-topped tent and regained some stability, but it wasn't over. This battle was only just beginning.

I rose up again, my eyes fixed on the scene above me. Several of the ravens were attacking Laoch, pecking at him and smashing their bodies into his. Every time he tried to get away, another one went for him. I ignored the pain in my back and frantically beat my wings so I could join him and help. As I did so, I flashed an image towards the raven whose body I'd stolen and dredged up the memory of my earlier confrontation with Cadal Righ.

He will kill them all, I tried to tell the raven, reminding it of my purpose. *He will kill all the Mages if we don't stop him.*

I had no idea if my explanation worked because, a heartbeat later, three of the ravens attacking Laoch peeled away in order to turn their attention to me. They swooped down, claws and beaks outstretched. I wasn't big enough, strong enough or experienced enough to fight them; the only way I could survive was to escape. And the only way I'd do that was by thinking less like a bird and more like a human.

I held my breath and waited for the sinister trio to draw close. In the very last second, just before their sharp claws grabbed hold of me, I plummeted headfirst, allowing gravity to take its course. Behind me, the chasing ravens screeched and followed.

Resisting the urge to flap my wings, I waited until I was close enough to skim the tops of the tallest tents. Only then did I adjust my course, level out and pick up speed. I passed over several fabric-topped structures until I found a gap, then flew further down until I was veering in and out of tent poles, piles of bags and some very startled people.

It was dangerous flying so low. Except for the Mages,

nobody had any love for the ravens and a stone thrown by a human would bring me to the ground. I had to maintain both speed and momentum – and somehow find my way back up to help Laoch. I twisted left through a narrow gap between two flimsy canvas tents, then spun right and swooped over a cold firepit. I heard a screech behind me. The other ravens were gaining on me.

I quashed all my panic and focused. Glancing right, I saw my chance and drew in my wings an inch – I wouldn't make it otherwise. I felt a strange ache across my avian shoulders as I flapped even harder.

Something nipped at my tail and suddenly the raven's consciousness urged me on. It was in danger as much as I was. I conveyed silent agreement then, using all my remaining energy, I dropped another half metre and flew through the first tent and out the other side. A woman screamed. I ignored her and made my way to the next tent.

I would never have managed it if these had been proper shelters, but most people had created roofs from thin sheets and blankets and there were few walls. That meant I could flap from one interior to another, staying out of the other birds' sight. They were far too smart to risk coming this low among humans who might try to hurt them.

A child snatched at me, grabbed a fistful of my feathers and yanked them out. The pain was excruciating. I tipped to the left as the sudden loss temporarily affected my ability to balance in mid-air. As I did so, a man picked up a brush and advanced towards me. He raised it high and prepared to strike. I ducked, flapped out of the way in the nick of time and emerged from the tent. I couldn't tell where the other ravens had gone but I couldn't stay down here. It was time to rejoin Laoch.

I swung upwards, beating my wings to rise high in the sky. Silhouetted against the weak sun, Laoch was still fending off more of the black-feathered bastards. Shite. I didn't know what to do. We couldn't fight them all and time was ticking away. The Mages would soon be face to face with Cadal Righ and then—

I didn't know if it was my brief flash of panic or whether the raven whose body I'd commandeered grew more determined, but in that moment it took over. It pushed away my control with a silent, powerful caw that echoed inside my skull. While my mind scrambled, the bird pelted upwards, using a cold current of air to gain as much height and speed as it could.

The largest raven, who I'd already surmised was the leader, slammed into Laoch with such force that it was a miracle he remained in the air. My raven barrelled through the flock, knocking several of them out of the way and pushing aside one smaller bird. It swung around in a 360-degree turn, fixed on the glittering, beady eyes of the leader and inserted itself in front of Laoch like a black-winged bodyguard.

Mairi. Laoch's voice gasped inside my head. *What's going on? What are you doing?*

It was a struggle to respond. *I don't know. I don't have control.* The words stuttered out of me. My raven flapped its wings once with grim focus then darted at the leader with murderous intent.

I expected a fight, to be ripped apart, but the lead raven squawked once and moved out of the way. I thought it was a feint and tried to wrest back control but my bird was having none of it. It wheeled around and stared at the others. Although it wasn't the biggest or the most agile raven, it was certainly the most determined.

I heard the leader squawk a second time from a metre or two below me, then it slowly turned and flew towards the city gates. A heartbeat later, the rest of the flock followed.

They're leaving. Laoch sounded tired but also astonished. *I don't understand.*

The raven's consciousness preened with smug satisfaction before yielding again to mine.

Sometimes I guess it's not size or power that matters, I said, staring after the departing flock. *It's how you act that matters. Act like the bully and others will react to you as such.* I shouldn't have been surprised that a raven employed such a technique; it was exactly how its masters, the Mages, had acted for years.

Laoch was hovering in mid-air and seemed alright, despite several bald patches on his back where the other birds had ripped his feathers out. *How are you? Can you still fly?* I asked.

He circled around me. *I'm good. These birds are tough.*

Indeed. No wonder the Mages chose to command them. I glanced away from him to the horizon beyond. *We have to go.*

His answer was immediate and grim. *I know.*

CHAPTER

NINETEEN

Although we tried to fly as fast as we had before, we couldn't. The fight with the ravens had cost us both, we were flying against the wind and our energy was fading. The fight had also delayed us and, when I saw the black-cloaked Mages a mile or so ahead, I knew that it no longer mattered how fast we flew. We weren't going to make it.

Less than fifty metres from the Mages stood an entire swaying army of the Afflicted. There was no doubt Cadal Righ would be there also.

We're too late. The dull resignation in Laoch's voice mirrored my feelings. We both slowed to conserve our energy; there was no point in rushing now. We couldn't turn the Mages around – we couldn't even delay them. This scene was going to play out without our input.

I thought of the dead ravens we'd seen in Edinburgh. We'd have to keep hidden, too. If Cadal Righ spotted us, he'd zap us out of the sky in the space of a single breath.

Laoch took the lead and descended to the line of trees alongside the main road. At this time of year there wasn't much foliage and we'd have to stay still in order to remain out of sight, but it was better than nothing. The last thing I wanted was to play the role of silent witness but we had little choice.

I landed on a high branch and found a useful perch where I could watch the unfolding action. I felt the raven resist; it was unhappy at my lack of fight after our earlier bravado. I acknowledged its frustration but I stayed where I was, with Laoch on the branch directly above me. Tragically, this wasn't the time for ploughing in and making ourselves known.

Despite Aspen's earlier bluster and the over-confidence of their seniors, I was pleased to see the Mages showing some restraint. They had spaced themselves out along the road, with the largest group at the rear. There were a hundred or so of them, their cloaks wrapped tightly around their bodies for warmth. None of them were speaking but I sensed they were prepared to band together and draw on each other's power to produce a magical attack against Cadal Righ if it were necessary.

Maybe, I thought with a faint flicker of hope, their combined energy would be enough to beat Cadal Righ. This wasn't Edinburgh, and this time they wouldn't be taken by surprise. Perhaps they could hold their own.

Then the voice in my head answered me sarcastically: fat chance of that. I'd already seen what Cadal Righ was capable of. He had far more power than a dozen hastily scrambled Mage armies.

I eyed the thousands of Afflicted men and women. Some appeared to have been in that state for a long time; only a few scraps of clothing covered their dirty bodies, their ribs were visible and they had long, scraggly hair. Others must have been infected recently; if it hadn't been for the dull light in their unfocused eyes, they could have passed for healthy.

It wasn't the number of them that bothered me, although that was truly terrifying. It was their silence. By their very nature the Afflicted were a noisy bunch; even single Afflicted person would typically produce a cacophony of snuffles, grunts and groans. Here were thousands of them and they weren't making a sound. It was one of the eeriest things I'd ever witnessed.

I wasn't the only one who was disconcerted. I could feel Laoch's discomfort as he perched above me. Also, the more senior Mages, including the Ascendants from Perth, Dundee, Aberdeen and Inverness, were shifting from foot to foot while their nerves were being shredding by the second.

I sensed magic crackling and assumed they'd established an invisible wall between themselves and the gathering Afflicted. For the Mages' sake, I hoped it would hold.

My claws curled more tightly around the branch. With each second that passed, the tension grew. I could see it in the Mages' bodies and I certainly felt it in my own. The wind picked up and the grey clouds overhead drifted faster across the sky, as if they also wanted to get away from the impending disaster. Nearby branches trembled, and the silence continued to be deafening.

As the seconds drew into minutes, my plan to stay hidden started to dissolve. I communicated to Laoch. *If Cadal Righ doesn't emerge soon, maybe we have time to speak to the Mages and persuade them to pull back.*

Laoch didn't answer immediately but when he did, his words were heavy with frustration. *They won't retreat, Mairi. But if we return to our human forms and confront them, perhaps we can encourage them to make the right choice. They're afraid. They know this could go very badly. Look at the Ascendants' expressions.*

I tilted my head to catch a clearer glimpse of their faces. I already knew from their body language that they were nervous. When I gazed at their expressions, I realised that Laoch was right. The Ascendants expected Cadal Righ to want his pound of flesh and knew that some of them might not make it beyond this meeting with all their limbs in the right places. Even so, they still believed they'd triumph in the end. They were too used to their own success.

Despite what had occurred in Edinburgh, and the brutal, sudden loss of the Ascendant and the city itself, they didn't believe that Cadal Righ would kill them all. The Mages simply couldn't conceive of a world where they weren't top of the food chain.

They started murmuring to each other, persuading themselves that Cadal Righ was striding forward to talk to them because he was scared. Having looked him in the eye, I didn't think that Cadal Righ was capable of any emotion other than blind fury. I doubted he was pacing up and down in the centre of the Afflicted army because he was worried about what the Mages might say or do; it was more likely that he was enjoying ratcheting up the fear by delaying his appearance.

I dragged my attention away from the Ascendants and back to the Afflicted people. If I flew over their heads, perhaps I might spy Cadal Righ and find out what he was doing. I poised, preparing to throw caution to the wind, take off and do just that. A second or two before I could take to the air, however, one of the Mages took the initiative instead. It was the eejit who'd laughed at me in the dining hall: McAllister. He'd mocked the idea that women could wield magic; now he was being nudged forward by the others.

I dropped back onto the branch, relaxed my wings and watched as he passed through the magical barrier to confront the Afflicted horde. He stared at them and they stared back. When he threw his arms wide and shouted, his voice carried along the wind until I was sure that even the poor souls hiding in Edinburgh would hear him.

'Cadal Righ!' he bellowed. 'We come to parley! We are not here to fight you. We want to talk. Show yourself!'

At first nothing happened but then I felt the air stir. The wind shifted in our direction, carrying a breath with it. The breath altered to a murmur. I doubted there was a single Mage who couldn't feel the foul magic contained in that soft, disembodied voice. I couldn't make out the words but I didn't need to; within a few moments it was obvious what was happening

It began with a cry as McAllister jerked and his mouth emitted a pained sound. His outstretched arms dropped to his sides and, as they did, I saw tendrils snake upwards from the dirt at his feet and twist around his ankles. They were roots, perhaps from underground plants, or maybe they came from the same tree that I was perched upon. It didn't really matter where they'd come from; what was important was the way they wrapped themselves up McAllister's legs, tightening their grip and cutting off his blood flow.

He screamed as his fingers reached for the tendrils, desperately trying to yank them away. His upper body writhed as he tried to run back to safety behind the invisible wall, but the roots held him fast. The tendrils continued to grow, curling around his knees and then his thighs. Within seconds they'd reached his stomach.

None of the other Mages moved. They appeared to be frozen, without the ability to speak or to stop what was happening to one of their own. I jerked. No matter who this bastard was or what he'd done in the past, I couldn't simply watch him be tortured like this.

But Laoch knew me too well and was already aware of what I was thinking. He hopped down from his branch and perched next to me. *No. You can't stop this. You'll die if you try.* He cocked his head in a distinctly birdlike fashion. *Anyway, he's not worth it.*

That wasn't the point. I drew breath, preparing to ignore

him and go to help McAllister, but the air shifted again. The masses of Afflicted people parted, creating a path between their stinking, rotting, swaying bodies.

McAllister was waving his hands and shouting '*Del var. Del var! DEL VAR!*', but his attempts at blocking the spell were useless. He was panicking too much and Cadal Righ's magic was far too strong. The tendrils stretched up towards his throat and his head. His face turned purple as his lungs constricted and he found the simple act of breathing difficult.

As the first tendril curved around his skull in a lethally tight caress, Cadal Righ finally appeared, sweeping forward through the path created by the Afflicted. He smiled benignly and strode to McAllister.

He eyed the choking Mage with a vaguely curious glint in his cold, red eyes. McAllister was almost two feet taller than Cadal Righ – but height was no indicator of power. 'There now,' Cadal Righ cooed. 'There's no need to be upset.'

A single tear rolled down McAllister's cheek.

'You're weeping.' Cadal Righ seemed surprised. 'Does it hurt that much? Aren't you supposed to be a man? Why are you sobbing like a child?'

McAllister opened his mouth to speak, but it wasn't a shout or scream that left his lips this time; it was nothing more than a croaked whisper. 'Please.'

Cadal Righ pursed his bloodless lips. 'Very well then.' He waved a hand. '*Chelta.*'

The tendrils, which seemed to have halted their attempts to smother McAllister for a moment, stretched and grew once again. Now they were moving with greater speed. I lurched forward out of the tree but I was already too late. Within less than three seconds, Mage McAllister was no more.

In his place stood a towering vine with thorns and twisted roots that pointed up towards the sky. It would have been more in keeping with an arid desert than a damp field in Scotland, but that would be no comfort to McAllister.

I fell back and landed with an ungainly crash on the same branch. Cadal Righ didn't glance in my direction. I had no idea whether he'd noticed that two ravens were watching him, or if he was aware of the daemon magic that had enabled us to enter their bodies. His focus was wholly on the Mages. Although I despised myself for my weakness, I was glad that he wasn't looking at me.

'Why have you come here?' Cadal Righ asked, addressing the closest group of Mages. 'Unless you are planning to hand me the keys to the city of Glasgow and join my other children,' he indicated the ever-watchful Afflicted masses, 'I cannot imagine why you want to talk to me.'

This time none of the Mages rushed forward to speak. The Inverness and the Dundee Ascendants took a step backwards. Cadal Righ tutted, apparently annoyed by the lack of an immediate response. He sniffed and turned his red gaze on them. '*Sel ez.*'

I spotted the flicker of blue flame at his fingertips before both Ascendants started to splutter. I shook my head. *Sel ez?* That was the magical word for water, but there was no water nearby, magical or otherwise. Unless...

I stared at the two Mages. They were drowning. They were drowning on dry land as a result of Cadal Righ's spell. He'd cut through the Mages' magical barrier as if it didn't exist and he was using his powers to fill the Ascendants' lungs with fluid.

'Stop!' A third Ascendant jerked forward. 'Enough! I will answer your questions!'

Cadal Righ raised his right hand and, with a slow deliberate movement, extended his index finger. I thought for a moment that he was planning to point at the Ascendant and kill him too, but instead he stuck the tip of his finger in his ear and wiggled it around to suggest he was hard of hearing. All the while, the two drowning Ascendants choked and spluttered. One fell to his knees before pitching forward onto the hard ground. The second one quickly followed.

'I'm sorry,' Cadal Righ said, not sounding sorry at all. 'I'm quite old, you see, and sometimes rather deaf. What was it that you said?'

The third Ascendant swallowed and repeated his words. 'I will answer your questions. Let them go. Release the spell.'

Cadal Righ removed his finger and gazed at the two fallen Ascendants, who twisted and writhed before falling still. He shrugged. 'Too late.' He winked. 'Oh well. What's your name, boy? Who are you?'

Perhaps it was the boy epithet that reminded the Ascendant of his status. He looked away from the bodies of his two comrades, straightened and met Cadal Righ's gaze without flinching. 'My name is Alastair Reyworth,' he said icily. 'I am the Ascendant for the proud city of Aberdeen. You have demonstrated your power and we know what you are capable of. Now it is time for *you* to act like a man and negotiate.'

My muscles tightened at the implied insult. Rather than react with anger, however, Cadal Righ threw back his head and laughed. The cold sound echoed around us, more chilling than another show of magical violence would have been. 'Negotiate? Me?' He laughed again. 'My dear boy.'

'I am not a boy,' Reyworth bit out.

Cadal Righ waved a hand dismissively. 'You are to me. I've been alive longer than you can imagine.'

'If that's true, then where have you been all this time?'

The answer was swift. 'Sleeping. Waiting for the right moment when I could claim Scotland as mine. You helped me a great deal, you know. I might not have woken for several more decades, but your deeds helped to give me power in the same way they helped you. You pulled on magic from the corpses you killed. When you buried them, their power leeched into the ground and drew towards me.' He flexed his fingers. 'It was quite delicious. Perhaps I shall continue the custom with your mutilated bodies.'

Although Reyworth was visibly taken aback by Cadal Righ's revelation, he didn't allow the threat of death to intimidate him. I was beginning to see how he'd risen to the position of Aberdeen Ascendant; he wasn't easily cowed, even in the face of overwhelming odds. Maybe he had some extra tricks up his sleeve, or maybe he was still idiotic enough to believe that he could bargain with Cadal Righ. Either way, he folded his arms and regarded his opponent with an implacable gaze. 'You're welcome. I think that proves that we can have a mutually beneficial relationship.'

'Mutually beneficial?' Suddenly Cadal Righ was no longer laughing. He stepped towards Reyworth, who took a step back. 'Everything that you are, everything that you have enjoyed in your entire pathetic life is thanks to me,' he sneered. 'If I had not given you the tools to rid yourselves of the female Mages, you would not be in charge now. If I had not created the Afflicted, you could not have kept the population under control. You have lived a charmed life because of my actions. And now you suggest you deserve respect for that? There is nothing mutually beneficial to be had here. You have reaped all the benefits! You should be bowing at my feet, not raising yourself to my level! Impudent pup.' He glared at the Mages. 'All of you!'

Reyworth had realised his error. His shoulders were dropping and he suddenly appeared far more nervous. 'We can give you Glasgow. Today. We'll give you Glasgow and everyone inside it.'

'I will *take* Glasgow,' Cadal Righ shouted. 'I do not need you to give me it!'

'You can have Aberdeen too,' Reyworth stammered. 'My gift to you.' He glanced at the two drowned Ascendants. 'And Perth. And Dundee. They're all yours. But leave us with Inverness. We'll stay there. You might need unAfflicted people in the future and we can provide them. You might want to have people who can still hold a normal conversation. You might want—'

'I am *so* bored with talking.' Cadal Righ sniffed. 'And I am still waiting!'

Reyworth stared at him. 'Waiting for what?'

'For you to fucking bow!' he roared. 'All of you! Why are you not yet bowing?'

Bloody hell. I felt myself tremble at Cadal Righ's rage – even the branches on the tree seemed to shake. I watched wide-eyed as Reyworth lowered himself to his knees. One by one, every other Mage did the same.

'Lower!' Cadal Righ shouted. They dipped further. 'Lower!'

By this point, most of the Mages' foreheads were touching the ground. Maybe I should have felt some momentary exulta-tion that they were getting the same treatment that they'd doled out to us for so many years. And yet, I couldn't feel pleased. Reyworth had offered up every person in four cities as sacrifice to Cadal Righ; he was still only interested in the Mages' survival. And if the Mages fell, we all fell.

'As I said,' Reyworth mumbled from his prone position, 'we will do whatever you want. Allow us to keep Inverness and—'

Cadal Righ interrupted him again. 'All of Scotland will be mine. I did not sleep for more than a hundred years and put all these plans in place to be content with only a slice of it. It is all mine!'

I watched Reyworth rather than Cadal Righ. His body slumped for a moment then he straightened his back and stood up. 'Then you leave us with no choice,' he said. He gestured at the other prostrate Mages. Most – but not all – also got to their feet. '*Belzac.*'

A plume of flame shot from Reyworth's fingertips, jetting out towards Cadal Righ and his silent army of the Afflicted. The other Mages followed suit.

'*Belzac.*'

'*Belzac!*'

'*BELZAC!*'

The raven's muffled mind managed a hiss of satisfaction but I couldn't match its feelings. Cadal Righ blocked the first few spells easily but it wasn't long before I couldn't see him at all as dark smoke and bright flames engulfed the scene.

The Mages didn't let up. They threw the same spell at Cadal Righ over and over again until they were chanting the word together like a strange, destructive song. *Belzac. Belzac. Belzac.*

I can't see anything, Laoch. Is Cadal Righ still there?

His response echoed in my head. *I don't know. I can't see anything either, and I can't sense anything with all the damned magic flying around.*

I heard a shriek. A figure came running towards us, screaming, from beyond the thick smoke. It was one of the Afflicted – and his whole body seemed to be on fire. He sprinted forward but his sight was so obscured that he had no idea where he was going. He smacked into the trunk of the tree where Laoch and I were perching and fell backwards.

His blackened chest heaved for several more breaths before it stopped. I stared down at him. Half of his body had been burnt to a crisp though the other half was unharmed. There was a crude tattoo inked onto his upper arm: *Mum.* I half-closed my eyes. That poor man.

Nobody else emerged from the flames and swirling smoke. My eyes were stinging but I still tried to peer through the murk to see what had happened to Cadal Righ. I couldn't hear him or see him. Had the Mages' combined spell actually worked?

Reyworth, smoke swirling around his upright body as if he were the centre of a hell-spun maelstrom, raised his right hand. One by one the Mages fell silent and stopped their barrage of fiery attacks. None of them moved. All eyes were on the smoke-filled spot where Cadal Righ had been standing.

A gentle breeze filtered through the trees. As it picked up, it brushed away the edges of the acrid smoke. Finally, it billowed away from the epicentre of the attacks. Laoch's single word said it all. *Shite.*

Cadal Righ remained on his feet, arms folded and his expression akin to boredom. He was completely unruffled; in fact, he wasn't even singed. Neither did many of the Afflicted army behind him appear to have been affected. I spotted a couple of charred bodies and a few infected figures whose clothes were still aflame, but most of them were standing exactly where they had been before, waiting and watching Cadal Righ.

He sighed heavily as if he were disappointed. 'Is that it? Is that all you've got? I'd have expected more from Scotland's finest.' He tutted. 'Hey ho. Now I know the best that you can do, it's only fair that I show you the best that I can do. Unfortunately, it means you're about to die. I hope you said goodbye to your loved ones before you came here.' He raised his hands and grinned. 'Cheerio.'

TWENTY

Some of the Mages recognised the danger and whirled away to flee but most were stupid and held their ground, waiting for Reyworth to tell them what to do. Cadal Righ didn't wait. He looked Reyworth in the eye and cheerfully murmured a single spell, '*Folis.*'

It wasn't the magic I'd been expecting. Reyworth's body rose in the air and he twisted, yelling out the words to block the spell. It was to no avail; Cadal Righ's hold was too strong.

A few of the other Mages reached for Reyworth and tried to pull him down through sheer force, but as soon as they touched his body they were flung backwards by some sort of violent, magical energy. Reyworth was held there, suspended five metres in the air.

Cadal Righ gestured towards the Afflicted behind him and a dozen of them let out a loud whoop, the first sound I'd heard any of them make since we'd arrived. A moment later, they bounded towards Reyworth.

Remnants of the Mages' magical wall still held and the twelve Afflicted men and women slammed into it and fell back.

They immediately turned to Cadal Righ, who gave them a soft, almost indulgent smile. '*Desh mar.*'

The air crackled and the spell fell away, removing the invisible wall entirely. It had taken Cadal Righ no effort whatsoever. Then the Afflicted were on their feet again, passing through the spot and launching themselves at the suspended body of the Aberdeen Ascendant.

The first to reach him was a woman. It was hard to judge from the grime coating her thin body but she was probably no more than a teenager. Her youth was no barrier to her appetite, though. She grabbed Reyworth's ankle and latched onto it, sinking her teeth into his flesh. Reyworth screamed but she didn't so much as blink.

Another of the Afflicted took his right arm and ripped away his cloak to get to the bare skin underneath. The twelve Afflicted people attacked Reyworth as if he were a pig on a spit, hanging there purely for their delectation.

A few Mages started to run to his aid but they changed their minds when they saw Cadal Righ's red eyes watching them and sprinted away in the opposite direction. It suddenly seemed that it was every Mage for himself.

'*Ins veil.*' Cadal Righ barely whispered the words but at least thirty of the fleeing Mages were thrown to the ground. Almost immediately more Afflicted peeled away from the army to launch themselves at the fallen bodies.

The raven's mind stirred and I knew it was right. We had to act. Despite my intentions only to bear witness, I couldn't just sit here and watch. Scotland needed as many Mages as possible if there was to be a fighting chance against Cadal Righ.

Can you help them? I projected to Laoch. *The Mages?*

I can try.

Good. I held my breath then I ejected myself from the raven's body.

Laoch's voice reverberated in my head. *Mairi! You bloody eejit!*

I crashed through the branches and landed in a heap at the foot of the tree next to the burnt body of the Afflicted man. I picked myself up and brushed myself down, then I responded calmly, *I will delay Cadal Righ. You get as many of the wankers as possible back to Glasgow.* I paused. *Anyone who's not Afflicted needs to get inside the city walls.*

This is a fucking terrible idea, Laoch retorted.

I smiled sadly. *We've got nothing else.* I turned and looked at him. Even though he remained inside the raven, I could sense his will. He was scared for me but he understood my determination. He nodded once.

I glanced across at the raven who had been a part of me until moments ago. It glowered at me with characteristic malevolence. 'Thank you,' I said aloud. Then, without waiting for it to react, I marched towards Cadal Righ.

There was almost nothing left of Reyworth when I passed his suspended body. The Afflicted were still gnawing at him and there were puddles of blood on the ground beneath him. Nothing alive remained of the man himself.

It was probably a good thing that all I could smell was the smoke from the Mages' fiery attack. I avoided looking at Reyworth's body and swept past, making a beeline for Cadal Righ. I would borrow a leaf from the raven's book and play the part of the bully. I wouldn't beat him, but maybe I could divert his attention away from the eejit Mages for long enough to have an impact.

Sensing my approach, Cadal Righ turned his head. He'd already opened his mouth to bark out a new spell but the words faltered on his lips when he saw me. Confusion marred his expression and I realised he was trying to identify me. 'Wait,' he said. 'I know you, right? You're that daft woman from Edinburgh. How on earth did you get here?'

I tried not to let my triumph show on my face. If he was talking to me he wasn't attacking the Mages, and right now every second's delay counted. I stopped in front of him, closer than Reyworth had been, and smiled. 'I walked,' I said. 'It's a fair distance but it's not that far. How did you get here? Did you fly?'

Cadal Righ's brows snapped together and I realised I'd erred by mentioning the word fly. His gaze rose towards the tree where Laoch and I had been hiding and he registered the ravens. I didn't think he'd made the connection between the ravens and me but he wasn't stupid. I needed to divert him.

Without waiting for an answer, I continued hastily. 'I don't suppose how either of us got here is important. What is important is why you're doing this.' I looked beyond him to the Afflicted army, most of whom were still waiting patiently for their turn to attack. 'Is this what you truly want?'

'Of course it is!' He bared his teeth. 'I'm the King of Scotland and I need to rightfully claim what is mine.'

I inhaled. 'Why should an entire country belong to you?'

He said simply, 'Why shouldn't it?' Then his eyes narrowed. 'You're brave, you know. There are not many who would dare to come this close to me and demand answers.' He jerked his thumb at Reyworth. 'You saw what happened to the last person. And he had magic. As a woman, you—'

He stopped mid-sentence. Uh-oh. His eyes flicked once more to the tree then to me. 'No.' Cadal Righ shook his head. 'Say it isn't so.'

'Say what?' My nerves were starting to get the better of me but I had to hold my ground. I had to give Laoch and the Mages the best chance possible.

'Those stupid fucking bastards.'

I swallowed. 'Who?'

'Them. Those black cloaks. That's who.' Cadal Righ's fists clenched – he was genuinely angry.

I watched his expression closely. No, it wasn't only anger. I saw a flicker of fear as well and my body tensed. What was he afraid of? What was it? I searched his face desperately for an answer.

'I gave them everything they needed to get rid of every woman with magic,' he spat. 'And yet here you are, standing right in front of me.' His lip curled. 'I should have known.'

'There are no female Mages,' I told him. Was it women that scared him so much? If so, why?

'Perhaps not,' Cadal Righ growled. 'But there are females with magic. Right?'

When I didn't answer, his cheeks grew red and he shouted. 'Right?'

I gazed into his eyes, trying to decipher the different emotions flitting across his face. Then I hummed. *Meshar al.*

I wasn't sure what I'd expected to happen when I directed the spell. Theoretically, it would turn a body limp and defenceless. Perhaps I'd hoped that the nature of my sex would somehow cause my power to affect Cadal Righ in a way that the male Mages' spells had not; maybe that was why he was scared of my existence. But when my magic reached him, he reacted with little more than a frown and batted it away easily. He didn't so much as stagger.

'Huh.' He cocked his head. 'You didn't speak – but you do have magic. Quite a considerable amount. How does that work?' He advanced towards me.

I reminded myself yet again of the success that one bullying raven could achieve and forced myself to hold my ground. Somehow I allowed a smile to spread across my mouth. 'I guess we've evolved since your day,' I said. 'Near-total annihilation tends to cause people to find new ways to survive.' I nodded at the swaying Afflicted hordes. 'You would do well to remember that.'

He gazed at me, considering, then wrinkled his nose. 'Nah. I'm not buying it. You're an anomaly, an exception to the rule. There's bound to be some. You're nothing to worry about.'

My smile turned into a snarl. 'Let's see about that, shall we?' I hummed once again, this time throwing every iota of energy I had into the spell. I didn't use my magic against Cadal Righ, however, I used it on myself. *Bish var.*

It took but a moment. Within a single breath, I felt my entire body being imbued with the extra strength the spell had given me. It was only temporary, but I didn't have much time left.

As soon as I knew it had worked, I lunged for Cadal Righ, curled my right hand into a fist and punched him on the side of his pinched, pale head. He reeled backwards. The flash of satisfaction I experienced at finally doing something that affected him adversely was amazing, though unfortunately it didn't last long.

Before I could hit him again, he cast an attack of his own. '*Ins veil.*'

I'd never felt power like it. I'd been attacked by plenty of Mages but nothing they'd done was like this. It wasn't so much the spell itself, although that threw me backwards by at least twenty metres, it was the casual strength attached to it that took my breath away. In that instant I couldn't see how anyone, no matter how well we worked together or what we did, could best Cadal Righ. He was simply too strong.

My back crashed into the ground, jarring my spine and making me cry out. Several of the Afflicted who'd been so intent on chewing Reyworth's bones turned their heads with interest.

Cadal Righ ordered them back. 'No,' he instructed coldly. 'This one is mine.'

Dazed and in agony, I raised my head as he approached me again. Desperate to slow him down so that I could recover, I hummed. *Vaz.* Alas, my invisible wall gave him no more trouble than the Mages' wall and he stepped through it without pause. I shouldn't have wasted my energy.

He strode towards me. As I struggled to my feet, doing everything I could to push away the pain, he peered at me unblinkingly. 'How many more are there like you?' he demanded. 'How many more women are there who can do magic?'

I hawked up a ball of phlegm and spat it at his feet.

He raised an eyebrow. 'How very uncouth,' he murmured. 'In my day, ladies were far more refined.' He sniffed. 'Answer the question.'

No chance.

'Answer the question.'

No.

'Answer the question.'

Fuck off.

He sighed as if my resistance were nothing more than a vexing irritation. Then he shrugged to himself and muttered, '*Sel ez.*'

It was the magical word for water; he was doing the same to me as he'd done to the two Ascendants. I gasped for air, pulling as much into my lungs as I could. It didn't help; I could already feel the liquid filling my body, constricting my airways and overtaking all that I was.

I gurgled and spluttered. The dull pain in my chest started to expand, crushing my very bones and forcing away rational thought. My vision blurred and I felt myself falling. Then, inexplicably, Cadal Righ released the spell.

On my hands and knees I choked out water while he bent down and put his face next to mine. 'Let's try that again, shall we? How many other women can do magic?'

I glared at him and spat out another mouthful of foul, brackish water. 'I don't know,' I hissed. 'But there are lots. I'm not an anomaly. Women like me have stayed hidden for years, so there could be any number of us.'

Although I'd given him the true answer, I didn't expect him to believe me. Somehow, though, he knew I wasn't lying.

He wasn't as concerned as I'd thought he might be. 'Hidden? So you've not spent a great deal of time comparing notes? You've not learnt from each other. You've not properly studied the art of magic and you've concealed your powers. Is that why you hum? Are all female Mages like that now?'

I pushed away my damp curls and again refused to answer.

'Do we need to do this every time I ask a simple question?' Cadal Righ tutted. '*Sel ez.*'

The second time was worse. I knew what to expect and cloying panic overtook me before the spell had even taken root. I felt the water rise up in my lungs again. No. Oh no. My chest was still burning after the first semi-drowning and this time the pain and the fear were excruciating.

Tears sprang to my eyes and my fingers scrabbled desperately at my clothes, as if tearing them off could possibly help. I managed half a hum, desperately stretching my magic in a frantic bid to throw away the spell but, as with the Mages earlier, either my panic was too great or Cadal Righ's magic was too strong. My hum had no effect. I gasped for air, but none was forthcoming.

Make it stop. Oh God, make it stop.

He released me a moment later. While I choked and cursed, he asked the question again. 'Do you all hum?'

Bastard. The pain in my chest was too much and I couldn't

bring myself to speak. Instead, I slowly shook my head. The Gowk had been tortured by the Mages for weeks, months, even; I'd been tortured by Cadal Righ for a few minutes and I already wanted to give up. I didn't think I could bear being drowned for a third time.

'Good girl.' He patted my head as if I were a pet dog. 'Now, there's only one more question. After you answer it, I'll set you free. That will be good, won't it?' He smiled. 'Soon there won't be any more pain or suffering. All you have to do is tell me if there's anything unusual about your powers. Is there anything you can do – that you've learned to do – that the Mages cannot?'

I pinned my mouth shut. What I wouldn't have given at that moment to be mute again. I knew deep down that I wouldn't be able to stay quiet for long and I started to shake.

I still had some energy left inside me; if I directed more of my magic at myself, perhaps I could do something before I was forced to answer. I searched my brain for the right spell but I wasn't sure that any of them would work in the way I needed them to.

I pushed myself up and managed somehow to get to my feet. Cadal Righ put his hands on his hips as he waited for his answer. I held up my hand to indicate that I needed time to get my voice back.

I had one play left. There was little hope that it would work but I had to try. I gave Cadal Righ a look of total defeat, then I grabbed every ounce of magic left inside me. *Desh mar tun desh mar.* It was the same spell that had driven the magic permanently out of Noah; maybe it would have the same effect on Cadal Righ. It was all I had.

The power flew out of my body and into him. His eyes widened and something flared in their crimson depths, but then I felt the magic bounce away from him uselessly, dissipating into nothing.

'Well,' he said, 'I think that answers all my questions. Thank you. And nice try.' He bared his teeth. 'Although now you've got nothing.'

He raised his hands and I knew it was over. He was right: I had nothing left to give and I was out of options.

All of a sudden, a black shape hurtled down out of the grey sky above us and threw itself into Cadal Righ's face. I gaped, genuinely surprised. Then hands were grabbing me, hauling me backwards. Laoch scooped me up against his chest and started to run, speeding away from Cadal Righ as fast as his feet could carry him.

'No,' I mumbled. 'He'll come after us. He'll hurt you too.'

'I've managed to persuade some of the Mages to help,' he grunted without dropping his speed for a second.

A blast of magic rippled the air, pushing past us and towards Cadal Righ. It wouldn't do much damage but it might hold him back for a few minutes.

'The raven—'

'It did that of its own accord,' he said. 'Don't ask me how or why. Birds are going to do what birds are going to do.'

I nodded, then I closed my eyes and gave in to the pain and blessed relief of unconsciousness.

TWENTY-ONE

I wasn't out for long. When my eyelids fluttered open, I was still cradled against Laoch's chest and he was still running. Now, however, Glasgow was within touching distance.

Laoch sped past row upon row of tents. I could hear cries and shouting up ahead.

'What...?' I croaked. 'What's happening?'

'They're letting everyone into the city.' He kept moving. 'Cadal Righ's Afflicted army is right behind us.'

I swallowed hard, then wished I hadn't because it reminded me of the agony in my chest. 'The walls,' I whispered. 'They won't hold him back.'

'I know.' Laoch sounded grimmer than I'd ever heard him before. 'And there's likely as many infected people as healthy citizens being allowed inside.'

'What else can we do?'

'Nothing.' He didn't pause. 'We're all fucked.'

He started to slow. I told him that I could walk, he didn't have to carry me all the way, but he only tightened his grip. I didn't insist. Here in Laoch's arms I felt protected, even if that feeling was only temporary.

I let him carry me towards the throng pushing through the city gates. The people around us were terrified – there was no doubt about that – but there was a strange sense of calm as well. I realised it had sprung from relief that the inevitable was finally upon us. We'd all known it would come to this. Now the end was here and Cadal Righ was on our heels with his thousands of Afflicted souls, the waiting was over. The business of dying could begin.

I shivered despite Laoch's warmth. He glanced down at me with sudden concern and I managed a shaky smile in return. It didn't reassure him; it didn't reassure me either. Then we passed through the gates and into the city itself.

As soon as they were through the entrance, most people darted down the streets determined to put as much distance between themselves and the advancing army as they could. Not that it would help.

Laoch looked at me questioningly and I shook my head. He nodded, then carefully lowered me.

I wobbled slightly and rubbed my chest. 'I'm alright,' I told him. 'Honestly.' I looked around. The guards seemed to have abandoned their posts for good. I pushed my matted hair out of my eyes. 'I need to see,' I said.

Together, we pushed through the last few stragglers. While the city gates were closed and people dragged furniture out of their houses to add to the barricade, Laoch and I headed for the guard tower nearby. We climbed the stairs so we could watch our impending doom for ourselves.

The best view from the guard tower wasn't from the window that looked out of the city; that was only a tiny opening through which it was hard to see anything. The largest window faced in the opposite direction because the guards' role had been to watch the people *inside* the city, not the dangers that might come from outside.

I hissed in annoyance, kicked the larger window open and started to clamber out. My strength was returning but it was still an effort to heave myself out and climb up to the pointed roof so I could edge around and get a proper look.

Laoch followed me, less than half a foot away at all times, prepared to catch me if I fell. But the height was the least of our problems. The moment I caught sight of Cadal Righ and his Afflicted followers, I sucked in a sharp breath and only just managed to bite back a cry of dismay.

From up here, things somehow seemed even worse than they had been when I was face to face with the red-eyed bastard. The Afflicted army appeared more formidable as they shuffled forward with inexorable intent while Cadal Righ marched at the helm. He'd do what he did in Edinburgh and blast his way in as if he were slicing through warm butter.

I clenched my jaw. We had to do something, to put up some sort of a defence. He was less than a hundred metres from the first line of makeshift tents.

I cast around until I saw a group of huddled Mages gesticulating frantically at each other. I turned to Laoch. 'Are they the ones who helped you?'

He nodded. Good: I shouldn't have to persuade them to get involved, then. I waved downwards and shouted. 'Oi!'

The Mages were too caught up in their own discourse to hear me. I cleared my throat and tried again. 'Oi!'

This time several of them looked up in my direction and I noted flashes of relief on several of their taut faces. Under any other circumstances that would have amused me. The knowledge that they could be pleased to see me and believed I might yet save their sorry arses should have been delicious. But there wasn't any time to savour the moment; there was barely any time to breathe.

'We need to work together!' I called. 'We need to make a wall that can stop him.'

'We tried that out there. It didn't work.' The Mage who answered flapped his hands. 'We can't stop him. We can't do anything.'

We could always do *something*. We could at least try.

'A combination,' Laoch bit out. 'Two spells together. *Vaz* for wall and...' he met my eyes '...*belzac*?'

'The Afflicted don't like fire,' I agreed. 'It's a good idea. I don't have any magic left though – I threw everything I had at Cadal Righ and it had no effect. I'll need the damned Mages to make the spell work.'

'Aye. We do.' He held out his hand. I took it and, using Laoch's magic, we floated down to the ground and ran to the Mages.

'I have an idea.' I said, the words bursting out of me as soon as we were close. 'I'll need your magic. I'll need to borrow power from all of you.'

Half of the Mages appeared to agree immediately but the other half looked dubious.

'It's a trap,' one of them warned, throwing back his black cloak. 'It has to be. The bitch is probably working with him. She'll betray us in a heartbeat and we'll end up like the Ascendants.'

For fuck's sake. 'Don't you get it? Can't you see what's going on here? Cadal Righ doesn't need me. He doesn't need anyone! He will enter this city in the next five minutes if we don't do something to stop him! I don't want to die any more than you do. It might have escaped your notice, but I don't want anyone in this city to die. I'm on their side. But if Cadal Righ comes in here, we all know what will happen.'

'What can *you* do?' the Mage sneered.

'More than you.' I drew myself up. 'I know you. Your name is Brian, right?'

His watery blue eyes narrowed. I had no idea why he was surprised that I knew his name; as a servant, I'd cleaned up after him and his damned chums for weeks. I'd learned far more about him during those days than he'd ever want them to know.

'You're a Mage.' I didn't break my gaze. 'You can only perform three spells. No matter how hard you try, everything else is beyond your reach. Until recently, you told the others that you were working on a way to purify the water that runs through the city, but you actually spent all your time in your study drinking whisky and perfecting the art of making paper aeroplanes.' I gazed at him. 'Your magic is negligible. You can piss off. You won't be able to help me.'

'I've got plenty of magic!' he blustered. 'Of course I can help!'

I put out my hand. 'Then prove it.'

It was a testament to what the Mages were truly like that he was more concerned about his image than that I might stab him in the back and help Cadal Righ to over-run Glasgow. He slapped his hand into mine and glared. 'Go on then. Take what you need. There's plenty in there.'

Aye. Sure. I glanced at the other Mages. They quickly joined up, linking hands so that we were all bound together. Some did it because they believed in me, others did it because they were afraid of what secrets I might reveal about them. I didn't care what their motives were. I had to stop Cadal Righ.

I turned to Laoch. 'I need you to be my eyes.'

He didn't waste time answering but murmured a quick spell and threw himself up to the steep roof of the guards' tower so he could see what was happening. When I saw his face pale, I knew we had seconds rather than minutes.

I closed my eyes and reached into myself to prepare before tugging on the combined power of the Mages next to me. Magical energy surged through me, my heart rate increased and blood roared in my ears. There was nothing apart from me and the magic. I pictured the outskirts of the city in my mind, then I hummed for all I was worth. *Belzac vaz. Belzac vaz. BELZAC VAZ.*

'Higher,' Laoch shouted. 'It needs to be at least a metre higher. And focus on the left side. It's a bit sparse at the far end.'

I concentrated and tried harder. I felt several of the Mages down the line waver, their control slipping as I continued to draw from them. My heart was hammering so fast now that I feared it would burst out of my chest. I ignored it and focused on the wall of fire.

Belzac vaz. Belzac vaz.

My body wobbled as I grew more light-headed, and I swayed from side to side.

'You've got it, Mairi!' Laoch shouted. 'You've bloody got it!'

And then, above the noise of my heart, the roar of the fire and the ragged cheers from the fleeing people who'd stopped to see if this would work, another sound arose. It was a scream, louder than anything I'd ever heard, filled with raw fury and frustrated impotence. And I knew who had made it.

Gasping, I fell to my knees. We'd done it. At least for now, we'd done enough to hold Cadal Righ back.

***

It took a surprisingly short time for dozens of other Mages to appear. They'd sensed the huge burst of magic and, recognising it came from their side and not Cadal Righ's, they ran towards us to help.

When I heard a familiar voice by my side urging me to relax, I almost cried. I turned to Angus and commanded my legs not to give way. 'You're not dead.'

'Not for want of trying, lass.' He grinned but I could see it was an effort. 'The perimeter spell is established now. Others can maintain it. You can release your hold.'

I tilted my head upwards and my eyes met Laoch's concerned green gaze. He nodded in agreement. Stumbling backwards, I let go of the magic.

I gazed down the line of Mages who had lent me their power. Some were doubled over and retching and at least three had passed out. To my surprise, Brian was still on his feet. 'There, bitch,' he said with a satisfied grunt. 'I'm no weakling.'

Apparently not. I gave him a tired nod and allowed Angus to help me move aside, where I sat down and tried to recover.

Laoch descended and joined us. 'You're amazing,' he said, kneeling down in front of me and cupping my face in is hands. He leaned in and his mouth descended on mine. I returned his kiss, and his physical energy endowed me in a similar way to how the Mages had imbued me with their magic.

'You two.' Angus clicked his tongue and sighed. 'Always with the public displays of affection.'

I ignored him and enjoyed Laoch for as long as I could. Finally I pulled away and we both looked at him. 'Andy?' I asked.

'He's conscious. The lad headed straight for the library as soon as he was able.'

'Aspen?' Laoch growled.

'He's being contained. You've done good, lass. I don't think anyone else could have done this.'

I appreciated the words but I didn't need compliments. 'The wall won't hold forever,' I said. 'We've got a day or two at best.'

Angus looked away from me. 'We'll come up with an alternative by then.' There was a distinct lack of conviction in his voice. We all knew where we stood; we had gained some breathing space but it wouldn't last for long.

'Mairi!' A small shape barrelled towards me, all flying hair and gangly limbs. I stood up, confused for a second as to who it was. When she stopped short in front of me, not yet ready to engage in a hug or any physical contact, I realised it was Isla. She'd had a bath, was wearing fresh clothes and looked like a different person.

'I like Glasgow!' she declared. 'And your friends are braw!'

I glanced over her shoulder, noting with another surge of happiness that she wasn't alone. Behind her stood Belle, Twister, the Gowk, Ailsa and Fee. It felt like a lifetime since I'd last seen them. More tears pricked my eyes and this time I didn't hold them back. 'It's good to see you all again,' I sniffed,

'Aye, well,' Belle replied. 'I suppose it's good to see you, too. It's nae been that long, though.' Twister muttered at her but I spotted the twinkle in her eye.

'Gimme a hug, lass,' the Gowk said gruffly, extending his claw-like hand. My smile widened as I opened my arms and clapped him on the back. I did the same with the others.

'I hear you almost won,' Fee said. 'You almost beat all those fuckers. You could be the Glasgow Ascendant.'

I pursed my lips. 'The Ascendancy Challenge didn't finish – and Ascendants these days tend to have a short lifespan.' I didn't want to be Ascendant any more now than I had before I'd left Glasgow.

Ailsa's expression was dark. 'Aye,' she said. 'Belle has filled us in on most of the details. Apparently she was quite the hero and saved your life on three separate occasions.'

I snorted. When I looked at Belle, she suddenly appeared genuinely embarrassed and could no longer meet my eyes. I cleared my throat. 'Actually,' I said, 'I think it was four times, not three.' So I was capable of lying after all.

Belle's eyes widened and I smiled slightly. 'What happened while I was gone?'

The Gowk's lip curled. 'What you'd expect. The Mages did everything they could to find us, but they didn't. There are more people than ever with us, prepared to stand against them.' He looked at the large cluster of Mages and I sensed he was prepared to attack them as soon as I gave the word.

I cleared my throat to draw my friends' attention. 'We can't stand against them. We need them.'

Fee glared. 'We dinnae need them at all. Trish, Lottie, Flora and Jane are nae here because they're rounding up all the women who can do magic. An' there's another woman called Maggie fae Edinburgh who's doing the same. We've got the power and the energy and,' she paused for effect, 'the will.'

I looked away. 'It won't be enough.'

'But—'

Laoch repeated my words. 'It won't be enough.'

I pulled back my shoulders. 'That man out there – if you can call him a man – is more powerful than anything you can imagine and he has only one goal. He wants to take all of Scotland for himself.'

'He cannae be worse than the Mages,' Ailsa said.

'He is.' My voice was flat. 'He wants to rule over a country of the Afflicted. Only then can he be sure that we'll all toe the line.'

The Gowk sucked in a breath.

Isla coughed. 'Uh ...'

'What is it?'

'There's a lot of them now,' she whispered. 'Inside the walls. We passed hundreds who have the Affliction eating away at them.'

I wasn't surprised, but her words still dismayed me.

'Without us, the Mages can't win against Cadal Righ,' I said. 'And we can't win against Cadal Righ without the Mages.'

The silence suddenly became uncomfortable. To my surprise, it wasn't one of my ragtag group who broke it, it was Brian. 'So,' he said, rubbing away the sweat on his brow, 'how do we win against him?'

I wished I had an answer.

TWENTY-TWO

The City Chambers' dining room had seen a lot of action in its day but I was sure it had never been as packed as it was now.

Ailsa looked nervous; she hadn't been inside the building since the day we'd run from it after I killed the Glasgow Ascendant – and she'd certainly never sat down on one of the chairs. She lowered herself nervously, but her expression altered from anxiety to disgust, when she looked around.

'Look at the state of this place,' she said. 'There's a cobweb in that corner! And the edges of these chairs haven't been wiped down properly for weeks. That's … that's…' She pulled a face. 'That's dried gravy on the floor! How long has that been there?'

Everyone stared at her and she stared back. 'Whit?' she demanded. 'I spent years keeping this place clean. I'm allowed some professional pride, aren't I?'

Morag, who had remained at the City Chambers, sent Ailsa an icy glare. 'It's no' my fault! I've got a skeleton staff! Half the building is in ruins and the world is in uproar! I've done ma bloody best!'

Ailsa bobbed her head vigorously. 'An' I bet nobody has ever bothered to say thank you. Nobody sees how hard the likes of us has to work.'

Mollified, Morag agreed. 'Exactly! It's no' a battle trying to keep this place clean, it's a damned war.' The Gowk reached across the table and patted her hand.

Isla had other concerns. 'If this is the dining room,' she asked, 'are we going to get fed? I'm kinda hungry.'

Fee refused to sit down. 'I thought it would be grander in here,' she said. 'With more gold.'

'And tartan,' Belle said, adding a tart sniff for emphasis. 'I thought there would be a lot more tartan.'

Aspen was in the corner, tied up with rope and flanked by Alan, Morag and Teasag who looked more than ready to smack him on the head if he dared to try anything. He gave a derisive snort. 'Glasgow is over-run by the Afflicted,' he said. 'A villainous bastard intent on destroying us all is at the gates, our country is on the brink of annihilation and these *women* are thinking about cleaning, their stomachs and interior design.' His voice was heavy with disgust.

'You don't get it, do you?' A cold smile curved my lips.

He gazed at me blankly. 'Get what?'

'For you Mages, this is the apocalypse. It's the end of the world. For us,' I indicated my group, 'it's Tuesday. We've felt like this from the day we were born. Our lives have been on the line every day we dared to draw breath. And as far as we're concerned, Cadal Righ is just another Mage who's not all that different from you.'

Angus frowned. 'I'm not sure that's fair.' I raised my eyebrows and he shrugged. 'Just saying.'

The Gowk put his hands on the table. Many of the Mages glanced at his misshapen left hand, deformed by the torture he'd endured at their hands many years earlier, and some of them winced. There was a steely glint in his clever eyes. 'Let's put the politics and the verbal attacks aside, shall we, and focus on the matter in hand? How do we beat Cadal Righ?'

Laoch spoke first. 'We know from the diary Mairi found and the way he reacted when he discovered she has power that he's terrified of women who have magic.'

'I very much doubt he's terrified,' one of the older Mages muttered.

'But he is,' I said. 'He's terrified and he's angry, although we don't know why. I attacked him with all the magic I could muster up and he didn't flinch. I tried everything I could and nothing had any effect. It's not women alone that worries him, it's something else.'

'It's because you can combine spells and pull the magic from a person,' Teasag said. 'He's afraid you'll do the same to him. If you take his magic, he'll have nothing left.'

'Pah!' Aspen rolled his eyes and looked at me. 'She's been face to face with Cadal Righ twice. Twice you could have done that to him and twice you didn't. Either you don't have the ability to do it and you're lying about this spell combination, or you don't *want* to do it.' He wriggled against his ropes. 'We need to stop listening to this bitch and solve the problem of Cadal Righ without her!'

Alan raised his fist. As casually as he might have quaffed a beer, he whacked Aspen on the side of his head. 'She's not a bitch. Say that word again and I'll rip off your arm.'

Several Mages rose to their feet in protest and the room descended into chaos again. Once again, the Gowk brought it to order. 'Enough! Mairi, can you answer his concerns?'

'Bring me an Afflicted Mage and I'll prove that I can pull away someone's magic.' I looked down. 'But when I tried it with Cadal Righ, I couldn't do it. There's a chance that it might work if I can draw on others' magic as well, but at this point I don't think it will. His defences are too strong.'

'See?' Aspen sneered. 'She's just proved my point. She can't do half of what she says she can. She's useless.'

Isla stood up and started to walk slowly around the room like a basking shark. There weren't enough chairs for all the Mages, so a number of them were standing. She circled them, pointing at several of them in turn.

'I'd have tapped on you on the shoulder, but I don't want to become infected too.' She spoke breezily, her tone entirely at odds with the atmosphere. 'You eight Mages are Afflicted. It'll show within the next twelve hours or so, but there's no doubt.' She shrugged at me. 'You can heal them, I suppose, if you really want to – and if these bampots need to see it to believe it.'

I'd rarely seen the Mages move so quickly. Within seconds, everyone else had backed away from the eight supposedly Afflicted men. Those nearby were covering their mouths and noses with their sleeves.

'I feel fine!' one of them shouted.

'So do I!' said another.

'She's lying. We're not Afflicted.'

'It doesn't matter whether they're Afflicted or not,' Laoch said through gritted teeth. 'In a day or two, we'll all be either Afflicted or dead. Cadal Righ will break through that fiery wall and enter the city.' His voice took on a sarcastic edge. 'I don't know if you've noticed, but he's already got one or two Afflicted people with him.'

One of the younger Mages burst out, 'So we retreat! We leave Glasgow and all of us who are healthy head to Perth.'

The first Mage whom Isla had singled out glared at him. 'And what about those of us who aren't healthy? Will you leave us here to die?'

The young Mage sniffed. 'You should have been more careful. It's not our fault you're Afflicted.'

Fucking hell. 'How long do you think it will be before Cadal Righ marches on Perth?' I demanded.

'Then we'll go to Dundee.'

'And after that?' Belle enquired. 'When he arrives outside Dundee?' The Mages exchanged glances; they could all see where this was going.

'We need a permanent solution,' the Gowk said. 'Not a temporary one.'

I heaved in a frustrated breath. I wasn't the only one to do so. Even with our combined minds and strength, we couldn't think of anything that would work.

There was a flicker of movement in the doorway and I felt a wave of relief when I saw Andy hovering there. 'Andy!' I exclaimed. 'You've found something in the library?'

He looked anxious, pale and drawn. He wasn't smiling and his shoulders were slumped. 'I've scoured the shelves,' he whispered. The room was suddenly so quiet that his voice carried easily to every corner. 'I can't find anything.'

No. Misery clawed at me. 'There must be something. The books written by those old female Mages...'

'They've been destroyed. Burned. I found a few scraps of legible paper but nothing useful.'

I stared in horror at the Mages. 'Why? Why would you burn books just because they were written by women?'

Andy shook his head. 'It wasn't us who destroyed them. It was during the uprising when the building was stormed. Somebody tried to set light to the library.'

Aspen let out a bark of satisfied laughter. 'Hoisted by your own petard, *Queen* Mairi.'

Alan raised his fist again but I held up my hand. 'Don't.' There was no point.

'I would have kept looking,' Andy continued. 'There's always a chance there's something in a random chapter in one of the other books. but there's something outside that I thought you should see.'

I stiffened. What now? Andy nodded towards the door and I looked at it warily. I dreaded to think what he wanted to show us. Swallowing hard, I stood up. 'Is it dangerous?'

'No,' he hedged. 'But...' His voice trailed off. He tried again. 'You need to see it for yourself. It's right outside.'

I steeled myself then walked past him and out of the dining room. As I crossed the entrance area to the front door, Laoch's hand reached for mine. Our fingers entwined and we walked outside.

At first, I didn't see anything; the open area in front of the City Chambers appeared to be the same as always. I scanned from left to right, confused, until my eyes fell on a skinny tree bereft of leaves. It was across the street, less than thirty metres from the front door of the Chambers. I squinted. Oh.

'That's the same raven,' Laoch murmured. 'Right?'

I stared at it. Aye, it was the bird into which I'd injected my consciousness in order to reach Cadal Righ and the Mages; it was the same bird that had attacked the red-eyed wanker so I could escape.

It was definitely that raven, though it looked different now. It was holding one wing awkwardly and missing many of its glossy black feathers. It also appeared to have lost an eye.

I watched its bedraggled, pitiful form for a moment or two, then I said, 'That's paper in its beak.' At first I'd thought it was a twig or, heaven forbid, a bone. But the more I examined it, the more I was certain it was rolled-up parchment.

'I think it's a message,' Andy said awkwardly from behind me. 'The raven tapped on the library window until I noticed it, and it had the paper in its beak. There's only one person it could have come from.'

'Fae Cadal Righ?' Belle squawked. 'Cadal Righ has sent a

message?'

I didn't answer. Instead, with Laoch still by my side, I straightened my back and walked to the bird. It didn't attempt to fly away or peck out my eyes; it didn't look as if it had the energy to do either of those things even if it wanted to.

I stopped in front of it and focused on its beak. It was holding a neatly rolled piece of parchment. 'You need to rest,' I told the bird.

It blinked at me with its one good eye; it seemed to be telling me that rest wouldn't be enough and that it was already at the end of the road. It opened its beak and dropped the parchment at my feet. Before I could stoop down to pick it up, the raven fell off its perch and smacked onto the ground.

I reached for the bird first and cradled it gently in my cupped hands. It was already dead. I closed my eyes in silent apology. I was more upset than I'd have thought possible at the passing of a black-feathered raven.

Laoch scooped up the parchment and unravelled it. While he read it, I laid the bird at the foot of the tree and stroked its feathers. 'You were brave,' I told it quietly. 'Very brave indeed.'

Laoch's face was set in a stiff mask as he handed me the parchment. It was brittle, already disintegrating at its yellowing edges. Cadal Righ had probably found it in the pocket of a long-since infected Afflicted person and taken it for his own purposes. I glanced at the loping, scrawled script and felt sick. Blood, I realised; he'd written his message in blood.

My fellow Mages,

Upon reflection, and after reconsidering your suggestion, I have decided to change my mind. I will grant you the city of Inverness and a five-mile radius of land around it. I will not venture there and neither will any of my beloved Afflicted children.

In return for this most gracious boon, you shall present to me the head of the red-haired bitch, together with the heads of all other females who possess magic. Failure to do this will result in the destruction of all your cities and your own painful deaths.

Most kind regards and felicitations,

Cadal Righ, the true King of Scotland

Frustration built inside me as I read and re-read the words. This wasn't about misogyny; there was some other reason why Cadal Righ wanted to destroy all women with magic but I couldn't work it out. The answer felt as if it were almost within my grasp but it remained too nebulous to decipher properly.

Laoch's voice echoed in my head. *If they see this, they will do it.*

When I lifted my gaze, I saw that everyone from the dining room had followed us outside. The Mages were standing on the steps of the City Chambers watching my every move. They'd hauled Aspen out with them and his narrowed eyes continued to spit hatred.

When I saw his lips move as he spoke to the Mage next to him, I knew Aspen was trying to persuade him to loosen his bindings. The Mage didn't react; it appeared that Aspen's colleagues were becoming as irritated by him as I was.

My friends, standing to the side, all looked nervous. The same question was written on every face, Mage or not: what does the message say?

I answered Laoch silently. *You mean that if the Mages see this note, they'll cut off my head without a second thought and present it to Cadal Righ on a silver platter.* It wasn't a question.

Aye. His tone was dark. *And before you harbour any thoughts of martyrdom, this isn't a deal we can accept. It won't just be you who dies, or any woman who possesses magic. It'll be thousands of people in Glasgow, Dundee, Perth and Aberdeen — and that's assuming Cadal Righ keeps his word, which I very much doubt.*

I didn't argue because I knew he was right. I passed a hand over my eyes, sighed audibly and let the parchment drop from my fingers. I reached for Laoch's hand again and squeezed it.

'For fuck's sake, lass!' Angus yelled. 'What does it say?'

I didn't answer. Instead, I jerked my head to indicate that we were leaving.

Isla got the message immediately and trotted over. 'What's going on? What does he have to say to us?'

'I'll tell you once we're away from here.' I watched as my other friends crossed the street and joined us. A moment later, Andy and Morag also came over. Fearful of what their colleagues might do to them, the eight men whom Isla had identified as Afflicted darted off in the opposite direction.

Aspen shrieked, 'She's going to run away! Somebody has to stop her! Find out what that fucking message says and put that bitch in irons!'

Only one Mage moved: Brian marched forward with swinging shoulders and a hard expression. He bent down and picked up Cadal Righ's message, read it silently then looked at me. A muscle jerked in his cheek. I felt Laoch tense beside me.

'You're right,' Brian said eventually. 'I can only do three spells – but I can do those three spells very effectively and I have plenty of power inside me.' He licked his lips. 'But I know that I don't have enough magic to stop Cadal Righ. I felt what you're capable of when you created that barrier around the city and I'm starting to believe you're the only one who might manage to kill him. And even that's a long shot.'

He looked again at the paper. 'However, you're right. You should run from here.' He paused. 'Now.'

I didn't need telling twice.

TWENTY-THREE

Nobody tried to stop us as we jogged away from the City Chambers, a tight close-knit group of determined escapees. It was a testament to the trust they all put in me that they didn't stop to ask questions; they merely followed, taking flight because I had deemed it necessary. I didn't allow myself to dwell on that thought too deeply because I still couldn't provide the solution they were hoping for so desperately.

Once there was some distance between us and the City Chambers, the Gowk took the lead and led us to a nondescript tenement building. He banged sharply on the door, giving an elaborate series of knocks. There was a pause then the door swung open and Jane's exhausted face appeared.

She hastily beckoned us inside. Moments later, within the depths of that dusty building, I explained what Cadal Righ had written. The response I received wasn't an explosion of dismay but rather a show of muted despair.

'It's no' all bad,' Flora said, doing her best to lighten the mood. 'While you lot have been running around, we've gotten hundreds of women with magic ready to move at a moment's notice.' She received a few faint shrugs and dull smiles.

Jane stepped in. 'The people of Glasgow have proved themselves to be strong. I cannae think of a single household that hasnae taken in refugees from Edinburgh.' But then her shoulders slumped. 'Of course, they're likely hoping they'll receive the same response when we have to flee here for Perth.'

Twister, who had wrapped himself around Belle and appeared unwilling to let her go, piped up. 'Maybe we should leave now. Cadal Righ is out there to the south, but if we head north we can get out of Glasgow while it's still possible.'

'It doesn't matter which corner of Scotland we go to,' Teasag told him. 'Cadal Righ will find us all sooner or later. We should make a stand here.'

Alan placed an arm around her shoulder and Teasag leaned into him. The sight of a city guardsman comforting a daemon was extraordinary. It was kindred spirit like that which we needed to survive.

'What do we do, Mairi?' Isla asked.

Everybody looked at me and the weight of their gaze was immense. 'The fire wall will hold until morning,' I said. 'Right now, I'm exhausted. I can't think straight. I need to get some rest.' My magic needed to recuperate and I needed some space – and silence.

'There's a room upstairs with clean sheets,' Lottie said. 'I'll show you where it is.'

I smiled at her gratefully and raised my eyebrows at Laoch. He nodded and we followed Lottie. The fearful tension emanating from my friends dogged every single step.

Once the door closed behind us, I wrapped my arms around Laoch and burrowed against his broad chest. Somehow he understood that I didn't want to speak. Strange as it may seem,

I wanted the familiar comfort of remaining mute; I needed to rely on feelings and sensations instead of mere words.

We remained like that for several moments as the heat of Laoch's body warmed mine. He rested his head against my shoulder, then eventually started to use his long fingers to tease out the matted snarls in my hair, unravelling it and carefully working out the snags.

I pulled back. With my fingertips, I gently traced the outline of the tattoos that curved across his cheekbones. Even after all this time, I still marvelled at their intricacy.

Laoch traced the same shapes on my skin as if he were creating a mirror image. The base of his thumb dropped to my mouth and he brushed it across my lips before lowering his head to kiss me. His mouth was soft at first, almost tentative, but as I leaned in he increased the pressure. The rough stubble on his unshaven jaw pricked my skin but the sensation wasn't unpleasant. It only added to my pleasure.

The electric energy between us increased, akin to the build-up of magic before a powerful spell. But this energy, this feeling, wasn't borne out of a need to defend or attack or control. There was nothing between us beyond mutual desire and the desperate need to provide comfort and love to the other.

I moved my hands to Laoch's chest and unfastened the first button of his shirt. He did the same to me, our slow, deliberate movements only heightening the emotion. To begin with, I took care not to touch his skin, wanting to suspend the moment somehow and delay my pleasure. But when his hand reached for my breast and cupped it through the fabric of my old bra before grazing his fingers across my taut nipple, I couldn't hold back.

I pressed my palms flat against his chest, marvelling at the sensation of his heart thudding beneath his ribcage. His breath caught. As I trailed my hands down towards his stomach, he lowered his head to my neck, nipping at the soft flesh until I couldn't stop the moan from escaping my lips.

I curved one hand around his back, moving my fingers from one nub of his spine to the next, while my other hand toyed with the waistband of his breeches. He moved away, and the sudden absence of his body next to mine chilled my skin and worried my heart. But when I looked into his eyes and saw the heat there, all I could do was smile.

Laoch gazed at me as he removed the rest of his clothes and dropped them on the floor in a grubby pile. When he was naked he took a step back, encouraging me to admire him.

I didn't require any prompting. My eyes travelled slowly down his length, taking in the scars that marred several sections of his otherwise smooth skin and the smattering of dark hair across his chest, his stomach and below. I allowed myself a long, lingering look at his erect cock, drawing out the moment while Laoch's skin grew more flushed. Then he cleared his throat pointedly and raised his eyebrows.

I smiled softly. Taking my time, I peeled my blouse from one arm then the other and extricated myself from my bra. I stood bare-breasted and unmoving for several moments as Laoch's greedy gaze devoured me, then I removed the rest of my clothes.

In front of anyone else, I would have felt too vulnerable and too embarrassed. My clothes were filthy and so was my skin, but Laoch was probably in a worse state and it didn't diminish my lust in any way. From the glint in his eyes, he felt the same about me. I wasn't scared of him, or nervous. It was pride – and anticipation of what was to come – that filtered through my veins. The tension was becoming both exquisite and unbearable.

I gave a tiny nod. He returned it then we met halfway, pressing our bodies against each other. I hooked one arm around his neck and one leg around his waist. Laoch's eyes met mine, my lips parted and he entered me in one swift movement. We both gasped aloud. Liquid lightning. For several precious and far too short minutes, nothing existed beyond us.

We were the world. And the world was us.

***

Laoch's body was draped across me, one leg protectively over mine while his arm lay loosely across my waist. The heat of his skin was reassuring and I allowed myself a moment to appreciate the tingle of his masculine scent. It was a far cry from the rotting reek of the Afflicted that I'd gotten so used to lately. His chest fell and rose with the regularity of sleep and, as I listened to him breathe, I turned everything over and over in my head.

No matter how hard I tried, however, I couldn't connect the dots. I couldn't work out what exactly it was about women with magic that made Cadal Righ so afraid.

I shifted slightly and placed my hand over Laoch's before absently stroking his fingers and then his thigh. I watched the sky outside slowly lighten, changing from the cold night to the first glimpses of a warmer dawn.

I felt Laoch's breathing alter and his voice murmured in my ear. 'I wouldn't change this for all the magic in Scotland. No matter what today brings, I've found out how to be happy. You've shown me what it means to be truly free.' He nibbled at my earlobe. 'I love you so very much.'

I smiled softly. Then my smile vanished. 'Wait,' I said. 'What did you say?'

'I love you, Mairi Wallace. So very much.'

'Not that.'

'That's not enough?'

I turned and faced him. 'I love you, Laoch, with every beat of my heart. Now please tell me. What did you say before?'

A line appeared in between his eyebrows. 'I don't know,' he said, puzzled. 'I said you've shown me what it means to be free. And that I wouldn't change this for—'

I finished the sentence for him. 'For all the magic in Scotland.' I sat up, my mind whirling.

'What is it?'

I pulled away from him and reached for my clothes. 'Cadal Righ said that,' I told him. I yanked my blouse over my head, ignoring the stench that rose from the befouled fabric.

'That he wouldn't change lying next to you for all the magic in Scotland?' Laoch was still frowning.

I grabbed my breeches and shook them out. 'Not that.' I met his eyes. 'What he said was that as long as magic existed in Scotland, so would he. He said it to a Mage in Edinburgh right before he sucked all the sanity out of him.'

'So?'

I smiled, a long, slow, dazzling smile that wreathed my face. 'We can't take the magic from Cadal Righ because his personal defences are too strong, but we can take all the magic from Scotland. If enough of us band together and use each other's power, we can use magic to remove magic. *All* magic. Two spells combined together, which don't take magic from a person but take it from an entire land.'

Laoch stood up. I kept my eyes trained on his face, expecting him to disagree with my logic. Instead, he grinned. 'Magic sustains the Afflicted and is tied to their creation. You can take magic from a Mage and heal their Affliction. But a normal person doesn't possess magic. So you take it from the entire country and...'

'And the Afflicted will be healed.' I hedged my words. 'In

theory. And there will be no more Mages with magic that Cadal Righ can steal.'

Laoch was nodding. 'It makes sense, Mairi. It makes perfect sense. A broad approach instead of a targeted one might be what we need. Remember Cadal Righ also said that he grew stronger because he drew on magic that leeched from the corpses the Mages had buried. Take away all the magic and you might remove the Afflicted from the equation – you might also take away the source of Cadal Righ's power.'

His face shone. 'Only a combination spell could manage it and only women can perform those spells. That's got to be what he's afraid of. That's got be the way out.'

I nodded vigorously. 'I'm sure of it – almost sure of it.' I pulled a face. 'As sure of it as I'm sure of anything where Cadal Righ is concerned.'

He sucked his bottom lip. 'Can it be done? The power you'd need to draw on would be immense.'

'It's never been tried before so there's no way of knowing until we do. We'd need everyone. All the Mages. All the women. Anyone who has any magic inside of them. We need them all.'

'It might work.'

'It *will* work.' I paused. 'Hopefully.'

He picked up his clothes. 'Then let's get a damned move on.'

TWENTY-FOUR

'You want to take away all the magic?' Fee's eyes were as wide as saucers. 'Whit? All of it?'

I waved at her to keep walking. We had to get to the City Chambers as quickly as possible and prepare the Mages. I wasn't fooling myself about how they'd react to my suggestion. It would be extraordinarily difficult to persuade them that this might work or that it would be worth it.

Isla kept up with me, her legs moving quickly to remain abreast. 'You want to remove my magic?'

'Aye.'

'And Fee's magic?'

'Aye.'

'And the magic from everyone else? Forever?'

I twitched. 'Aye.'

Isla paused. 'And you want to remove magic from the Mages?'

I glanced at her. 'Aye.'

She nodded thoughtfully. 'Braw. I'm in.'

That had been easier than I thought it would be. I continued watching her. Aware of my curious gaze, she gave me a wide grin. 'Without their magic they are nobody,' she said. 'They have nothing – and everything will change.'

I reckoned that everything had already changed, but there was no point in saying that aloud.

Twister had stayed quiet until now. He continually touched Belle and sent her awestruck glances when he thought she wasn't looking, as if he were seeing his wife for the very first time. Now he cleared his throat. 'They might still try and cut off your head.'

I turned to Angus and Andy. They both looked grim. 'They probably will,' I admitted. 'But I'm hoping that the night has given them time to think over Cadal Righ's proposal and discard it as a waste of time.'

We reached the end of the street and the City Chambers came into view. The scaffolding was as silent and empty as it had been the previous day, and the rest of the building as terrifyingly imposing as it had always been.

'I guess we'll soon find out,' Alan muttered.

I addressed the group. 'All of you wait here. I'll approach the Mages and speak to them. Keep out of the way so that if everything gets messy, you have time to escape. Go north. Don't head to one of the cities.'

The offer that the Edinburgh Ascendant had once made to me flickered into my mind. 'There's an island,' I told them. 'It's on the west coast. If you can get a boat and make your way there, you might escape what's coming.'

Laoch snorted. He strode over from where he'd been walking next to Teasag and took up position next to me. A second later, she joined him – and so did everyone else.

From his position beneath Isla's clothing, Mungo's tiny nose poked out and he squeaked. She grinned. 'The mouse has spoken. We're with you all the way to the end, Mairi. Whatever that end might be.'

'You're thirteen years old. This shouldn't be your end.'

Her smile grew even wider. 'It won't be.' Not for the first time, I wished I had her confidence.

She'd seen enough and been through enough to be allowed to make her own decisions. We all had. This was freedom.

I drew in a deep breath and felt the cold air wrap its way around my lungs, then I squared my shoulders and raised my head. There had been many occasions in the past weeks when I'd needed words to aid my fight. None of them seemed as crucial as this one.

I held my head high and marched towards the front door of the City Chambers. Before I came close, it swung open and the Mages filed out. I felt a sickening lurch when I saw Aspen was leading them and they were all dressed in freshly pressed black cloaks. They wanted to remind themselves of their position and power, and they wanted to remind me, too.

I opened my mouth, hoping to pre-empt their demand that I present them with my bare neck ready for an axe's blade, but Aspen got in first.

'Well, well, well. Look what the cat dragged in. I'm glad to see that a good night's sleep has shown you that handing your-self over is the best way forward. Your country won't forget you.' Some of the Mages winced at the mocking sneer in his voice. I didn't.

'I'm not here to give you my head, Aspen.' I rolled my eyes to emphasise the ridiculousness of the idea. 'If I thought that it would save the people of Glasgow, Dundee, Perth and Aberdeen, I would hand you the axe myself. But if you agree to Cadal Righ's demands, they will die as well as me. I'd be condoning genocide.'

Aspen wasn't surprised by my answer, but that didn't stop him from making a show of shock. He threw his hands in the air and stepped back in apparent dismay. I couldn't imagine who he thought he was performing for; nobody here was under any illusions about his true feelings.

'Your selfishness never ceases to amaze me,' he drawled. 'You truly believe that your life is more important than the future of this entire country? Some of us will still survive. We'll go to Inverness and *it* will survive. In time, we can make Cadal Righ see that our way is better. We'll reclaim our country.'

'You don't honestly believe he'll let Inverness to remain free, do you?' I eyed the other Mages' expressions. Most of them looked doubtful; they knew it was a long shot.

Aspen sighed loudly and placed his hand over his heart. 'What other choice is there?'

It was a rhetorical question and he certainly wasn't expecting me to respond.

I smiled and raised my voice. 'I'm very glad that you asked because I have the answer to all our problems.'

He blinked. For the first time since we'd abandoned Edinburgh, I saw uncertainty in his expression. The audience of silent Mages behind him stared at me, several of them displaying delighted anticipation. I spotted Brian watching expectantly, not bothering to disguise his sudden optimism. I could do it, I realised; I could change minds and alter fates.

'Go on then,' Aspen called. 'What's your grand plan?'

My smile remained but I held my breath. 'We remove all the magic from Scotland.'

It took a moment or two for my words to sink in before all hell broke loose. I'd been prepared to give them time to digest what I was suggesting but they didn't take it.

Three young Mages sprang forward, spells of violence on their lips. Laoch was ready and murmured an incantation to block their efforts. Several other Mages ran forward, clearly planning to use physical violence where magic had failed. This time it was Angus who moved in front of me. He threw his head back and bellowed, 'Listen to the lass! It might save all our sorry lives if you do!'

Four weeks ago, they'd have knocked Angus out and killed me together with anyone else who stood with me but Angus's words, combined with our unflinching stares, made them falter – at least for now.

I exhaled and then, before anything changed, quickly outlined my theory. By the time I'd finished speaking, not only had the Mages' fury increased, but so had their scepticism.

'You can't subtract the magic from an entire country!' one of them shouted.

I stayed calm, using faked confidence to bolster my argument. 'I believe I can if I have enough power behind me. Your power.' I gestured to my friends. 'And their power.'

There was a high-pitched shout from behind me. 'You have ours also.'

I turned my head. I'd been so intent on reading the Mages' reaction and so focused on persuading them to my plan that I hadn't realised Maggie was now behind me – with dozens upon dozens of women.

Aspen stared at them, his derision clear. 'Who the fuck are you? Get out of here! There's a curfew in place!'

A stooped old woman shuffled forward. She was using a stick to help her walk and her face was lined with years of experience and decades of pain. When she opened her mouth, little more than a whisper came out. '*Vair al.*'

Aspen staggered. He tried to say something, to yell, but the woman had removed his ability to speak.

She sniffed, adjusted her headscarf and addressed us all. 'My name is Rhona. I have lived in this city for my entire life and I've never set foot outside those gates. I've borne three children. I lost one to the Affliction and one to an accident. I've got five grandchildren. And I've had magic inside me since the day I was born.'

It was a strain to hear her but nobody interrupted, not even the Mages. We all leaned forward to hear her words. 'All magic has ever done for me is cause me pain. I dinnae ken who you are, Mairi, and I dinnae ken if I can trust you. I dinnae care. This is worth the risk. You have my power.' She hobbled towards me and held out a hand. I took it. I didn't dare not to.

It was Laoch's turn. Sunlight glinted off his horns and his green eyes glittered. 'You all know me,' he said to the Mages. 'I was your creature for years. You stole me from my kind and forced me to be your slave for no good reason other than to boost your own power.'

I moved an inch closer to him, lending him my support, my heart aching for all that he had gone through at the Mages' hands. He flashed me a crooked smile and continued.

'I'd rather be a slave for the next hundred years than Afflicted. I imagine all of you would say the same. You're refusing to countenance Mairi's plan because of your own selfish fears about your magic and your authority.'

He shrugged. 'We can't alter your innate selfishness with one conversation, so I'm not going to try. What I am going to tell you is that if we don't do this, you will all be Afflicted too, whether you run to Inverness or not. You know it will happen. And I know that you'd prefer to be slaves than experience the Affliction eating you from the inside out for one single day.'

A surge of hope lifted my spirits. At least some of the Mages were nodding; at least some of them were listening.

'May I?' Andy asked politely. Laoch nodded. The young Mage, who'd already stood against his friends and colleagues, twisted his trembling fingers. 'It doesn't matter what you think of Mairi,' he said. 'It doesn't matter if you think she's a bitch.'

Laoch growled and I sent him a warning look.

'It doesn't matter,' Andy continued, 'if you don't believe that any woman should be allowed to practise magic, or if you think you deserve to live blameless lives with all your riches and authority because you do a difficult job. None of that matters because you are Mages. *We* are Mages.'

He pointed at me. '*She* is a Mage.' He pointed at Rhona, at Teasag, at Laoch and at Maggie. '*They* are all Mages. And a Mage's sole task is to protect this country. We're a step away from annihilation. We have to do this because Cadal Righ and his Afflicted Army will destroy everything if we do not.'

More of the Mages nodded as they warmed to his words. But not all of them.

'There's no guarantee it'll work! What if she takes away our magic and leaves us with nothing, but the Afflicted still exist and Cadal Righ still comes for us? We'll be left with nothing! We'll have no defence!'

A male voice piped up from around the far corner of the City Chambers. I stiffened and my body turned ice cold. 'You already have no defence.'

Laoch looked at me. 'You have got to be fucking kidding me.'

Stooped, covered in dried blood and caked grime, and with an attitude and air that reminded me starkly of the raven whose body lay but a few metres away, Noah dragged himself forward.

He was missing his left hand and his right ear. His once smooth, perfectly coiffed hair was in matted clumps. I could smell him from a distance and it was far from pleasant. But he lifted his head and, with what appeared to be considerable effort, managed to smile. 'Did you miss me?'

TWENTY-FIVE

'Is anything going to kill that wanker?' Pale faced and wide eyed with shock, Laoch stared at Noah.

He wasn't the only one. My jaw was hanging open. 'How ... how ... how...?'

'How did I survive?' Noah tried to shrug but it clearly caused him great pain and a spasm of agony crossed his face. 'I'm as surprised as you are. I got myself away from the nuck-alavees, then I got myself here. Anything else is just window dressing.'

There was a whole world of stories within that single statement but he was right. Noah was just one man and we were dealing with the fate of a nation.

Angus had more practical concerns. 'How the fuck did you get into the city, lad? The fire wall. Is it—?'

'It's failing,' Noah croaked. 'It has an hour before it gives way entirely. Probably less. I only got in because I remembered an old smugglers' route through the sewers. I caught some people using it in my first few months as a Mage.'

Belle started forward, rage lighting her face. 'Not now,' I hissed. She whipped around, glaring at me. 'Honestly, Belle.

Leave it.' She looked as if she were prepared to strike me but she subsided and fell into line next to Twister.

'Noah.' I shook my head, still barely able to believe he was here and he was alive. 'I—'

He interrupted. 'No. I'm not here to talk to *you*.' He turned to the Mages. 'You all know who I am and what I used to stand for. Many of you saw me before when I was—' He hesitated, seemingly unable to say the word Afflicted. He shook his head. 'It is worse than you can imagine. Believe me.'

'But why aren't you Afflicted now?' a Mage called out.

'She drew it out of me,' Noah said simply. 'With her magic.'

Brian looked at me. 'You weren't lying?'

'No,' I said. 'I wasn't.'

'It can be done?'

I nodded. 'It can.'

Noah drew in a long, guttural breath. 'The Afflicted exist because of Cadal Righ's magic, and he exists because of theirs.' He met my eyes. 'When I was with him, I could feel his thoughts as he could feel mine. And I can tell you all that Mairi Wallace is right. If the magic is removed from this country, Cadal Righ will lose his power. That's the only thing he is afraid of – and that's the only thing that will stop him.'

Nobody said a word; nobody stirred. All eyes were on Noah – apart from Isla's. 'You were right,' she said to me. 'He is the fucking saviour of Scotland after all.'

A hysterical giggle bubbled out of my mouth. I couldn't help myself.

Aspen, still under Rhona's silence spell, flapped his arms frantically then jumped once, twice, three times. When he landed heavily on his right leg and stumbled against another Mage, I gestured to Rhona. 'Release him.'

She bared her teeth. 'He doesnae deserve to speak.'

'Nobody should be denied a voice,' I said quietly.

Her jaw tightened and Laoch sent me a swift glance, but Rhona waved a resigned hand and removed the spell.

'Bullshit!' Aspen screamed. 'This is all bullshit! We know how to deal with Cadal Righ! We give him her head and he gives us Inverness! It's a negotiation between men who know what they're doing. These other people shouldn't be involved. And you!' He flung a disgusted hand towards Noah. 'You should be dead! You're probably still Afflicted and you don't realise it!' He turned to the Mages. 'We stick to the plan. We kill her and then—'

I didn't hear what was supposed to happen after my death, although I could guess. Aspen's words were drowned by a loud roaring and I felt the ground shudder beneath my feet. There was an odd cracking sound and the air vibrated.

'The wall,' Laoch hissed. 'The fire wall is breaking.'

Rhona let out a sob of terror. When I saw what she was looking at, I did the same. A ball of fire was hurtling through the sky and heading straight for us. It was enormous, at least three metres wide, and glowed white hot at its centre. To say nothing of the trail of flames and sparks that followed it...

I wasted no time. I hummed, focusing on it with all my energy while around me people darted for cover. If I could use magic to push it off course and send it spinning towards the river to the east, I could keep us safe. Laoch's magic joined mine; Fee added hers and so did the Gowk. I heard Isla mutter the same words.

Ins veil. Ins veil. INS VEIL.

It should have worked – but we weren't the only people using magic to divert the massive fireball. Opposite us, on the steps of the City Chambers, the Mages also invoked their magic and chanted the words *ins veil*. Instead of trying to fling the fireball east towards the river, they chose to divert it west. Perhaps they were aiming for the nearest park, hoping to send it thudding into grass and trees where nobody would be hurt and no buildings would be destroyed.

I didn't get the chance to find out. Their magic collided with ours and the lethal ball of fire in the middle was pulled one way and pushed the other. There was no hope. A heartbeat later it hurtled down towards us.

I held onto Rhona's hand and Laoch grabbed mine. We turned and fled away from the fireball; it was too late to do anything other than take cover. Isla sprinted past me, and I caught sight of Belle and Twister, holding hands and running.

And then, a split second later, the force of the blast ripped me away from Laoch and Rhona and sent me flying forward. I must have been thrown at least a dozen feet through the air.

I raised my head as a cloud of belching dark smoke overtook me. My body felt battered and bruised and there was a strange ringing in my ears. Laoch was already scrambling to his feet, his anxious green eyes searching for mine. I gave him a tight nod to indicate that I was unharmed then I looked for Rhona.

She was in a heap next to a doorway. With my heart in my mouth, I ran towards her. I heard her groan and felt a sag of relief; at least she was alive. That was something. 'Are you alright?'

'Dinna fash yourself, lass. I'm braw.' She choked and tried to stagger to her feet. I reached down and helped her up.

'Get inside,' I urged. 'Take cover.'

She glared at me. 'Why? Because I'm a woman? Or because I'm old?' She tossed her head in a gesture that seemed oddly familiar. Then I realised why I recognised it. I often flicked my head in a similar fashion. 'I ain't going nowhere.' She cracked her knuckles and turned to look at the devastation behind us.

I saw Laoch brushing away sooty grime from Isla's wide-eyed face, then I turned to look at what remained of the City Chambers. At first it was difficult to see anything at all because of the thick smoke. Apart from the ringing in my ears, it was eerily quiet. I had the sickening sensation that this was merely the calm before the storm.

A gust of chill wind blew in from the street to my left and I could make out some ghostly shapes. I thought the City Chambers was still standing but, as another gust rattled through and more smoke cleared, I realised I was wrong.

When the people of Glasgow had taken it upon themselves to attack the Mages so many weeks ago, only a small section of the building had collapsed. Cadal Righ had been far, far more successful.

Twisted scaffolding snaked from where attempts had begun to rebuild the initial damage. No amount of scaffolding would do any good now. The fireball had landed in the very centre of the building, sending a shockwave through the entire structure. There were fallen bricks and debris. There was a blazing inferno in the middle, where the fireball had made direct impact, and smaller fires had sprung across the rest of the collapsed building. Only one back wall and half a staircase were still standing.

A distant part of my mind registered the stairs as one of the servants' thoroughfares, that I'd used regularly during my time working there. Before the thought had fully formed, there was a loud rumble. As if in slow motion, both the staircase and the charred wall it clung to collapsed.

I took a step backwards, shaking my head, barely able to believe my eyes. That was when I started to hear the dim screams and calls for help. The Mages, I realised. Dozens of them hadn't been able to move quickly enough.

Beside me Laoch muttered. '*Indah sal.*' A strong breeze lifted through the air, clearing away more of the smoke. '*Indah sal.*'

I wiped my stinging eyes with the cuff of my jacket and looked at Angus's grim face. Beside him, Andy added his voice. I saw Noah stagger upwards and open his mouth to add to the spell but something pained flashed across his face and he closed it again. Noah no longer possessed any magic; his words wouldn't help.

He started forward, heading for the nearest moans. I watched him for one long, strange moment, my feet planted to a spot on the dark cobbles as if glued there, then I too walked determinedly forward. I wished the ringing in my ears would stop; I'd need to use all my senses to remain alert for danger. I knew that more would come – it was only a matter of time.

The first Mage I reached was already a corpse. An older man, who had once slapped me for allowing the fire in his study to die out, was staring sightlessly up at the sky. Half of his skull had been destroyed. I turned away. There was no time to be sickened.

I lurched towards the next body and checked for a pulse. I felt it flutter against my fingertips and inhaled deeply, then reached for the large stone that was crushing the lower half of his body. I hummed, drawing on just enough magic to imbue myself with a flash of extra strength. *Bish var.* A moment later, I pulled the stone away from him. His eyelids fluttered as he regained a flicker of consciousness and his mouth opened in a silent scream.

I placed a hand against his forehead. 'Relax,' I murmured. 'It will be alright.'

He stammered out a croaking whisper. 'No. No. No. No.'

'Hush,' I said gently. 'Don't panic.' But then there was another whooshing roar from the sky and every atom of my being clenched in fear, resisting my own instruction.

I looked up and spotted the second fireball through the billowing smoke. This time it didn't head for us but roared past over our heads. I felt others find the magic within themselves to direct it elsewhere and this time they worked together, casting the damned thing away to safety.

I dared not relax, however. There was another heart-sickening roar and I spied yet another ball of flame launch upwards from the edges of the city where Cadal Righ waited. Then there was another one. And another.

I heard a high- pitched scream from across the street and recognising the sound immediately. Belle. A second later Isla's screech filled the air. 'Do something! You're fucking Mages! Fucking do something! Stop this!'

She was still yelling when the ground started to tremble. It was barely noticeable at first but the sensation grew until the tremble became a shudder. I staggered sideways, almost falling flat on my face. I spun around, desperately concerned about what this new threat might be.

Teasag's soot-blackened face appeared in front of mine. Her coiled horns, normally iridescent with sparking colour, were now almost as black as Laoch's. 'Cadal Righ's army has entered the city,' she hissed. 'The Afflicted are heading this way. I can sense them.'

My stomach dropped. The Mage on the ground next to me moaned. 'Do it,' he whispered. 'You have to do it. There's no other choice.' His eyes fluttered closed and his chest, which had been barely moving, stuttered to a halt.

I gazed at his slack face. 'There was never a choice,' I told him sadly. I straightened up and met Teasag's anxious eyes. 'Find anyone with magic who is still standing and bring them here now. We have to act before it's too late.'

TWENTY-SIX

We were standing across from the ruins of the City Chambers. There were more of us than I'd have thought possible given all that had occurred in the last half hour. Many Mages had escaped the destruction of their home and were clustered together, their expressions tense. At least two-thirds of them had discarded their swirling cloaks; whether that was by accident or to hide their identities and escape Cadal Righ's impending appearance, I didn't know. What I did know was that I no longer had to argue my case. Everyone was aware that we were out of options.

A further smattering of Mages was dotted nearby, holding themselves apart from their colleagues. Aspen was cowering at the far edge. Something had struck him on the side of his head and the wound was bleeding profusely. His expression was dazed, as if he still couldn't believe it had come to this despite all he'd witnessed in Edinburgh. Lord Aspen couldn't accept that he was the underdog in this fight, that he was on the losing side. At least he was no longer talking and I was grateful for that small mercy, if nothing else.

I gazed at the group of people to my right. Isla was there

with Fee, Jane and Flora. Next to them, heads held high as they watched me and waited, were Angus and Andy. Behind them was a sea of faces, young and old, and I marvelled at the numbers. Naturally, most of them were women though a surprisingly large percentage were men – ordinary folk who had eschewed what the Mages stood for and kept themselves and their abilities concealed. Waves of fear were emanating from the Mages but these people had the same expressions of quiet, determined defiance. The people of this city were far, *far* stronger than anyone gave them credit for.

I looked at Maggie and then at the Gowk, both of whom stood at the front. They didn't require words or fine speeches, not this time. I nodded and they nodded back.

By my side, Laoch murmured, 'Half the city is on fire. A lot of people are fleeing north – but a lot of them won't make it.'

Belle and Twister were standing silently beside Ailsa, Alan, Trish, Lottie and many others. None of them had magic but none of them were going anywhere. They'd fight tooth and nail to the end with nothing more than their bare hands. Glasgow had cowered under the Mages' yoke for decades; the bravery I was seeing now was in stark contrast to that long-suffering past.

'The Afflicted army is less than a mile away,' Teasag said. 'If you're really going to do this, you need to do it now.'

I caught sight of Noah, who was standing silent and pale-faced next to Andy. He raised his hand and saluted. I almost smiled, then I steeled myself and took Laoch's hand, feeling the warmth of his fingers. It was time.

Teasag gripped my other hand tightly. In an act that took my breath away, she extended her other hand towards the largest cluster of Mages. They hesitated for a long-drawn-out moment, while flakes of grey ash fluttered down from the grey sky and the horizon glowed with the fires that had broken out across Glasgow. She beckoned them again with only the merest hint of impatience.

Before any of them moved, however, Isla harrumphed loudly and stalked across the street to Laoch's side. The sight of a scrawny, dirty girl taking her life into her hands did the trick. The Mages stopped prevaricating and joined Teasag. Within moments I felt the trickle of their magic as we joined together through the simple act of touching.

The Gowk joined us, and Maggie, and hundreds upon hundreds of women. In less time than a single hanging would take in George Square, I was surrounded by a thousand people, all of whom possessed magic and all of whom were prepared to help me banish it from Scotland forever.

Finally Aspen pursed his lips and marched over. He was glowering but he didn't say a word. He took the hand of the Mage nearest to him and, in doing so, added his power to everyone else's.

I sucked in a shaky breath. If this didn't work – and there was no guarantee that it would – it would spell all our doom. Laoch felt my anxiety and squeezed my hand reassuringly. *You can do this, Mairi. I'm with you all the way. And so is everyone else.*

I managed a tremulous nod. Raising my head, I spotted a shuffling group of Afflicted men and women emerging from the side streets to watch us silently. These were the bedraggled, disease-ridden souls who'd always been within Glasgow's walls. They were waiting for their kin to join them and for Cadal Righ to end our resistance before they acted.

I had to take advantage of this pause. I dug deep, pulling all that I had from inside myself before drawing on the energy of the people around me. Magic suffused me, building up and up and up into a crescendo of power. That was when I finally started to hum.

Desh mar tun desh mar.

The spell burst out and filled the air. I heard a collective gasp; even those people who possessed no magic felt the surge of energy.

Desh mar tun desh mar.

I gritted my teeth, Power flowed out of me, hurtling in all directions.

Desh mar tun desh mar.

The sky started to change colour from insipid grey, marred by the streaks of Cadal Righ's black destruction, to a luminous purple. Night herself seemed to have decided that it was time the world altered forever.

Desh mar tun desh mar.

Still waiting for their false king, the Glasgow Afflicted started to sway from side to side, their hands and arms flapping frantically as they felt the shift in the atmosphere.

Desh mar tun desh mar.

I focused straight ahead, seeing nothing but noticing every-thing. I felt several faltering stutters as some of the Mages stag-gered and fell away, but others quickly pulled together to fill the gaps. The power returned with more strength than before.

The ringing in my ears finally stopped; now all I could hear was a steady throb as the ground beneath my feet started to pulse. The rhythm grew in speed and intensity. As if from a great distance, I heard myself cry out. Laoch's body leaned against mine, supporting me as best as he could. And a heart-beat later, Cadal Righ's army came into view.

Even here, where the cramped streets and narrow thor-oughfares blocked most of them from view, it was obvious that their numbers were extraordinary. For a moment the magic faltered, stumbling in the face of the terrifying sight, then the people around me rallied and again the power flowed out of me like floodwater.

Desh mar tun desh mar.

Some of the Afflicted closest to us, those who had already been within the city walls, fell to the ground. Their bodies twisted and writhed, and they screamed in anguish and horror. I blocked out the sound and gave everything I had to the magic.

Cadal Righ's army stampeded towards us. Wherever the bastard was, he knew what was happening and he had sent his cannon fodder to stop us. I felt the fear of those around me but I held firm. We all did.

Some of the Afflicted near the front fell and were trampled on by others and I watched impotent rage flash across the faces of the front runners. Two hundred metres, that's how close they were. I could smell their rotting forms and their fury. But I could also smell a faint scent of lingering hope.

I yanked one last time, taking everything from everyone until there was nothing more to draw on, before dragging in a final gasping breath. The Afflicted were barely a hundred metres away. I lifted my head towards the sky, opened my mouth and screamed, '*Desh mar tun desh mar.*'

The world shuddered and time seemed to stop. Teasag's hand fell away from mine and a second later so did Laoch's. They collapsed beside me and I realised that everyone else had done the same.

I saw Belle, Twister, Noah and a few others hug themselves and pull out of the path of the marauding Afflicted. The purple sky flashed once, twice, three times and there was a dissonant boom.

I exhaled the breath I'd been holding and tried to take another, but it felt like all the oxygen had been sucked away and there was none left. I tried again, but again I could draw nothing into my lungs. Panic clawed at my throat. I tried to breathe once again and my chest expanded. Pure, beautiful Scottish air filled me and, as if knocked down by a single, giant, godly hand, the Afflicted army collapsed.

My legs gave away and the ground rushed up to meet me. For several long seconds, all I was capable of doing was breathing. I didn't twitch or think or try to accomplish a single thing beyond bringing air into my exhausted lungs. I might have stayed that way far longer if a pair of shoes hadn't swum into view.

A familiar face ducked down and peered at me. 'Well?' Belle demanded. 'Did it work?'

'Give the lass some space,' Twister said – but then he also crouched down. 'Did it work? Are we free? Are we saved?'

I coughed half-heartedly and struggled up to a sitting position. The fallen people around me were also stirring. Nobody seemed to have died, which was the first positive point, but then I looked at Laoch . His face was etched with lines of pain and fatigue, though his emerald-green eyes were shining. 'I have no magic left, Mairi,' he said. 'There's nothing there.'

I reached inside myself and found that I was empty too. The power had gone and there wasn't a drop of magic lingering in my bones. When my magic had been drained during the Ascendancy Challenge, it had taken me a full day to recover; until this time tomorrow, we wouldn't know if the magic had gone for good.

Even so, I smiled at Laoch before anxiously scanning the masses of fallen Afflicted. Were they...? Had they...? It was impossible to tell from this distance.

From the side, I heard a gasp. Isla straightened up and stared. 'Whit is that fucker doing now?' she muttered.

I followed her gaze and stiffened when I saw Noah, of all people, march towards the first of the Afflicted bodies.

'He's dead,' Maggie said from further down the line. 'They'll rip his flesh from his bones in an instant.'

I wasn't too sure. Based on past performance, Noah possessed an uncanny knack for staying alive. Still, I watched his progress with my heart in my mouth. When he finally reached a dark-haired Afflicted man, stopped and looked down, I had to bite back the urge to shout and ask him what he saw. His lips moved but I couldn't hear what he was saying.

Angus hissed, '*Tinza*,' the magical word to enhance hearing. As soon as it left his mouth, he grimaced. 'No magic,' he muttered. 'No point.'

I stared at Noah. 'It doesn't matter,' I whispered. 'We don't need it.' I swallowed the lump in my throat. 'Look.'

It happened in slow motion. Noah stretched out a hand towards the man. In turn, the man stretched his own hand upwards and Noah helped him to his feet. Although he staggered on the way up and was standing bow-legged with hunched shoulders, the man was neither groaning nor attempting to attack. Instead, he appeared to be chatting to Noah. My jaw dropped.

It felt like an age but eventually Noah called out, 'This gentleman's name is Ian Mc...' He looked again at the Afflicted man, who said something to him.

'Ian McIlvaney!' Noah shouted. 'It's been seven years since he last remembers holding a conscious thought of his own. He's been Afflicted since then. He has a wife called Norah and—'

There was a loud scream. I whipped around, frantically searching for the source of the noise. A thin figure burst forward from the large group of women who were with Maggie. It was a middle-aged woman with long brown hair tied into a messy bun and a grubby skirt, the hem of which dragged on the ground behind her.

She must have been exhausted because she was one of the many people who'd given me her power. Even so, she sprinted towards Noah and Ian McIlvaney. She slowed when she drew close to them then threw herself forward. McIlvaney's arms wrapped around her while she kissed him full on the mouth.

As they continued to embrace, more of the fallen figures behind them stirred. They stumbled up and gazed around with dazed expressions as if they were seeing the world for the very first time.

I moved forward, my eyes welling with tears that I dashed away with my fist. I wasn't ashamed of crying but I didn't want to blur my vision of all these people. Not a single one of them was slack-jawed or drooling; although there were groans and grunts, they were healthy sounds, not the animalistic sounds of creatures who didn't know their own names.

When I was close enough to look properly, I could see that their eyes were clear. They weren't Afflicted. It had worked. It had bloody well worked.

Laoch joined me. 'You did it,' he breathed. 'You did it, Mairi!'

I turned to him with shining eyes. '*We* did it,' I told him. 'We all did it.'

And that was when the air was filled with yet another loud whooshing roar.

TWENTY-SEVEN

The fireball hurtled towards us. The purple-tinged sky altered colour immediately as the flames shot through it. I yelled and waved my hands, shouting at everyone to take cover before grabbing Laoch's hand and sprinting away from the middle of the street. Cadal Righ wasn't done yet. He'd kill us all first if he could.

My frantic, flailing mind assumed he'd aimed the fireball directly at the largest group of people, all those thousands who had been but were no longer Afflicted. Cadal Righ would want to punish them for daring to grow healthy again and leave him.

Laoch and I reached the dubious shelter of a narrow doorway and turned to watch the massive ball of flames' unstoppable approach – but it swerved over the heads of the ex-Afflicted. It didn't even fly towards the fatigued, magic-less Mages. Instead, it came to a halt and hovered above our heads. I felt sick to my stomach as I stared at it. This fireball wasn't like the others. Something about it was different, and I had a horrible inkling that I knew what it was.

It started to spin on the spot, shooting out jets of flame. Several flew in my direction and their intense heat licked my face. Laoch snarled and jumped forward but I pulled him back. A moment later, the fiery creation slammed down into the ground less than twenty metres away from where we were standing. This wasn't over – not by a long shot.

From somewhere within the black smoke, a voice boomed out. 'You think you're so clever, don't you?' It was Cadal Righ himself. Whether he'd been part of the fireball, or whether he'd somehow transported himself here after it had dropped, I didn't know. Either way, it was clear that the bastard still had plenty of magic to call his own and none of the rest of us did.

My stomach lurched sickeningly with fear. Had I consigned us all to imminent death?

'All you've done,' Cadal Righ continued, his body still concealed in the soot-laden cloud, 'is fuck yourselves. Now you've got nothing and I've got everything.' He stepped forward. His red-eyed glare was as intense and cold as ever and power rippled from him in unceasing waves. He swivelled until his eyes met mine. 'I'm going to guess,' he said, 'that this was your stupid idea.'

I stared at him, my tongue cleaving to the roof of my mouth. Speech, it appeared, had deserted me yet again.

Cadal Righ sneered. 'What? Cat got your tongue? Nothing to say for yourself?' He turned to the others. 'Is this the person you've assigned to be your leader? You ought to have done better, you know. This is why this country needs someone like me in charge.' He paused. 'Wait. No. Not someone *like* me. *Actually* me.' He bared his teeth in what I supposed was meant to be a smile. 'But don't think I will show you any mercy for your poor decision making. You will all burn.'

Laoch nudged my elbow sharply. 'Why aren't we burning already then?' he muttered. 'He still has magic and we don't. He could have already destroyed us all. Why is he wasting time on chatter?'

Ego, I imagined. I looked around, desperately wondering if there was anything I could do or anything I could use that would defend these people against him. Against his immense power, however, I came up with nothing.

A figure emerged from the other side of the street and strode towards Cadal Righ. It was Aspen; of course it was. Something inside me collapsed as I waited, expecting the bastard Mage to prostrate himself and offer Cadal Righ his undying allegiance.

'Don't worry about her,' Aspen said, stopping only metres in front of Cadal Righ. 'She's only a woman.' He didn't look at me. 'An annoying woman at that. She holds no sway here. Kill her if you want. In fact, it would be my pleasure to hold her down while you do so.'

'I will murder that fucker,' Laoch spat. 'I'll slit his throat and—'

Aspen coughed delicately as he waved away the smoke that was billowing towards his face in gentle, wispy waves. His attention was wholly on Cadal Righ. 'No,' he said. '*She*'s not what you have to worry about.'

Cadal Righ crossed his arms over his thin chest and crooked an amused eyebrow. 'Go on,' he said. 'Who should I be worried about then?' His voice dripped with derision. 'And please don't say you. You might have had power before, old man, but without magic you're nothing.'

Aspen didn't flinch. 'Oh, I am well aware of that fact.' He jerked his thumb towards me. 'It's her fault. I would appreciate it if you did kill her.'

I knew without a shadow of a doubt that he was telling the truth.

'Traitor!' somebody screamed and I realised with a start that it was Brian. He was still on his feet, albeit with streaks of blood and soot covering half of his face. 'Traitor! You're supposed on our side! Not his! We need to work together, Aspen! We need to—'

'*Sesh voy*,' Cadal Righ said calmly.

Brian clutched at his throat. His eyes bulged and almost popped out of his skull. He fell to his knees while others around him rushed to his aid and blocked my view. Seconds later, they stepped back again. I didn't need to look down to know that Brian was already dead.

Aspen didn't glance at his former colleague. I leaned towards Laoch and whispered. 'We should rush him together. He'll kill us in an instant, but if we're fast we might do some damage.'

Laoch replied. 'Wait. If it comes to it I'll martyr myself, but wait a moment first.'

I frowned, then I realised he wasn't watching Cadal Righ; he was watching Aspen.

Aspen spoke casually, as if the tragic scene with Brian hadn't happened, 'My own frailty isn't the only thing I'm aware of. You see, our powers have been waning for years – that's why we were forced to draw power from corpses. We had to bolster our magic somehow. To maintain the Mages' control, we've had to incite fear in every heart. We couldn't allow anyone to think we were growing weaker, not for a moment.

'I know exactly what it takes to show power and remain in charge. I know how desperation can make you do extraordinary things. And,' he smiled placidly, linking his hands together in front of him, 'because of all those things, I know that your power is failing too.'

He nodded at the hundreds of ex-Afflicted people standing nearby, Noah included. 'You drew your magic from them. It's the only way you could have sustained your own life for so many years. Now that they are no longer under your control, you have no source left. Once the magic within you is used up, there will be no more. Not for you, not for any of us. I understand the power of propaganda and fear better than anyone. You thought you could use the last of your power to beat us into submission.' He gave an approving sniff. 'To be fair, I'd have done the same in your situation. You can't win, though. It's over.'

Cadal Righ roared. 'It's not fucking over!' And at that very moment, I knew that Aspen was right.

Cadal Righ flung his arms out towards the Mage and bellowed, *'Kall moy!'* The effect was instantaneous. Aspen started to choke, gasping for air as the oxygen was driven out of his lungs.

'You liar!' Cadal Righ screamed. 'You're a fucking liar! I will always have magic! I will use it to destroy you all!' He spun towards the masses of ex-Afflicted men and women. *'Ins veil!'*

They were all thrown backwards, knocked down by an invisible tsunami. Before most hit the ground, another figure broke away from the crowd on the opposite side: Angus.

I caught my breath then ran forward to attack Cadal Righ myself before the old Mage reached him, but I was too late. Cadal Righ had already spotted him and once again he yelled,

'Ins veil!'

Angus was thrown up into the air then jerked back with extraordinary force. His limp form barrelled into another cluster of Mages and sent them flying to the ground. A second later, someone launched a small grey projectile. It missed Cadal Righ by less than a metre and thudded into the ground by his feet. I turned to see Isla, reaching down to pick up another of the fallen stones from the collapsed City Chambers. *No.*

'Laoch,' I whispered. 'If he attacks her—'

'I'm there.' He ran past me, making a beeline for Isla to block her from Cadal Righ's view.

I sprang towards the red-eyed bastard. He snarled at me, '*Belzac.*'

Fire coalesced from nowhere, attacking my front, my back and my sides. I yelped and threw myself down, rolling on the ground to stop my clothes catching fire. My body smacked against Aspen's. He was on the ground too, his face purple and his fingers clawing desperately at his face and his throat.

As Cadal Righ strode towards us, he opened his mouth to utter another spell. I braced myself. That was what we needed; we needed him to use up his magic as quickly as possible. Regardless of the consequences, anything that would drain him was worth it.

Before he could say anything, Aspen's hand shot out and clutched his ankle.

Cadal Righ hissed and kicked him away. 'You think you can lead this country?' he screamed at me. 'You think you can be queen? You don't have it in you. *He* could have managed it.' He lifted his foot again and stamped on Aspen's hand but the Mage was too far gone to do more than whimper.

'You, woman, aren't ruthless enough. You need to be strong to be a ruler. You need to be like me. Without me, Scotland will fail. I'm the only one who deserves this country. I'm the only one with the power left to lead her.'

Aspen gave another splutter then his body stilled. I knew he was dead. I looked up at Cadal Righ and whispered, 'I don't want to lead Scotland. I never did.'

'Then why do you keep getting in my fucking way?'

'Because you don't deserve us.' I raised my chin. 'Do it. Do what he told you to do and kill me.'

Cadal Righ's eyes flashed. 'With pleasure.'

Another stone flew out of nowhere and hit him on the centre of his forehead. It was swiftly followed by another, then another and another. I wasn't standing alone; this time I was the person with an army at my back.

'*Vaz!*' Cadal Righ shouted to create a magical wall to protect himself from being hit again. The air shimmered as magic flowed forth from him. More stones were thrown but now they bounced away uselessly. Several people ran towards him, abandoning the safety of the crowd to throw themselves at him, but they hit the wall too and fell away.

My eyes met the Gowk's as he sprawled only a metre away from me. We may as well have been a mile apart; the magical wall that Cadal Righ had created to protect himself had inadvertently surrounded me, too. I gazed at the Gowk as his lips moved. 'It's on you now, lass. It's all on you.'

I nodded and forced myself to my feet. 'You know you've already lost,' I said. 'You had one play left and you failed. How long did you spend sleeping, waiting for the moment to become king? More than a hundred years? Countless people have died to get you to this point. The whole country has suffered because of the Affliction.'

I shook my head. 'And it got you nowhere. You can kill me, but you still won't win.' I gestured beyond the invisible wall at the people who used to be Afflicted, the men who used to be Mages and the women who had been neither. 'They won't let you.'

Cadal Righ howled, '*Kall moy!*'

I choked and my chest tightened. I knew this feeling...

I gasped for air – and immediately felt my lungs inflate. The spell hadn't taken. Cadal Righ's magic was running out. He'd squandered too much on time on posturing and showmanship and now he had hardly anything left.

I couldn't waste the opportunity. I barrelled into his thin body and knocked him to the ground. He squealed, kicking and writhing to escape me. His hands reached for my face and he pressed his thumbs towards my eyes in a bid to blind me. I lifted my head and slammed my forehead into his. Pain ricocheted through me, reverberating into the depths of my skull, but I knew that Cadal Righ's agony was greater.

'That,' I said in a clear and distinct voice, 'is what we call a Glasgow kiss.'

He spat at me. He wrinkled his nose and focused his eyes, and I knew he was reaching for the last dregs of his power. '*Ins veil.*'

I was thrown away from him and my spine slammed into the magical wall. But the wall was wavering; it wouldn't hold for much longer. All I had to do was hang on.

Then he was on me, his fists clenched as he punched my head over and over again.

I opened my mouth and bit down hard onto the knuckles of his right hand. Blood filled my mouth. It wasn't much of a wound but it forced Cadal Righ to hesitate.

I jerked up my knee with all the energy I could summon and it connected with his groin. He shuddered as pain flashed through him and I managed to wriggle away.

The ringing in my ears had returned with a vengeance. I grimaced and shook my head, but it only made it worse. I heaved myself up. 'I told you,' I said. 'You cannot win.'

Cadal Righ's face was a mask of fury and hatred. 'Then neither of us will.' He half-closed his eyes. '*Belzac.*'

I knew the fire he'd summoned would be weak and the magic inside him wouldn't sustain the spell for long, but it didn't matter. We were both trapped in a small space and it didn't require much power for the area at our feet to fill with flames. They lapped at my toes and I felt my skin blistering.

The fire wasn't the problem; the choking smoke would get me long before the flames did. I coughed then stamped around to put the fire out. Before my vision was almost completely obscured, I glimpsed Laoch on the other side of the wall banging his fists uselessly against it before he vanished from my sight.

An involuntary cry left my lips. No. I wasn't ready to leave him yet. I wasn't ready to abandon the future we could have together that was now within touching distance.

I closed my mouth, held my breath and leapt in Cadal Righ's direction. He was already on the ground being attacked by his own fire spell. I stumbled over him and fell to my hands and knees. I wouldn't wait for the fire to claim us both. I would survive.

As I grabbed his head, flames attacked my feet and started to burn my clothes. I wrapped an arm around his neck and heard him moan in protest, but I closed my ears to the sound.

I squeezed Cadal Righ's neck with everything I had. I couldn't hold my breath for much longer, so I had to do this now. I felt the air alter as the magic wall snapped out of existence and the flames subsided. Laoch's strong arms hauled me away from that death zone, and I knew it was finally over.

***

A thready voice called my name. I raised my head and saw Ailsa by Angus's side. She was smoothing his forehead with the palm of her hand and her expression was heavy with concern.

I bit my lip and limped across the street, avoiding the debris and blackened stone that littered my path. My feet were in agony but the pain was scarcely a distraction. 'Are you alright?' I asked.

'I'm fine,' she said. 'But I'm worried about Angus.'

Blood trickled from the side of his head and his skin was deathly pale. I knelt by his side while Belle walked over and peered down.

Angus grasped my hand. 'Promise me, lass.' His voice was weak. 'Promise me you won't let things go back to the way they were. The world has to change now. It has to be different. Without magic, you can all start afresh.' He coughed. 'I won't be there to see it, but I'll be looking down on you from above. Always.'

I squeezed his hand. He shouldn't have been talking that way. It wasn't like Angus to give up.

'You bampot.' Belle rolled her eyes. 'Listen to you, wheezing on as if you're already deid. You've got a bang on the heid, nothing more. Honestly, men do like to make drama out of nothing.'

Something flickered in Angus's eyes: frustrated irritation. 'For goodness' sake, woman!' he snapped. 'Will you no' allow me my moment? I was a hero out there! The least you can do is let me make a wee speech and gain some well-deserved concern for my sacrifice.'

I pressed my lips together to stifle a smile. 'You'll need to get that wound properly cleaned. And you'll need some bed rest in case of concussion.'

He glared at Belle. 'You see? At least she cares about me!'

Ailsa shook her head. 'I thought you were dying.'

'We're all dying, woman!'

'Some of us faster than others,' she muttered.

I stood up and caught sight of Isla with Laoch. She skipped over to me. 'Is he deid?'

'Angus is fine.'

She frowned. 'Not him.'

Angus pouted enough to cause Belle to kick him in the shin.

'Cadal Righ,' Isla said. 'Is he really deid? Are you sure he's no' going to come back?'

'I'm sure.' Once I'd recovered enough, I had double-checked, then triple-checked, then ordered Teasag and Laoch and even a terrified Twister to check.

Isla searched my face for any hint that I was lying. Without warning, her eyes filled with tears that started to roll unchecked down her cheeks. 'That's … really … good,' she hiccupped.

Laoch wrapped his arms around her and gave her a tight hug. His eyes met mine over her shoulder and he smiled slightly. I smiled back.

'What about the Mages?' she asked, her voice muffled. 'Will they come back?'

'No,' Laoch told her. 'They're gone too.'

I nodded resolutely. Andy was standing over Aspen's body. Suddenly he looked forlorn. 'Give me a moment,' I said, kissing Laoch's cheek.

Andy didn't look up as I approached but I caught a flicker of a smile on his face and I knew he'd noticed me. 'It's the last thing I ever thought he'd do,' he murmured. 'At the very end, Lord Aspen proved himself braver and smarter than all of us.'

I stared at Aspen's body then knelt down and gently closed his unseeing eyes. I strongly suspected that his actions had been borne out of his unwillingness to live without magic or power rather than selfless sacrifice. Perhaps he'd hoped that at the end, when he recognised himself in Cadal Righ, his name would go down in the history books as a hero and not a villain. Perhaps I was being uncharitable but I doubted it. 'He won't be forgotten,' I said simply.

Andy nodded slowly as Alan approached. Next to him was a familiar face. I smiled suddenly when I recognised Keith, the other guard who had been identified as Afflicted by Isla. 'Hi,' he said weakly. He waved at me awkwardly before sniffing. 'You did it. You kept your promise. You found a way.'

'The Affliction has gone,' I said. 'For good.'

Keith started to cry as Alan patted his shoulder. 'What happens now?' Alan asked. 'What do we do?'

'We rebuild our country from the ground up,' I said.

I touched Aspen's arm and stood up. Then I noticed the shoot of green by his cooling fingers. A little thistle plant was sprouting through the cobbles. Under the right conditions, thistles could be excellent anti-inflammatories – and a lot of people here were badly injured. I plucked it and started to scan around for more. There was a lot of work to do, a lot of healing.

A shadow fell across my face. 'Can I help?' Laoch asked.

I smiled. 'Always.'

TWENTY-EIGHT

The potent reek of the tincture made my eyes water. I'd gone overboard with the quantity and would have to be careful how much I doled out to my patients; too much would kill them. At least I had plenty to go around.

The simple act of mixing, pounding and boiling the herbs had given me hope for my future. A lifetime ago I'd dreamed of becoming an alchemist, making medicines to heal the sick. Now it wasn't only potions that were brewing; the flickers of my old ambitions were stirring.

I glanced out of the window. Laoch had his top off as he strained and heaved building materials from one side of the street to the other with Andy and Alan beside him. We were recreating our country in so many ways and improving it in so many others.

I allowed myself a moment of lewd drooling for Laoch, then I grinned and headed for my first patient. Noah was sitting up, propped against several pillows. His skin remained pale but the spark in his eyes suggested he was on the mend. He offered a brilliant smile when I entered and a dimple formed in his cheek. So much had changed in such a short space of time.

'Hey,' I said.

'Hey.' He glanced at the bottle in my hands and looked slightly abashed. 'I bet you never thought you'd be tending to my needs like this.'

I gave a short laugh. 'No, it's not what I imagined I'd ever be doing.' I leaned across and carefully removed his bandages to examine his wounds. He was healing nicely, although he'd never grow another ear or hand. It still amazed me that he was alive.

He winced as I cleaned each wound but he didn't complain. Once I started bandaging them again, he relaxed and grew chattier. 'How are things going out there?'

'Good,' I said. 'It's incredible what can be achieved through will and teamwork.' I smiled. 'It helps that we have a lot of people. Many of those poor folk who were Afflicted have joined in the re-building efforts across the city. I think they feel guilty, although goodness knows they have nothing to feel guilty about. None of it was their fault. They couldn't control themselves.'

Noah didn't return my smile. He looked down at the stump at his wrist. 'It's a terrible thing to have no control,' he said quietly. 'It will never happen to me again.' He looked up, his eyes suddenly blazing with fierce determination. 'I can promise you that.'

I finished replacing the last dressing. 'You've been through a lot – and you've achieved a lot. If it were not for you, I'm not sure I'd have convinced the Mages to help remove the magic even when those blasted fireballs were destroying half the city. None of the other ex-Afflicted I've spoken to felt any real ink to Cadal Righ. They were desperate to please him and would have laid down their lives for him, but none of them felt his thoughts like you did.' I shrugged. 'It must have been because you were a Mage. The magic probably created a stronger bond.'

Noah raised an eyebrow. 'You're talking about when I said I knew the only thing he was afraid of was you taking away the magic.'

I nodded. 'Aye.'

'I made that up.' His smile returned. 'But you're welcome.'

I blinked. 'Pardon?'

'I was hardly going to allow those bastards to continue swanning around with all their powers intact when I had none left, was I?'

I stared at him.

'Don't worry, Mairi. I don't blame you for what you did. Taking away my magic was the best thing to do at the time. It worked – it saved me.' He grimaced. 'Though it's a horrible sensation to lose all that you ever had. Even with death on our doorstep, I wanted the others to feel the way that I had.'

Fury flared in his eyes for the briefest of moments. 'They didn't help me when I was Afflicted. Quite the reverse, they treated me like a fucking animal. They deserved to suffer in the same way that I had.'

Uh-huh. I turned away to prepare the tincture; at least with my back to Noah, he couldn't see my expression. 'How did you get away from the nuckalavees?' I asked. Even to my own ears, my tone sounded too casual.

'There was another guy, some farm boy. I think he'd been following you for some time. It's all a bit hazy but I remember some part of me being aware of him. He was watching from the trees and I directed the nuckalavees away from me and towards him. It was the only way to save myself. It was a shame, but I know you'll agree that my life is more important than a peasant's could ever be. As you said, you couldn't have persuaded the Mages without my help. It was survival of the fittest. And the best.'

Blood rushed to my head. John-not-John; that was the farm

boy Noah was talking about. He must have changed his mind about staying on his own and come after us, and that decision had ended his life. Noah had made that decision when he was human; he couldn't blame it on the Affliction.

Tears pricked the back of my eyes and I held my breath until I could force them away. 'You were lucky,' I said, still not turning around.

'Aye. But I'm like you, Mairi.' His voice was smug. 'I make my own luck.'

My hands were shaking as I drew a few drops of the tincture into a small cup. Then I asked, 'So what's next? What will you do now?'

'I've got plans.'

'Mmm?'

Noah smacked his lips. 'Scotland is no longer the same country and things will have to change. For one thing, we can't have each city led by a different person. We need an overall leader who can bring everyone together. Nobody has magic any longer. I've tried over and over again and there's nothing inside me. My power has gone for good. But I've got the experience and the lineage, not to mention the intelligence. I can use what happened with my own Affliction to bring everyone to my side. I'll be the everyman for every person.'

I looked down at the contents of the cup. 'You want to become the leader of Scotland? The … king?'

He chuckled. 'It has a nice ring to it, doesn't it?' He paused. 'You're concerned and I can understand why, but it won't be like it was before. I'll give you a place at the table. You'll have a voice – you can be the female voice of reason that helps to keep the rest of us men on the right track.'

'That's good of you.'

'It's the least I can do. You can advise on a lot of weighty matters.'

I added a few more drops of the tincture to the cup and swirled them around. Then I added a few more. 'Such as?'

'Ordinary people will feel better about the future when they see that the past has been laid to rest. We'll start with the Mages. You can help with a list of names. Anyone who dissented or who didn't agree with the plan to take away the magic in order to defeat Cadal Righ can be first.'

'First?'

'To hang in George Square. We'll string them up and let everyone see that justice has been done. Then there are the guards who stopped the Edinburgh refugees from coming into the city.'

'That was at the Mages' order.'

'That's no excuse. Glasgow won't stand for soft-heartedness and neither will Scotland. I need to show that I can be strong, even if I don't have all my body parts. One-Handed Noah, the even-handed choice.' I heard the smirk in his voice. 'The country needs to know that I'll be fair and am prepared to punish everyone equally. That will restore law and order and allow everyone to see that control has been re-established.'

I turned towards him and handed him the cup. 'Here. Drink this. Make sure you take every drop.' I watched as Noah lifted the cup to his lips and swallowed the contents. Bile rose in my mouth. Not everything had changed – but it could.

He met my eyes. 'You could still be my queen, Mairi. It doesn't have to be over between us. You can keep the daemon on the side. I understand why you like Nicholas so as long as you keep your relationship with him quiet I'll allow it to continue. The two of us together would be a force to be reckoned with. Scotland needs people like us.'

I didn't break our gaze. 'I'll have to think about it. Cadal Righ told me I wasn't ruthless enough to be a leader.'

Noah laughed. 'Who cares what Cadal Righ thought? He's

dust. We're the survivors. You're more than ruthless enough, and a leader has to be ruthless. It's one of the job requirements. Compassion is nice for the common masses, but it doesn't help anyone make the tough decisions that allow a country to prosper. Besides, you won't be the leader.'

He smacked his lips. 'That will be me. If you don't want to give orders, you can work on ways to bring back the magic.' His expression took on a thoughtful edge. 'Perhaps the bodies of all those Mages can be put to use. We can create another garden, a new one, a better one. We can bury them and draw whatever latent power is there to enhance our own strength. I'm sure you can come up with something. You're resourceful.'

I took the cup from him and glanced inside it. It was empty. 'We'll have to see,' I murmured. 'Although maybe you're right. I am ruthless enough.'

He grinned. 'You are, I know it. You wouldn't have gotten this far if you weren't.'

I scooped up my things and left, closing the door behind me. As I did so, I heard Noah suddenly choke.

I passed a hand in front of my eyes and sighed. He wouldn't come back from the dead this time. I headed down the hallway towards my next patient.

Isla found me a few hours later, sitting outside with my back against the tree where the raven had once perched. It was a miracle it was still in one piece with nothing more than a few charred branches to show what had happened nearby. When I tilted my head and gazed upwards, I saw a few buds emerging. Life would find a way sooner or later, no matter what else occurred.

'Mairi!' She danced over. 'I've been looking for you everywhere!'

'Is everything alright?'

Isla beamed. 'Aye. It's braw.'

I peered at her face. It would take a long time for Isla – and for all of us – to recover from what had happened, but her crying was done for now. So was mine. We had to look to the future and not the past.

There was a frustrated yell from across the street. Isla and I glanced over. There were four ex-Mages, all lined up next to each other. '*Belzac*,' the nearest one hissed. '*Belzac!*' He flicked his wrist. Nothing happened. The Mage next to him yanked off his black cloak and threw it on the ground before stamping on it in some sort of ceremonial fashion that made sense only to him.

'Everywhere I go,' Isla said cheerfully, 'I see black-cloaked bastards doing that sort of thing.'

I smiled. She continued. 'It felt proper strange when it first happened, when the magic first left. It was like a part of me had been removed.' She touched her heart. 'Part of my soul.'

Her expression altered and she lowered her voice. 'There's something I have to show you.'

'You don't have to show me, Isla.' I already knew.

She was insistent. 'I do. I do have to show you.'

I pushed my hair away from my face. 'Go on then.'

Isla focused upwards at the nearest branch. Then she whispered, '*Chelta*.'

The air around us stirred. A moment later, a tiny bud that had been sprouting started to blossom, growing in front of our eyes.

Isla wasn't watching it. She was watching me. 'It came back,' she said. 'I felt it come back.'

I looked at the Mages. Two of them had sat down in the middle of the road and buried their faces in their hands. The other two stood next to them, their shoulders slumped. 'It's not come back for them,' I said.

'No.'

I hummed. Isla's body rose momentarily in the air and hovered several inches above the ground before returning to its original position. Her eyes shone.

Laoch appeared from around the corner and his expression lightened when he saw us. He patted one of the Mages on the back as he passed. 'Not to worry,' he said. 'It's the same for all of us.' He paused to allow Rhona to pass in front of him. There was a huge grin on her lined face as if she were holding a great secret. She trotted out of sight.

'What are you two smirking about?' he asked.

I stood up and dusted myself off, then leaned across and placed an arm around his waist. I gave him a long, lingering kiss. Behind me I heard Isla making fake retching sounds.

I'll tell you later.

He started to nod then he stopped and stared. 'Wait,' he said. 'Did you just—'

I kissed him again, halting any further conversation. There would be time for that later.

ABOUT THE AUTHOR

After teaching English literature in the UK, Japan and Malaysia, Helen Harper left behind the world of education following the worldwide success of her Blood Destiny series of books. She thanks her lucky stars every day that she's able to do so.

Helen has always been a book lover, devouring science fiction and fantasy tales when she was a child growing up in Scotland.

She currently lives in Edinburgh with far too many cats – not to mention the dragons, fairies, demons, wizards and vampires that seem to keep appearing from nowhere.

Also by Helen Harper

The *FireBrand* series

A werewolf killer. A paranormal murder. How many times can Emma Bellamy cheat death?

I'm one placement away from becoming a fully fledged London detective. It's bad enough that my last assignment before I qualify is with Supernatural Squad. But that's nothing compared to what happens next.

Brutally murdered by an unknown assailant, I wake up twelve hours later in the morgue – and I'm very much alive. I don't know how or why it happened. I don't know who killed me. All I know is that they might try again.

Werewolves are disappearing right, left and centre.

A mysterious vampire seems intent on following me everywhere I go.

And I have to solve my own vicious killing. Preferably before death comes for me again.

Book One – Brimstone Bound

Book Two – Infernal Enchantment

Book Three – Midnight Smoke

Book Four – Scorched Heart

Book Five – Dark Whispers

Book Six – A Killer's Kiss

Book Seven – coming Summer 2023

* * *

The complete _Blood Destiny_ series

"A spectacular and addictive series."

Mackenzie Smith has always known that she was different. Growing up as the only human in a pack of rural shapeshifters will do that to you, but then couple it with some mean fighting skills and a fiery temper and you end up with a woman that few will dare to cross. However, when the only father figure in her life is brutally murdered, and the dangerous Brethren with their predatory Lord Alpha come to investigate, Mack has to not only ensure the physical safety of her adopted family by hiding her apparent humanity, she also has to seek the blood-soaked vengeance that she craves.

Book One - Bloodfire

Book Two - Bloodmagic

Book Three - Bloodrage

Book Four - Blood Politics

Book Five - Bloodlust

Also

Corrigan Fire

Corrigan Magic

Corrigan Rage

Corrigan Politics

Corrigan Lust

* * *

The complete *Bo Blackman* series

A half-dead daemon, a massacre at her London based PI firm and evidence that suggests she's the main suspect for both … Bo Blackman is having a very bad week.

She might be naive and inexperienced but she's determined to get to the bottom of the crimes, even if it means involving herself with one of London's most powerful vampire Families and their enigmatic leader.

It's pretty much going to be impossible for Bo to ever escape unscathed.

Book One - Dire Straits

Book Two - New Order

Book Three - High Stakes

Book Four - Red Angel

Book Five - Vigilante Vampire

Book Six - Dark Tomorrow

* * *

The complete *Highland Magic* series

Integrity Taylor walked away from the Sidhe when she was a child. Orphaned and bullied, she simply had no reason to stay, especially not when the sins of her father were going to remain on her shoulders. She found a new family - a group of thieves who proved that blood was less important than loyalty and love.

But the Sidhe aren't going to let Integrity stay away forever. They need her more than anyone realises - besides, there are prophecies to be fulfilled, people to be saved and hearts to be won over. If anyone can do it, Integrity can.

Book One - Gifted Thief

Book Two - Honour Bound

Book Three - Veiled Threat

Book Four - Last Wish

* * *

The complete *Dreamweaver* series

"I have special coping mechanisms for the times I need to open the front door. They're even often successful..."

Zoe Lydon knows there's often nothing logical or rational about fear. It doesn't change the fact that she's too terrified to step outside her own house, however.

What Zoe doesn't realise is that she's also a dreamweaver - able to access other people's subconscious minds. When she finds herself in the Dreamlands and up against its sinister Mayor, she'll need to use all of her wits - and overcome all of her fears - if she's ever going to come out alive.

Book One - Night Shade

Book Two - Night Terrors

Book Three - Night Lights

* * *

Stand alone novels

Eros

William Shakespeare once wrote that, "Cupid is a knavish lad, thus to make poor females mad." The trouble is that Cupid himself would probably agree…

As probably the last person in the world who'd appreciate hearts, flowers and romance, Coop is convinced that true love doesn't exist – which is rather unfortunate considering he's also known as Cupid, the God of Love. He'd rather spend his days drinking, womanising and generally having as much fun as he possible can. As far as he's concerned, shooting people with bolts of pure love is a waste of his time…but then his path crosses with that of shy and retiring Skye Sawyer and nothing will ever be quite the same again.

Wraith

Magic. Shadows. Adventure. Romance.

Saiya Buchanan is a wraith, able to detach her shadow from her body and send it off to do her bidding. But, unlike most of her kin, Saiya doesn't deal in death. Instead, she trades secrets - and in the goblin besieged city of Stirling in Scotland, they're a highly prized commodity. It might just be, however, that the goblins have been hiding the greatest secret of them all. When Gabriel de Florinville, a Dark Elf, is sent as royal envoy into Stirling and takes her prisoner, Saiya is not only going to uncover the sinister truth. She's also going to realise that sometimes the deepest secrets are the ones locked within your own heart.

* * *

<u>**The complete *Lazy Girl's Guide To Magic* series**</u>

Hard Work Will Pay Off Later. Laziness Pays Off Now.

Let's get one thing straight - Ivy Wilde is not a heroine. In fact, she's probably the last witch in the world who you'd call if you needed a magical helping hand. If it were down to Ivy, she'd spend all day every day on her sofa where she could watch TV, munch junk food and talk to her feline familiar to her heart's content.

However, when a bureaucratic disaster ends up with Ivy as the victim of a case of mistaken identity, she's yanked very unwillingly into Arcane Branch, the investigative department of the Hallowed Order of Magical Enlightenment. Her problems are quadrupled when a valuable object is stolen right from under the Order's noses.

It doesn't exactly help that she's been magically bound to Adeptus Exemptus Raphael Winter. He might have piercing sapphire eyes and a body which a cover model would be proud of but, as far as Ivy's concerned, he's a walking advertisement for the joyless perils of too much witch-work.

And if he makes her go to the gym again, she's definitely going to turn him into a frog.

Book One - Slouch Witch

Book Two - Star Witch

Book Three - Spirit Witch

Sparkle Witch (Christmas novella)

* * *

The complete *Fractured Faery* series

One corpse. Several bizarre looking attackers. Some very strange magical powers. And a severe bout of amnesia.

It's one thing to wake up outside in the middle of the night with a decapitated man for company. It's another to have no memory of how you got there - or who you are.

She might not know her own name but she knows that several people are out to get her. It could be because she has strange magical powers seemingly at her fingertips and is some kind of fabulous hero. But then why does she appear to inspire fear in so many? And who on earth is the sexy, green-eyed barman who apparently despises her? So many questions ... and so few answers.

At least one thing is for sure - the streets of Manchester have never met someone quite as mad as Madrona...

Book One - Box of Frogs

SHORTLISTED FOR THE KINDLE STORYTELLER AWARD 2018

Book Two - Quiver of Cobras

Book Three - Skulk of Foxes

* * *

The complete *City Of Magic* series

Charley is a cleaner by day and a professional gambler by night. She might be haunted by her tragic past but she's never thought of herself as anything or anyone special. Until, that is, things start to go terribly wrong all across the city of Manchester. Between plagues of rats, firestorms and the gleaming blue eyes of a sexy Scottish werewolf, she might just have landed herself in the middle of a magical apocalypse. She might also be the only person who has the ability to bring order to an utterly chaotic new world.

Book One - Shrill Dusk

Book Two - Brittle Midnight

Book Three - Furtive Dawn